THE BLUE CONDITION

TYLER

COMPTON

Tyler Compton
Los Angeles, CA 90046
www.tylercomptonbooks.com

Publisher's Note: This is a work of fiction. Names, characters, places, and incidents are a product of the author's imagination. Locales and public names are sometimes used for atmospheric purposes. Any resemblance to actual people, living or dead, or to businesses, companies, events, institutions, or locales is completely coincidental.

Book Layout ©2013 BookDesignTemplates.com

Ordering Information:
Quantity sales. Special discounts are available on quantity purchases by corporations, associations, and others. For details, contact the "Special Sales Department" at the address above.

ISBN 978-0-9893845-8-2 (paperback)
ISBN 978-0-9893845-9-9 (ebook)

For Morgan, Colby, and Ashley

I love the old way best, the simple way
Of poison, where we too are strong as men.
—Medea

To Detective David Parks, LAPD—

The time has come for us to move on to the next
chapter of our story. We have been through so much
that I feel we will always be bonded. In ways that even
we may never truly know. We both have been tested. And
while you came out the victor, I now understand where
my failings were. Nevertheless, there is always next
time.

Which is the true purpose of this letter. I know
there was a reason why you were "chosen" to be my partner in this journey we call life. Unfortunately, I can
never truly finish the tasks appointed me so long as
you are not vanquished. Therefore, I apologize, right
now, in advance, for what is coming your way. I hope
you do not suffer too much. That is the only instruc-
tion--nay, the only order that I made unconditional.

Then again, one never knows what life will bring.
Maybe, just maybe, if you are as good as I feel you
might be, we will meet again--one day--face to face.
But if you're not, then I am sorry, but it was not meant
to be. Until that time, which I really do hope happens,

Your friend, confidant, and trusted companion,
Lewis Hayward

MONDAY

ONE

Dr. Jacqueline Isley could feel her heart beating throughout her body, every vein pulsating as blood coursed through her being, her head an echoing reminder as she stood posed, her SIG-Sauer P230 aimed at her approaching target.

She wanted to brush the strand of crimson hair out of her face, away from her emerald-colored eyes as she tried to focus, making sure her attention wasn't diverted. But if she turned away, let herself become distracted, so much as blinked, the outcome could be disastrous for her.

A sheen of light sweat began to build along her forehead and above her lips, and she could smell the pungent salty odor as her body dealt with the uncomfortable situation. She knew what she had to do. This was it. There was no turning back.

Jackie Isley calmly sucked air in through her nose, filling her lungs and stretching her fuchsia-colored blouse across her chest. She could do this. Had done this hundreds of times. She knew what she needed to do and how to do it. Efficiently. She was a professional. Always had been, and always would be. She exhaled and then, with all surety, squeezed the trigger.

"So?" Amy Tanaka, the assistant chief medical examiner for the county of Los Angeles, had snuck up behind Jackie in the parking lot of the LA county coroner's building and startled her into almost dropping either her briefcase or morning cup of coffee. Luckily, she managed to hold onto both, though the mug of scalding beverage spilled a few drops on her hand. She winced in pain, holding back the urge to scream, and slowly turned around, her eyes glaring at the woman who was one of her closest friends going on eight years now. Tanaka had been with the city for over a decade, working her way to assistant chief, while Jackie had begun working for the city of Los Angeles in 2004 as a criminologist and assistant forensic toxicologist, moving her way up to lead forensic toxicologist, in charge of the toxicology lab. She had done it the same way she had accomplished everything in life: through sheer determination, hard work, long hours, and the refusal of defeat. Working out of the same building, the two women had become close, seeing each other day after day, two women fighting to stay on top in a "man's world," though neither had ever really thought of the world they worked within as belonging to any one man. They had been there for each other, through the good times and bad, heartaches and heartbreaks, promotions and pass-overs.

"Imagine what would have happened if I'd had a gun in my hand just now," Jackie said as she closed her car door and turned to her friend, who stood a good six inches shorter than her, even in three-inch heels.

"Oh, yeah," Tanaka smirked. "I feel so bad for your *car*. Since that's the direction your jumpy ass was facing. Some parking lot strangler or rapist comes sneaking up behind you, and you take your frustration out on poor ol' Bessie here." Tanaka smiled as she rubbed her hand along the top of Jackie's 2013 Lexus RX and then pulled her hand away and sneered at the film of dust on her fingers. "On the other hand, ol' Bessie here's probably saying, 'Please, bitch, put me out of my misery. Woman can't even give me a proper cleaning.'"

"Is that what my car is saying?" Jackie said as she started away from the parking lot.

"Hey, it's your car," Tanaka said, keeping in step. "I can't help what she says."

The two walked in silence toward the coroner's office. Both women stepped aside as several construction workers made their way into the building. The county coroner's building had looked the same since the 1960s and was getting a remake, a facelift both on the outside as well as the in, including a new computer system and updated tools to help with criminal investigations. The carpet throughout the front reception area and the offices was ripped out, leaving a loud, hollow, echoing sound with each step the two women made in their high-heeled shoes. Fortunately, even though it was a Monday morning, the first of the month, and Labor Day no less, construction on the building still commenced the same as it had every day for the past two months.

"So?" Tanaka repeated, the reason for startling Jackie all but forgotten.

"So what?"

"Oh, don't you make me pry it out of you," Tanaka said, a smile still plastered across her face. "Have you heard yet? I mean, I'm sure you haven't. But how do you think you did? The tests? How did you do?"

Jackie shrugged and pressed the button for the elevator, facing the closed doors as she thought about the gun range where she had done exceptionally well just two hours before.

"Girl, I'm a gonna smack you," Tanaka said with a sigh. "How. Did. You. Do?"

Jackie turned to Tanaka and simply smiled, not being one to toot her own horn, yet feeling good about how she had done on her detective's exams. She just didn't want to jinx the outcome, and Tanaka could understand that.

"You do realize it's simply a citywide mandate to make all investigators who spend any decent amount of time out at crime scenes be field certified?"

"It's an excuse to carry a gun and arrest a mo'fo!" Amy said excitedly.

"Okay. Calm down there, Jackie Brown," Jackie laughed.

Though she would never admit it, and though Amy Tanaka could have guessed it, that was the real reason Jackie pursued this. The city had *desired* all field investigators become gun certified, had even promised the possibility of a pay increase, but no requirements had been made. So far.

The year before had been one of the toughest for Jackie, both professionally and personally. It had been the year of the Palisades Poisoner, a sociopathic madman who had managed to poison a dozen men and women around the Los Angeles area before being stopped. Unfortunately, the chaos he had spread had already taken effect, polluting the relationships with the two men she valued most in her life—that of the budding love of LA homicide detective David Parks, and that of her only son, Ricky.

Throughout the course of the investigation, Lewis Hayward, a detective with the LAPD turned bad, had managed to mislead the investigation, all evidence leading Detective Parks straight for her son. Though the truth had come out and Hayward had been apprehended, the damage had been done. The accusations made could not be taken back. The romance that had been building between Dave and Jackie had been tarnished and spoiled.

She had never fallen for a man like she had Dave Parks, not even Ricky's father. Parks was different from the other men in her life. He wasn't verbally or physically abusive, and he was always striving to better himself, even though demons from his past haunted him.

She knew why Dave Parks had accused her son. Lewis Hayward had done a pristine job at making sure there could have been no other option. And Parks hadn't been the only one to fall for the trap. Everyone else who had seen the evidence had thought the same. She knew that. It wasn't his fault. He was, after all, only human. There was only so much one man could do.

She had seen Dave from time to time at the coroner's office, usually conferring with Tanaka on a case. But he had never seen her. Each time she had made sure to stay out of his eyesight, and she had never approached him, still not sure what to say or how to apologize. She felt she might have been wrong when she had rejected him from her life. But at the time, she could see no other option, a mother's love for her son coming above all else.

Regrettably, that hadn't paid off either. The Palisades Poisoner had attacked Jackie and her son in their own home, leaving a psychological rip through their own security. Since then she had completely redecorated the house, from top to bottom, giving it the look and feel of a new home. Though ever since that night, Ricky had visited her with less frequency, preferring the dorms of the nearby university he attended, only returning home during semester breaks. This past summer, the first one since being at college, he had filled his free time with summer courses and more hours at work. She had seen him even less than before. She wanted to blame Lewis Hayward for the distance between her and her son. Hell, even blame Dave Parks. She wanted to blame any and every one she could. Nevertheless, at the same time, that was life. He was in college to do what he was doing. Life moved on; children grew up and carried on lives of their own. This was the natural progression, and she knew she needed to blame no one but herself for not being able to grasp onto the notion that her "little boy" was becoming a man, taking care of his own in life.

Unfortunately, this only left more free time in her life. And no matter how many hours she worked, books she read, or TV shows she watched, there was a void that could only be filled with reflection and self-doubt. An emptiness that she could not fill, no matter how much she worked, what men she dated, or what friends tried to keep her time occupied. Something had changed within her, and she didn't like it or know how to fix it.

That was what had led her that morning to the gun range. It was time to prove after months of studying and practicing, that she was more than proficient with a weapon.

"You did it." Tanaka smiled. "I know it. How could you not have? You're only like the most smartest woman I know."

"Most smartest?"

Tanaka winked, her joke getting across to Jackie, only to make sure she was listening.

"I know it. You passed. Then you'll be a—what? Junior detective with the Los Angeles Police Department? I mean, why not? You already have the badge and the authority. Now you'll also have the gun... And maybe—oh, maybe, what if you get partnered with...*him?*" Tanaka was of course referring to Dave Parks.

Tanaka had known Parks longer than Jackie and had been an advocate of the romance between the two from the start. She liked Parks for Jackie. Jackie needed a good man in her life, and why not Dave Parks? A woman could do far worse looks-wise, and financially, well, having been raised by Newport socialites never hurt anyone's stature within the community (something Tanaka considered of utmost importance). Tanaka continued before Jackie could reply.

"Imagine it. The two of you working as partners. Taking down crime in the City of Angels. Oh, it would be so romantic. Like Mr. and Mrs. Smith. I could see you two being the Brad and Angie of the LAPD."

"Didn't they spend most of the movie trying to kill each other?" Jackie felt that said it all.

"Yeah, but that was work related. *Before* they realized how much they loved each other and decided to work as a team. I feel a theme building here."

"Well, I know who our first target would be if we ever did join forces." Jackie glared at Tanaka before looking at her watch. "Wait, what are you doing just getting here? I thought you started earlier than this?"

"Oh, please. I'm just getting back from catching my second wind," Tanaka said, holding up her Starbucks cup. "Been here since five-thirty. Already knocked out three of 'em. But that doesn't mean I don't have dozens more to attend to."

The elevator doors chimed open.

"Speaking of which..." Tanaka smiled as she turned and headed down the hallway while Jackie stepped onto the elevator and pressed the button to go up. "Later, girl."

Upon reaching her floor, Jackie walked down the hallway to the toxicology lab, which looked nothing like what television often portrayed. The floor was not filled with state-of-the-art technology and cool, slick counters and toys to play with, all clean and pristine, but rather was like any office in America, with nothing much to distinguish it from the rest of the world. Jackie shared her duties with two other members of the department, all three of whom had offices in the center of the floor; the rest of the rooms surrounding their quarters contained the various equipment and tools used to help with their cases. In one room there were various microscopes, while another she passed by contained a gas chromatograph and a mass spectrometer.

In her office, Jackie began to dig through the pile of paperwork—another thing most of the TV shows usually forgot to show—while waiting for her computer to warm up. She moved files around, signed her name to the various reports and numerous requests made of her, and then began inputting information from the various tests that she had run on the cases she was working on, a backlog that reached so far even she could not see where it began or would end.

She was deep in the middle of a case, determining the sobriety of an off-duty cop who had shot a man suspected of being on PCP while beating his girlfriend's face in to the point of fracturing her skull, when a knock on her door interrupted her train of thought. Jackie jumped, though ever so slightly, and looked up to find Ryan O'Connell standing in her doorway. Though not her direct supervisor, Ryan had managed to work it into both his and everyone else in the department's minds that he ran every person and thing around there. Jackie usually just blew him off. The higher up the food chain he got, especially at such a young age, the more Jackie was reassured that a few light slams of reality were needed every now and again. And she was only more than happy to oblige.

"What is it, Ryan? I'm busy," Jackie said, turning back to her computer. When O'Connell didn't move or speak, she stopped and turned back to him, removing her red-rimmed reading glasses to stare through him. "What?"

"You're being requested," O'Connell said, smiling his Cheshire cat-like grin. "Out in the field. Double homicide. Or murder/suicide. Not sure yet."

"And?"

Why couldn't he just spit it all out at once? Why did he have to drag every damn thing on and on?

"And they think it's a poisoning. They want your expert opinion."

"A double poisoning?" Jackie asked, leaning back in her chair. She breathed deeply and stared off into space, focusing on neither O'Connell nor the words coming out of his mouth.

"No idea. Just know that you've been requested, and I'm passing the notification along. They didn't give me the specifics. I'm assuming it's something about the condition of the bodies. Or else there's a big ol' bottle next to them labeled 'Poison.'"

"Oh, those clever killers. They just think they can get away with anything, don't they?" Jackie leaned forward in her chair and saved her report on the computer. "Where is it?"

"The hills somewhere. Up Crescent Heights, I think," O'Connell answered. "Not sure. Tanaka has the address. She's going too. M.E. 'n' all that stuff. I think it's the *Double Indemnity* house."

"The what?" Jackie asked as she stood up, grabbed her coat and purse, and started out of the office, O'Connell on her heels every step of the way. She had to admit, though the cologne he wore lately was somewhat powerful, it was at least an enticing smell, neither overpowering nor overly manly. If she didn't know any better, she'd say he had tried dozens of smells until he'd found one she didn't find that repulsive and now wore that one every day. Just to distract her.

"The *Double Indemnity* house. You know. The house where what's-her-name lived in the movie *Double Indemnity*."

"Barbara Stanwyck," Jackie corrected as she stopped at the elevator and pressed the button. Again. "And the house that was used in that movie is over in the Hollywood Hills area. Near Vine Street and the 101. Not where you're sending me. If I'm going up Crescent Heights?"

"Well, I don't know about that," O'Connell said. "But I'm pretty sure it's the same house. It looks like it at least."

Jackie turned and stared at Ryan O'Connell for a moment, taking in what he had said, not letting his brown and yellow eyes or the smattering of freckles across his recently tanned nose distract her.

"And how, exactly, do you know what the house where an allegedly poisoned body has been reported looks like?"

O'Connell paused for a moment.

"It's okay," Jackie said, saving him the embarrassment. "I get it. You were talking with your good buddies, the patrol-men. We seem to be having a lot of that around here lately."

Leaks were always a problem the department had to deal with, even, apparently, in the coroner's office. Interoffice communication, or the lack of it, had also always been a problem within the LAPD divisions. But it was the leaks going to people outside of the LAPD that had everyone on edge. And for good reason. The LAPD rarely came out looking good.

"You want to get caught with your hand in the cookie jar one of these days, O'Connell, then just keep doing what you're doing. You're good at it."

The doors closed on Jackie, leaving Ryan O'Connell with a red face.

TWO

"So apparently we're going to the *Double Indemnity* house," Jackie commented from her seat in the back of the LA coroner's van. Tanaka and her assistant, Robert, were about to pull away by the time Jackie made it to the parking garage, so riding together seemed the logical thing to do.

"Oh, God, did he tell you that too?" Tanaka laughed from the passenger seat while Robert took the wheel of the medical examiner's vehicle, driving away from downtown LA, up the 101 toward Hollywood. "He's so creepy."

Both women were playing on iPads as they tried to complete some unfinished work while away from their desks. Just because they were out of the office didn't mean it was time to play. Company time was work time. And one thing neither woman cared for was work time spilling over into personal time. When the day was over, the job was put on hold.

"He's not creepy," Jackie said with a smile. "He just tries too hard. Has to be that Mr. Perfect Man type of a guy. He's always so well kept and manicured and clean and in everyone's face about the rules and what's what."

"His face is too narrow," Tanaka commented. She looked up, staring out through the front windshield, deep in thought.

"What?" Jackie laughed. "Like that's the biggest fault in life. Having a face that's too narrow. He's still a good-looking guy. Overall. He's just anal."

"No," Tanaka disagreed, pulling her Gucci sunglasses back down and going back to her electronic device. "I like a guy with a more classical look to his face. Like our good boy Bobby, here."

Tanaka tapped Robert on the shoulder and he slightly jerked away, not out of embarrassment or fright, but out of pain. Jackie noticed the flinch.

"Oh, did I tell you," Tanaka said, looking back at Jackie with a devious smile. "Our good boy Bobby, here, went and got himself a tattoo this weekend. Didn't you now, Bobby?"

Tanaka's assistant simply shook his head from side to side and continued to focus on the freeway in front of him, trying his best to ignore his two companions. The traffic was light by LA rush-hour standards, but the lanes were still full, and the vehicles were beginning to slow. Luckily, they were heading away from the downtown area, so it wouldn't get much slower than their current forty-five miles an hour.

Robert had been Tanaka's assistant for two years now, working his way through medical school to one day become a coroner himself. Barely in his mid-twenties, the shock of Robert getting a tattoo came more from the fact that to everyone else he looked too much like a bookworm or nerd, with his thick, black-framed glasses (which he never knew only enhanced his appeal to the women who stared at and gossiped about him). That and his old-fashioned Catholic values that he had been raised with, along with the seven siblings who had all been crammed into a single-story house near Echo Park after his parents made the trek north from Ensenada.

"He did not," Jackie said, trying to keep the laughter reined in. "Where? Of what?"

"Well, I don't know what of," Tanaka admitted, rapping her nails on the screen of her iPad. "He won't confirm that just yet. Or where it is. But I think I have it narrowed down to either his right shoulder or chest area, because I could tell by the way he carried our equipment to the van. He's a wittle sore, now, isn't he?"

Robert blushed, easily embarrassed.

"Come on, what is the tattoo of?" Jackie asked as she tapped Robert's shoulder.

"No," Robert replied, focused on the road as he took the Hollywood Boulevard exit and headed west.

"Come on," Tanaka laughed. "You can tell us."

Robert looked into the rearview mirror and caught Jackie's eyes. At a red light, Jackie undid her seatbelt and leaned forward, as Robert turned and whispered something into her ear. Jackie put on a shocked look as she sat back down and the van started forward again.

"What?" Tanaka said, looking from Jackie to Robert and back again. "What did he tell you? Why don't I get to be included?"

"Oh, my," Jackie said somewhat jokingly as she moved her shirt collar back and forth as if to fan herself. "Girl, you got yourself a wild one there."

Jackie winked at Robert as he looked back at her through the mirror again. She held back a smile as Tanaka stared her down, the knowledge that Jackie knew something she didn't getting to her.

"The only reason you're starting to get hot under the collar is 'cause Robert and his tattoo have reminded you of another man with tattoos who gets you hot under the collar."

Tanaka had to be the one with the last word on the subject. Mentioning Dave Parks was just the way to do it. And end the topic.

"So about this house," Jackie said, getting their minds back on the task that would soon be at hand. "The one that is *not* the *Double Indemnity* house, despite what our esteemed Mr. O'Connell thinks. Do we know anything about it?"

"Other than the two dead bodies there?" Tanaka asked. "Not a thing."

"And speaking of men with tattoos," Jackie said, hating to bring up the subject. "Do we know why we've been requested?"

"Do you mean, is he working the case?" Tanaka asked, referring to Parks again. "No. He's not. This one belongs to Detective Wilkes."

Tanaka always said "Detective" before someone's name if she wanted to keep it professional, all forms of friendship out of the equation, and Detective Mark Wilkes was one of the last people on the LAPD force that anyone considered a friend. Though Tanaka had worked with Wilkes on numerous occasions, Jackie had only worked with him once before—on the famed Palisades Poisoner case. Though she had never personally butted heads with the man, she had not only heard the many sordid details about his professionalism, but she had also seen his questionable behavior at work due to his interactions with Dave Parks and his team.

"Well, great," Jackie sighed. If there was any one person on the force she cared to work with less than the man she had dated, it would have to be Wilkes.

"We reap what we sow," Tanaka said quietly, trying not to add to the mountain of guilt building on Jackie's shoulders.

"More like Karma's a bitch," Jackie snipped. "And if I ever run into her, I'm gonna kick her ass."

"Amen to that one," Tanaka said, facing the front again. "Amen."

THREE

"Took you fuckin' long enough." Detective Mark Wilkes stood at the top of the stairs leading up to the house containing the crime scene, hands on his semi-skeletal hips, looking like he was seconds away from throwing a fit. "You get lost or something?"

Having been promoted to the rank of detective early in his career, thanks to his sister who happened to be married to the mayor, Mark Wilkes had an arrogance about him like an entitled brat that the department simply had to put up with. It was only his dogged pursuit to always be right that helped him close as many cases as he did and allowed him the breathing room to be the jerk he failed to see himself as. Physically, he was thin yet strong; Wilkes paid attention to his physical health more for what it could get him in life than out of a true, conscious, health-driven decision, which was probably why he smoked like a chimney on fire, adding to the coarseness of his voice. He was often unshaven, while his curly brown hair was usually pulled in a slicked-back position, adding to the oily, snake-like appearance that he gave off.

"I swear, with you and Robert keeping secrets from me and working for this jerk all day, I'm gonna shank someone before sundown.

Just you watch," Tanaka muttered to Jackie as the two of them made it up the three dozen flights of stairs that zigzagged up the hill leading to the house that did indeed look like the one from *Double Indemnity*. The house was large, two stories tall, and white with green trim around the doors and windows, while the front door, garage, and several second-floor balconies were made out of a dark-stained wood. The roof had that southern California/Spanish look that adorned so many houses in the Los Angeles area, while the required palm trees poked their tops out from behind the house, adding to the atmosphere. The front yard, if it could be called that, was mostly a hillside with bushes, as well as other flora and fauna, covering the otherwise barren bark-covered yard, as if the house itself was nestled on the shrubbery.

"No. We decided to pull over and take in some of the tourist sites, check out some of the stars' homes," Jackie sniped at Wilkes as she plowed straight ahead, not stopping to acknowledge his presence.

Tanaka tried her hardest to hold the laughter in, while Wilkes stood there, mouth agape, trying to figure out how to reply. Truth of the matter was Jackie didn't work for the same people Wilkes did, so there was little he could do to her professionally. And despite the fact that both of them worked for the city, people weren't exactly lined up for her spot in the coroner's department.

"No, we didn't get lost. It just took a while to get here. You going to show us what you got?" Jackie stood half a dozen steps above Wilkes, her hands looking like she would have had them on her hips if she hadn't been holding two cases containing her equipment. "Today." Jackie held up both of her cases, her eyes glaring through her dark amber sunglasses at the detective.

"Yes, ma'am," Wilkes said sardonically with a smile as he marched up the steps.

Though he had never said anything to her directly, and no actions had ever been made, it was obvious to most who spent more than a few minutes around the two that Wilkes lusted after her and was probably biding his time until he could or would make a move. The fact that she used to be with Detective Parks was the only thing that had held him off so far, and even that respect for a fellow officer was only going to last so long. If Wilkes didn't see fit to hold off sleeping with women besides the one he was married to, then there was little professionally to keep the man on the straight and narrow.

The threesome made it to the oversized, wooden front door, where Wilkes rolled his eyes at the officer standing guard who took Jackie and Tanaka's identification. The guard checked them in on his sheet before nodding over to two chairs where boxes of latex gloves and booties waited to be adorned by anyone entering the crime scene.

As Jackie assembled her coverings, she glanced around at her immediate surroundings. The front foyer was large and spacious, an open space with a stairwell that led to the second floor on the opposite side of the mustard yellow and dull brown room. The neighboring room appeared to be a living room of some sort, with books covering the wall from floor to ceiling. The footsteps of people walking around on the second floor echoed throughout the house, the sounds of boards creaking helping to give away the age of the house.

"What do we have here?" Jackie asked.

"Huh?"

"The victims."

"Oh, uh, Mary Delancy," Wilkes began. "Sound familiar?"

"No," Jackie said, putting on purple latex gloves as she looked to Tanaka who shook her head. "Should she?"

"Movie star," Wilkes explained. "From back in the day. Before your—*our*—time. Stuff in the sixties and seventies. B-movies mostly. Few TV movies and guest appearances and whatnot in the eighties. Then she disappeared. Moved here with the younger of her two sons. Some sick-ass shit if you ask me. Grown man living with his mother. That's some Norman Bates shit goin' on around here. Anyway, she hasn't been seen or heard from since. And barely by any of her neighbors either. Apparently, only the son who lives—*lived*—here went out. Him and the servants."

"So, she's a shut-in," Tanaka said, putting on her own latex gloves.

"I'm surprised there's not a lineup of news vans down the street," Jackie said, genuinely puzzled.

"Like I said, she hasn't acted in twenty-something years. Name isn't familiar. You two proved that. No one remembers her. But I'm sure once word of this gets out she will be. And not for her IMDB credits, either."

"Who called it in?"

"Neighbor. Claimed she hadn't seen or heard any evidence of anyone around for several days now, and she knows that the Delancys never vacationed and that her son lived here with her too, so she figured someone should have been making some sort of evidence of people living here. She came over to investigate, claims she has a key for 'emergencies' as she put it, and snooped around until she found the bodies."

There was a loud squawk from a neighboring room, and the two women almost jumped at the noise.

"What the hell is that?" Tanaka asked, controlling her breathing.

"Damn, flipping birds," Wilkes answered. "She's got several in the other room. Some white things that keep squawking and talking 'n' shit. Can't shut them up. May have to shoot them."

"How old are the victims?" Jackie asked, keeping them moving along.

"Sixty-seven and thirty-seven."

"And we're sure this isn't just a natural causes death?"

"Trust me. This is the furthest thing from a natural death. But you take a look at the bodies and tell me what you think. Plus, the place was trashed. I think someone was looking for something."

Jackie looked around again, waiting for Tanaka to finish. She noticed no personal photographs adorning any of the nearby walls. No family vacations, no evidence to show who might have even lived there. The only things lining the walls were framed movie posters from yesteryear, the victim's personal films, as her face and name adorned each one in varying degrees of age and size depending on when in her career each one was made.

"This place was searched?" Jackie asked. "Looks pretty clean to me."

"In there," Parks said, pointing to a neighboring room. Jackie walked over and peered in as Wilkes continued to explain: "It's the lady's office. I think. Papers thrown everywhere. Look like they're from her memoirs or something. I think that's what she was working on before she was killed."

Jackie turned from the room and eyed the front foyer once again.

"Those look new?" She pointed to an antique cabinet near the foot of the stairs on top of which was a photograph of two little boys that appeared to be at least thirty years old, a dish with several keys in it, and—the object she was referring too—a short vase containing several blue flowers.

"How can you tell?" Wilkes asked, not caring. "Other than they're not wilted."

"That's a Phalaenopsis orchid. They're rare. They come from the flower shop blue like that. I can tell it's new because when the plant re-blooms it isn't blue. It's white. They're dyed that color at the flower shops."

"Well, thank you, teacher. So what? Broad liked flowers. Or had a boyfriend or a fan or whatever. Or maybe the son put them there. Who cares?"

Jackie stared at the flowers, not sure why, only knowing they called to her for some reason. There was something about them. They meant something. Their rarity. They almost seemed out of place sitting there at the foot of the stairs. Somehow more elegant than the rest of the house.

Then again, thought Jackie, *maybe that's what Mary Delancy liked about them. Their elegance.*

"Where are we going?" Jackie asked, knowing she needed to keep them moving or else suffer the wrath of Wilkes.

"Master bedroom," Wilkes said, looking up the stairs. "Up them. Down the hall. Last door straight off the hallway."

Wilkes motioned with his head and led the two women up the stairs, almost hopping up them with glee as he guided them to the crime scene.

Jackie had to admit there was something familiar about the crime scene displayed before her, almost as if she had seen it—or one *like* it—before.

"The initial CIs seem to think that this is a simple case of tetanus poisoning," Wilkes explained from behind Isley. "But there was something about this one that made me think about calling you. Not sure what it is, or why, but I did. Maybe you'll prove me wrong, it simply is tetanus, and we can all go home. Hey, you know me. I would love nothing more than for this to be some sick, twisted mother-son lovey suicide-shit and we can all call it a day. Another closed case and my numbers are looking better by the hour. Know what I mean?"

"You think this was tetanus?" Jackie asked, not taking her eyes off the scene before her.

"No," Wilkes huffed. "Which is why I called you. I don't know why...but something's off about this one. Something...Anyway, so I called you."

"This isn't tetanus," Jackie said, staring at the woman lying on the bed before her. Mary Delancy had a look of sheer terror permanently plastered across her face, her eyes bulging and her mouth wide open in a grimace. Rigor mortis had already settled in. The victim's veins were a brilliant blue that bulged out against the off-yellow color of her skin, almost as if they were trying to break free. Her back arched, her head almost reaching around to her feet. The bed was a mess, the signs of the victim thrashing around in it wildly apparent with the sheets tangled amongst their bodies. The son was the same. Same expression. Same color to his skin. Same physical distortion. Though the two victims' legs wrapped around each other, only the mother was still on the bed. The son was half lying over the side of the bed, his head arched back around the bedpost toward their feet.

Jackie turned from the bodies to a nearby nightstand table where two glasses rested, mostly empty. She picked up a glass and sniffed it, jerking her head back as she sat it back down.

"Have these glasses collected and tested," Jackie ordered, not sure who would do her bidding and not really caring. Someone would see to it that her orders were followed. Usually, the initial team of Cis would have already cleared out the crime scene but with the introduction of a poisonous agent to the crime scene, various items that they deemed connected with said toxin were usually left behind for Jackie to evaluate.

"And what are they testing for, exactly?" Wilkes asked, eager to know the answer but not appearing upset at being held at bay.

"Strychnine," Jackie said softly.

"No shit? They drank it? Both of them?"

"I believe so," Jackie answered.

"Suicide?" Wilkes asked, as he kept his distance from the crime scene, hovering near the doorway.

"I've really no way to know that," Jackie said. "That's your area. This is your case. Your investigation work to carry out. I would think it would be impossible for them not to know what they were drinking, at least not that much, and not stop."

"Is it possible they accidentally drank too much, and it got to them so fast that they couldn't call for help?"

On the nightstand next to the bed, just past the glass, sat a telephone.

"Amy, when you do the autopsies, check for their last meals. See how long it had been since they had last eaten. The reaction time to strychnine is quite quick, but a little slower on a fuller stomach."

Jackie reached into her kit and took out two syringes and several vials. She began swabbing the bodies for tissue, skin samples, DNA, and blood samples. She was going to have to have every inch of both bodies inspected. She pulled a hair out of each body when Wilkes finally broke the silence.

"How long would you say they've been dead?" Wilkes cared less which woman could give him an answer.

Tanaka examined the mother's body and answered without looking up. "Rigor. Room temp. Couple of days, give or take."

"Well, am I giving or taking?" Wilkes shot back.

"I'd say no less than early last night and no longer than Friday night. That's the best I can give you right away. When I get something more concrete, I'll let you know."

"So now what?" Wilkes asked, though everyone knew he knew better than to do so.

Jackie stood silently, continuing to stare at the bodies, not wanting to look up at Wilkes for fear of the glare she would give him. Tanaka remained on the opposite side of the bed, looking up at Jackie while her face stayed pointed down toward the crime scene.

They always did this. Whenever there was a contaminant introduced at a crime scene, they acted as if a plague had been unleashed and that they were seconds away from catching it. Anthrax and Ebola hadn't helped her place in society either. They all stepped back as if she herself was also contagious. For most of them, for the first time in their lives even, they waited until the woman told them what to do next. Wilkes knew better. He was a pro. No matter that he was a professional pain in the ass, he was seasoned enough to know what to do next. He didn't need to ask. He shouldn't have, either. He was almost being patronizing, and both women knew it.

"Well, assuming the CS unit has gone over the scene and that you and your...um, flying solo today, are we?"

"Partner's in court today. I wasn't supposed to be up next, but they thought it was a simple suicide and I said I could handle it on my own."

"Of course you did. Well, assuming you have done your duty, there isn't much more to do here. Amy will do her job, we'll wait for test results to come back in a few days, and that's it."

"That's it?" Wilkes all but gaped at her.

That's it? What did he want from her? For her to solve this whole thing for him? He knew what to do. This wasn't his first rodeo.

"Well, if I was lead detective, and this was my case? I'd go have a chat with that nosy neighbor."

FOUR

The neighbor's name was Rosemary (pronounced Rose-Marie *not* Rose-Mary, as she had been adamant about when giving the detectives her name) Gibson, and she had been a neighbor of the Delancys for over thirty years now. She was in her early sixties, with grayish-blonde hair that had been recently dyed, so as to not be too obvious. She was overweight, carrying it mostly in her hips, though she had a pleasant way about her, with rosy cheeks and beaming eyes. It wasn't until she showed her teeth that one saw where the lack of personal hygiene was evident.

Jackie didn't know that Wilkes couldn't stand the woman's unsightly teeth any more than he could her rosy cheeks or upbeat demeanor. He hated witnesses. To him, it was one of the worst parts of the job. Having to interact with other people. Innocent people. He preferred the scum. The guilty. He knew how to relate to them. He knew how to rile them up and get the truth out of them. The good—the innocent—well, they were just a waste of time. He didn't know how to manipulate them. So to him, they were worthless.

"She had moved into the house in, what...? Seventy-nine? Eighty? Maybe even as late as eighty-one," Rosemary continued from her front door where she kept the two detectives, failing to see the need to invite them into her house. "But no later than that. I remember that she had had both of her children when they moved in. As well as her husband, of course. The little one, her youngest son I mean, the little one was only a year or two old. I remember she used to be real friendly. Used to talk for hours about her movies. And by her movies, I mean the movies she had been in. Not that she had ever, herself, made any movies. Director-wise I mean. My husband used to work in the business. So I know what I'm talking about when I say things like that. Not that I gossip. I'm not one of *them*."

Rosemary glanced past Wilkes and Jackie, up at the Delancy house, as if it was haunted, now simply a piece of property set there to lower the quality of the neighborhood. Something bad had happened there. Something even, daresay, trashy. People would talk. A former starlet had been found in her bed, with her son, both of them dead. Whatever could have happened? Had they been posed? Or murdered while already in those positions?

"They were real friendly?" Jackie nudged.

Jackie could tell Wilkes's temper was already short, and this woman had been babbling about nonsense for close to twenty minutes, the entire conversation leading nowhere. But she was the only neighbor to come forward with any sort of information, and everyone else's doors they had knocked on either weren't home, didn't know the victim, didn't care about what had happened, or had no comment.

"At first, yes," Rosemary continued, drawing out the 'e' in yes. "Always showing off her two little boys. Her and her husband. He was a looker. One of those foreign-looking types. Maybe Greek or Roman. The kind with money. You know what I mean? Not that I gossip. Lots of hair. And a nose. But always that nice golden tan. But they were friendly. Whenever we had get-togethers around the neighborhood, they were always there. Her and her family. Well, her and the children at least. Her husband was always off traveling. For work, I suppose. I believe that's what she told me. Back then at least. Before he died. Not that she was ever lonely, I suppose. She always had people over at her place. Friends mostly, I mean. Or I suppose. Not really sure. But usually, several at a time. Always throwing a party of some sort. She loved to throw dinner parties. Heaven only knows where the children were during all this. Some of those people—well, not that I gossip, I'm not one of those types, but some of them—they didn't exactly seem like the right type of a crowd for children. If you know what I mean."

Rosemary stopped, lost in the past. Jackie wasn't sure she knew what Rosemary meant, but felt it was her job to nudge the woman along.

Let them do the talking. Dave had always said that. *People love to talk. Love to gossip. Even when they're not helping, they like to think they are. You never know when one thing will lead to another.*

"Until...?"

"Until? Oh, until her husband died. Then everything changed." Rosemary nodded as she said this, as if even though they may not believe her, it was the gospel truth. "Once he passed away, God bless his soul, she just changed. We never saw them anymore. I mean other than through the windows of her house. They never left. They stayed in. Shut-ins they were called, I believe. Even the people who came for her little dinner parties stopped coming around. I noticed that too. She never left the house. Never had to. She always had people out running her errands for her. The groceries. New clothes for the children. Only time I ever saw them leave was on the bus to school."

Rosemary stopped as she stared over Jackie's shoulders at the

Delancy home.

"She planted all those flowers herself, you know? I mean at first. Not now. Well, not now that she's dead—but I meant, before she died. Not lately. When she first moved in, she planted all the flowers all around the yard herself. Of course back then there was only a white picket fence around the yard. I think that was to keep the boys from running out into the street. Not that we ever get cars up here. Mostly just people who lived up here coming home from work at night. But still the same, she had that little wooden fence. It wasn't until later that she changed it to the gothic iron thing she's got now. And for good reason. She's had a few lookie-loos over the years. I mean, back then people respected privacy better. Sure, people would come around, point at the house where *she* lived. But then they'd be on their way. Nowadays it's all about whose privacy they can invade and whose property they can destroy. No sense of self-respect."

Rosemary adjusted the barely visible glasses on the end of her pointed nose and continued without so much as a breath, as if the simple act of talking about her neighbor was enough to keep her going on in life. Rosemary Gibson. Mary Delancy's own personal biographer.

"Some...some are even worse." Rosemary tilted her head in a way that made Jackie think she should have known what the woman meant.

Wilkes stood off on the side of the porch, just out of Rosemary's line of sight, smoking a cigarette. He glared at the woman, and even when Jackie caught him, he did not care, simply sneering, hoping she would move the woman along already. This was pointless. He didn't want to stand around the neighborhood BBQ spreading gossip. He had a killer to catch.

"What do you mean? The paparazzi?" Jackie asked.

"The papa-wha? No. You know what I mean..." Rosemary looked around, as if being spied on and pulled in closer to Jackie. "The stalkers."

"Mary Delancy had stalkers?"

"Now mind you, Bud and I—that's my husband, Bud. Mind you, we have never actually seen any. But we've read about such stories in the papers. All documented there. On the Internet. That Wikipedia and whatnot. Some stuff even I never knew. And some of it, I'll tell you, some of it I call BS on. You know what I mean? I mean I'm her neighbor, and if I didn't know it, then it just isn't possible. Well, anyway, even though Mary wasn't one for public appearances, every now and again she'd wander out into the yard, pick a few flowers, and even strike up a word or two before disappearing again. And let me tell you, even though I'm not one for gossip, she'd said so. Stalkers. She had 'em. And why not? I mean she was a looker. Though not so much anymore. She'd put on the weight lately. But I mean the stalkers. She had the stalkers, even up until recently."

"Really?"

"Yes, ma'am. The police were even called out one night not so long ago."

"When was this?"

"Oh...let's see now. About a year ago. Last summer some time. Someone broke into their house. The son caught him. Or her. Or whoever it was. I don't remember. But someone broke in through the basement window. Which I wouldn't expect, because there's always someone home. But apparently they were all upstairs or something. Guy was down in the basement for almost two days before they noticed anything." Rosemary leaned in closer to Jackie, eyeing Wilkes and deciding he didn't need to be a part of the conversation any more. "Apparently, he finally had the gumption to sneak up the stairs and into the main house. Wandered around most of the first floor before the son came down and scared the guy. So the police were called and they came out."

"And?" Jackie asked, absorbed in the story. "What happened next?"

FIVE

66 I know what that woman just told you, but I'm telling you nothing happened next because there never was an intruder," Wilkes said in a tone that neither confirmed nor denied he believed what he said.

"What do you mean?" Jackie asked. Had she been in a different mood, she just might have smacked him.

"Just that. I've seen the files," Wilkes said as he drove them back downtown.

Jackie had told Tanaka to simply head back to the coroner's office when she and Robert had wrapped up their duties at the crime scene. She had optioned to stay behind and follow Wilkes around in hopes of learning something new, as she felt there was always room to learn something new. Now she felt she could have learned more by watching *Rizzoli & Isles* or *Murder, She Wrote*.

"They're in the back seat. In that white box. The police were called out, but when they got there and went over the place, they said there was no evidence that anyone had broken into the house. Let alone lived in the basement for several days. Yeah, that's right. I know what that nosy neighbor told you. I've read the reports. Gotta be the same thing, because this crazy Delancy broad told everyone the same story. But I'm telling you: they didn't find any proof of anything. They left the house swearing she made it up. And if you pull the history on her, you'll see it wasn't the first time. She had a habit of it. Calling in fake reports of stalkers. She was just a lonely old has-been who missed the limelight. So she did what she had to do to stay newsworthy. It happens. She's not the first to make shit up. And she won't be the last."

"How do you already have old case files on Mary Dela—" Jackie stopped talking as it hit her. "You took the time to do a search on the woman and pull her case files before you came out to the crime scene? You knew who she was."

"Sure I did. And yes I did. So what? Had to let the CIs finish their job before I could even get into the crime scene and do my part."

"But how do you know she made them all up? I mean, yeah, sure she could have made it up in the past. So what? Obviously this time it was real. I mean, there are two dead bodies in that house. Someone had to be keeping an eye on her."

"But who? And why now? Who gives a rat's ass about some old out-of-work actress? Plenty of hotties worth committing crimes over. And I'm telling you, she wasn't one of 'em."

Jackie mentally rolled her eyes to herself at Wilkes's comment. Of course he would say something like that. Because only attractive people were ever killed or worth killing. Young, fit, healthy people. At least that was how it was portrayed in the movies. So that must make it true. And of course Wilkes would believe something like that.

"Look," Wilkes continued. "We technically don't even know it was a homicide. Still could have been a murder/suicide. Right? Until we get Tanaka's report back. Or any other evidence that says to the contrary—"

THE BLUE CONDITION | 35

"I'm telling you—"

"And you were made a detective overnight without my knowing?"

Jackie remained quiet. There was no point in getting suckered into his mind games. She knew better. This is who he was.

"I'm telling you not from my experience as a detective but from my experience as a forensic toxicologist that those two people in that room back there were poisoned. Intentionally. Against their will. Not by choice."

"You feel like stopping and grabbing a bite to eat?" This question came out of nowhere and made Jackie want to punch Wilkes. In the arm. In the face. Somewhere. Anywhere. No, she didn't want food. Least of all with him.

"No," she answered in a controlled tone. "I don't want to stop and have a bite to eat somewhere. I want to get back. I have work to do. I need to examine the bodies with Amy. I need to run tests on the poison—"

"I thought you said it was strychnine? Now you're changing your results on me?" She could tell her putting him off miffed him. He probably felt teased by her, though how that could possibly be was beyond her realm of imagination.

"I said I believed it was strychnine, but in case you ever want this case to end up in court with a conviction, you might want an official reading on that," Jackie continued. "Besides, even though the symptoms were common of a poisoning by strychnine, there were still some differences. Some changes. I think it's possible the poison might have been tampered with. I just want to check and see for myself."

"Well, how long do you think it will take for you to get me your reports?"

"A few days."

"What? What the hell for? You sending them out in Morse code?"

"Look." Jackie breathed deeply.

"I bet if Parks was working this case you'd have a report typed out and on his desk before we even got back to the station."

Jackie kept her breathing steadily. *Keep it in control,* girl. Jackie turned from Wilkes and stared out the window at the passing cars on the freeway. They were passing Echo Park, nearing downtown.

"I know that this was a poisoning. And yes, that does usually put a slight rush on things. Especially after Lewis Hayward. But there are still priorities. And while poison is high up on that list, it's not up there alone. And this case is not exactly life-threatening to the general public. So far as we know. Lewis Hayward"—Jackie remembered that Parks had refused to call Lewis Hayward by his moniker, thereby giving him more power—"was threatening multiple people, without us knowing who or when. The whole city was at risk. We needed to protect the public, and with the mayor and everyone else breathing down our necks, more money was thrown at the problem and results were obtained faster. That's all. We have a double homicide of a has-been actress. There's no evidence of further contagion or poisonings, so you'll have your damn report when I get it to you. Understand?"

They drove the rest of the way in silence. Wilkes dropped her back off at the coroner's station and followed her in to see if Tanaka had any results for him yet. When she informed him that it would be another day or two before she even got to his autopsy, he stormed off, once again rejected and feeling sour about it.

The two women were in Jackie's office, giggling over their defeat of the great and horrific Wilkes-monster, when Ryan O'Connell stopped by to see what all the commotion was.

"Nothing, Ryan. Just women being women," Tanaka said with a droll infliction, as she turned back to Jackie and opened a file to make herself appear too busy for idle chitchat.

"You both have reports that need to be on my desk, ASAP, right?" Ryan asked, guarding the doorway like a pit bull.

"We're both well aware of what our jobs and duties are," Jackie replied. "Come on, Ryan. We've been out with Wilkes all day. We just needed a minute or two to cool off. You'll have your reports. I promise. Okay?"

She sat there, staring intently at him, knowing that she was breaking him down, second by second. He never wanted to appear the bad guy to her, and if she asked for something he always delivered. No matter how impossible or difficult. The problem was eventually, one of these days, he would expect something in return.

"I was about to head out and grab a bite to eat. Either of you care to join...or need something?"

"I'm all good," Tanaka said, giving Jackie a look that could only mean one thing.

It was her turn to "pay the bill."

"What exactly did you have in mind?" Jackie replied with a smile.

SIX

There was something, just something, about the crime scene that was, well, just *off*. She wasn't sure what. Or why. Nevertheless, there was still something—it all seemed so...staged.

Posed.

She wished she had had someone to talk to about this. Unfortunately, the lead detective on the case was Wilkes. And though she was positive he wouldn't want to hear anything about this case from her, she had a feeling he would be more than willing to meet up with her privately to "discuss" it if she really wanted.

What she really wanted—who she really wanted to talk about the case with—was David Parks, even if she wasn't willing to admit that to anyone. Discussing the case with Parks would have been good for her. He would have pushed her. Challenged her. But also supported her theories. He was good for that. And now that she found herself out in the field, she realized only how much she had been missing him lately. She had tried to move on. Had done so, really. Still...he would always be a part of her life.

This case wasn't helping. Too many similarities between this case and the Palisades Poisoner victims. It made her wonder...

Jackie finished her dinner with Ryan, her mind constantly wandering back to the Delancy murders being the only thing that got her through the ordeal. After they made their way back to the office, Jackie discovered Amy had called it a day already, so she wandered the hallways to her office, not yet ready to go home. Forty minutes later, feeling like the last person left on earth as she sat in the otherwise vacant building, Jackie decided to revisit the scene of the crime at night to get a feel for the surroundings as the killer would have seen them. Parks would have done just that, even if Wilkes had thought it foolish and a waste of time.

Jackie swung her flashlight around, the shadows dancing around on the walls and ceilings as she made her way through the main foyer. There, on the desk by the bottom of the stairs, still stood the blue orchid. Even if Wilkes thought it was nothing, something about that flower irked her. It should not have been there. It was too rare. Too exotic. From what she had learned about Mary Delancy and her son that day, she doubted that either one of them would have had that flower in the house.

Could it be? Could the killer have brought it? Like a calling card of some sorts?

"Get a grip on yourself, woman," Jackie scolded herself. This was not a movie or book. There weren't psycho-serial killers just killing people off and leaving calling cards.

Jackie pushed past the flowers and made her way through the ground-floor rooms, once again taking in each room, scanning for any sort of hints or clues. And once again, she came up empty-handed. Thirty minutes later, she made her way up the stairs, checking every room along the landing as she made her way to the back bedroom.

She flipped on the light switch to the room and took it all in.

There it was. The scene of the crime.

"Okay, girl, just breathe," Jackie said to herself. She had to admit that being at the scene of a double homicide, late at night, all alone, was spooky. "You can do this. You know what to do. Ignore what's been told to you. Just take the scene in. Top to bottom. And back again. What do you see?"

And? Parks's voice added.

"And what *don't* you see?"

Jackie looked around and then spent the next hour going over every inch of the room. Stepping around blood droplets, maneuvering without touching where everything lay, avoiding the fingerprint dust. When she finished, she felt no closer to discovering why the crime scene still felt off to her.

Maybe it was the bodies and not the crime scene? Maybe she would have to go visit Amy about what bothered her. There were always clues left on the bodies. That was how so many perpetrators were caught.

She started for the door when she stopped. No. There was something else. What had Parks told her? There was as much to be learned about the killer not only from *who* the victim was but *why* they were chosen. And *how* they were killed. And *where. Everything* led back to the killer.

God, she wished she could talk to him right now.

Jackie took out her-cell phone and considered dialing him. He could help her. And he might even be willing to do it.

No, dammit. Not this time. Not now. She could do this. She had the smarts for it. It was nothing against Parks. She needed to do this for herself. To prove that she could do this.

Jackie sat on the edge of the bed and looked around the room, hoping for something to jump out at her. She glanced over at the two nightstands and noticed that everything on the one on her side was knocked over. As if the nightstand had been moved, perhaps? But why? So what? That's not proof of a murder. Or that something in the room was even off. She looked below the nightstand and noticed markings on the floor. Had it been moved? Intentionally?

She opened each drawer in the stand and found a Holy Bible, a Sudoku and crossword-puzzle book, several pencils and pens, and a personal telephone book. The second drawer down contained a Yellow Pages directory and nothing more. She took everything out and then took the drawers out and inspected every inch of the nightstand.

Nothing. There was nothing. But it had been moved. And recently. But why? She moved closer to the ground for a better inspection, when she noticed that the bed too had been moved, leaving behind scrapings on the wooden floor.

Had the bed been moved? Or was that simply a result from the thrashing the victims had gone through as a result of their poisonings?

It's also about what isn't there.

What if—?

Jackie paused, breathed deeply and then dropped to the floor. She pulled back the covers and looked under the bed, almost expecting to find the killer still waiting for her. Florescent eyes glaring out at her from the darkness, large and hungry for prey. But there was nothing. It was empty. No signs of anything.

But what about...Jackie looked up at the headboard to the bed. What if?

Jackie moved the nightstand over to the side. She then grabbed hold of the bed and tried her best to move it. The bed was heavy. An old king-sized bed with a full metal frame. If the killer had intentionally moved the bed, why?

"If he had moved it," Jackie huffed as she tried to pull the bed to the side. Once she had it moved over three feet where she saw the scrapings were no more, she stopped. This must be as far as the killer moved the bed. But so what?

She looked up at the bare wall, the now exposed area behind the headboard, and saw nothing. No hidden messages. No calling cards. No 1-800-CALL-ME-IM-YOUR-KILLER message. Nothing. What had she been expecting? Really?

You have more senses than just sight.

Jackie flinched at the words. They were Parks's words again. So audible in her mind, it was as if he were there, standing right next to her. But he had been right. She walked over to the wall, put her hands up against it, and rubbed them along. Nothing there, either. It was a singular, painted-over wall. Nothing appearing to have been altered or changed.

She—could she? She leaned in closer to the wall and took a sniff. This was stupid. Not even Parks would have done thi—and that was when she smelled it. There it was. She didn't know what it was or what it meant, but she knew this was it. It was faint. Hardly noticeable. A slight, floral smell. As if flowers had been rubbed up against the wall.

But why? And how could she see what exactly had been rubbed up against it?

What if—but that was just silly. She laughed at herself. Her ideas.

She left the room and walked down the stairs and out of the house, back to her car. She opened the trunk and dug through her bags until she found her black light. She locked up her car and stopped, looking up and down the street, feeling as if someone were watching her. She pulled her hair back out of her face and walked back up the steps to find the front door was now open, when she had made a point of closing it behind her. She stepped into the house and stopped, listening to her surroundings before deciding that she was still all alone.

She went back upstairs and stood there, in the doorway, exhaling deeply as she considered this. This might be stupid, but who would know? No one else was around. Just turn off the lights, see that there was nothing to see, and leave. She closed her eyes, took a deep breath, and then flipped off the switch. She remained motionless for what felt like a minute or two before she slowly opened her eyes. Even with the shades pulled shut, some light still seeped into the room from the streetlights outside. She took a few steps toward the wall and then held up the black light and turned it on.

Jackie Isley almost jumped back at the sight revealed before her. She had been right. This was big. Bigger than even she had first thought. Probably bigger than she could even understand.

It looked like that phone call to Parks she had kept putting off was finally going to be made. This killer had a calling card after all.

One she wished she could unsee.

One she knew would wreak havoc on the city like it hadn't seen in over a year.

This killer—who had taken the lives of two innocents less than twenty-four hours earlier—had a message. And Jackie Isley was the first to see that this was just the beginning.

TUESDAY

SEVEN

Detective David Parks knew who was on the other end of his ringing cellphone despite the fact that the number had come up as Unknown. Lately only one person dialing him was coming up Unknown, and he just wished the caller would take the next step and speak to him instead of constantly hanging up.

"Parks," Parks answered as he looked around the station at the hustle and bustle of the other detectives, rushing around as they went about their daily activities. There was no reply from the other end, not even the sound of breathing, which Parks could make out every now and again. This was the fifth call he had received in the last two weeks, and he had finally figured it out. Had even spoken to the boy's mother about it once, not angry about the calls, just wishing the boy would actually speak to him after making all the effort to reach him.

"Joshua?" Parks asked calmly into his cell. "Joshua, you know you can talk to me. If you want. I'm here. If you—"

The line went dead before he could get another word out. Hell. At least it was more than he had been able to say the other times. It had taken three calls before he had identified the boy, and last time when he said his name the child immediately hung up.

Joshua Levinson was the seven year-old son of Parks's former partner, Aaron Levinson, who had died on the job just one year before. It had actually already been a few weeks over a year, and Parks realized that was just around when the calls had begun. He wasn't entirely sure why the kid was reaching out to him, though he was familiar with the boy, as he had seen him around his partner's house from time to time for family dinners and when he had joined his partner at Joshua's Little League games.

The year before had been a rough one for the Levinson family. First Aaron had been killed by Peter Kozlov, a notorious child serial killer, but then shortly after Parks had arrested the man for his crimes, it had been uncovered that Aaron had been in the process of planting evidence to make sure the killer not only got locked up but remained so for the rest of his life. Though a member of the LAPD had been caught manufacturing evidence, with children being Kozlov's primary targets, people weren't sure whether to praise Aaron's deeds or condemn him. The department, on the other hand, did not see the situation as one to glorify. Especially when Kozlov's lawyers began to come after both the department and Parks for mishandling the case and filed corruption charges in the hopes of getting their client free.

As the court was throwing out most of the evidence built against Peter Kozlov, Parks had reached out to Kozlov's estranged wife, Natalie, who had been horrified to learn of her husband's activities.

Fearing what she might reveal, despite knowing nothing legally beneficial, Peter Kozlov had reached out to his brother Victor and had his wife silenced.

Permanently.

While the case against Peter Kozlov murdering children with razor blades was tainted by the devious Aaron Levinson's manipulations of the truth, the facts surrounding Natalie Kozlov's death were not. And both Peter and Victor Kozlov had thus been subjected to an arduous, two-month trial, which had finally ended just five months before and had resulted in both brothers having a new permanent residence up north in the state's illustrious prison of San Quentin.

In the middle of the all the chaos that ensued during the Kozlov trial, Aaron Levinson's activities had been permanently decided upon by the department, resulting in a denial of spousal benefits to his bereaved wife, Susan, and six-year-old son, not to mention the newborn Susan had delivered just two months after her husband's death. Tired of the looks and whispers, Susan had packed up her family and moved back to Arizona to be with her parents, who could help raise the children.

Dave Parks had been there for his partner throughout their five-year partnership, and he had stood by Aaron's family after his death, doing all he could that was physically, emotionally, and financially possible. And Susan had been more than thankful for all that he had offered to her family. They had stayed in touch after the move, with the occasional phone call here and there, but life was life and it moved on. It had been four months since Dave had spoken to Susan when he started getting the phone calls from Joshua.

After figuring out who was calling, Dave had called Susan, and the two had spoken for over an hour, both catching up on life and deciding what was going on in the seven-year-old's head. The best the two had been able to come up with, along with the help of the department shrink Doctor Black, was that the boy was looking for both a connection to someone who had known his father before his death (most likely with the anniversary of the man's death triggering this need) as well as some sort of a father figure, which Susan had assured Dave was not currently in the boy's life.

While Dave wished the boy would reach out and talk with him, both adults had decided that the child would finally do so when he felt comfortable enough. Baby steps. Dave figured he'd give the kid a few more rings before maybe he'd Skype with Susan and, sometime during the conversation, work a way to get the kid on the line. Maybe a face-to-face would be easier than just a voice.

"Parks!" barked a voice from behind the detective.

"Sir!" Parks looked up to find Chief Jane Hardwick hovering over him.

Jane Hardwick had begun with the LAPD right around the same time as Parks, and so the two had formed a mutual admiration for one another and the careers each of them had carved out with the force. Though Hardwick hadn't outwardly favored Parks over any of her other detectives on the force, with Hardwick being twenty years Parks's senior, there was a definite mother/son vibe to the relationship between the two, and there had been a time or two when she might have stuck her neck out an inch or two more than she would have for anyone else who worked beneath her. A few of those times, it had almost cost her the job or positions she had aspired to and worked so hard to get. Which was why, four months prior, Parks had been removed from Homicide Special Section, and Hardwick's direct supervision, and now reported to Robbery Homicide.

Parks felt it was simply politics as usual within the LAPD and that within a year he could very well be reporting to someone entirely new.

"What are you two working on?"

"Just wrapping up the Bell homicide," Parks said as he held up a folder. He wasn't sure why Hardwick cared what he was working on or why she was even asking, as she ran a different division than the one he was a part of.

"Anything else?" Hardwick pushed on.

"We've a few more open cases. Always do. Why? What's up?"

"Got you—oh, hello," Rachel Moore nodded to Hardwick as she walked up to her desk and set a coffee down on the edge of Parks's desk.

Dave and Rachel had been reassigned as partners after the dissolution of Parks's team four months before, of which Rachel had been a member of. After the other members of the team had been reassigned to their various positions within the department, only Parks and Moore had been left standing within the detective's division, and rather than reassign two other detectives new partners, the higher-ups had simply decided to keep the two as a duo.

Parks and Rachel's desks faced one another, just one of a dozen sets on the floor of the Robbery Homicide division of the LAPD in glorious, downtown Los Angeles. The building had been renovated a few years previous, and while it had started pristine and inviting, it had begun to revert to the classic, claustrophobic, old-fashioned detectives' squad feel. Most were fine with that. It was, after all, only a work environment. Even Parks, with his obsession for cleanliness and organization, had grown accustomed to the way things were. Not that he had been so accepting at first. However, having gone from leading a squad of LA's finest at one time to, as he put it, "being back in the trenches" had not been easy for anyone. Parks was just lucky, and happily accepted that he still had a job, even if it was down a floor.

"Two—" Hardwick paused as she realized Rachel was still sitting at her desk next to Parks's, within earshot.

"Should I leave? I can—" Rachel began as she stood back up, when

Jane held her hands up to stop her.

"It's okay," Hardwick said calmly, still looking around the room. No one else was around. "Word about this will get out soon enough, and you're partners. I'm sure Dave will talk to you as soon as I leave anyway, so why not hear it from me first. And you guys know how to keep your mouths shut. Always did."

"What's up?" Dave asked getting somewhat nervous.

"Rumor has it, and now mind you this is just a rumor, but I have it on good authority that you're going to be hit with a lawsuit within the week. Early next week at the latest."

"Lawsuit? What for? From whom?"

"Adam Wolfe's filing it," Hardwick answered. Parks was more than aware of the defense attorney and who all he represented. A rogue's gallery of some of L.A.'s nastiest.

"On whose behalf?" Suddenly a name came to Parks. "Katherine Norton? Aren't they about to go to trial though?"

"No. And yes. Not her. The Kozlov brothers."

"What?" Rachel all but wanted to shout in frustration.

"What for?" Parks's frustration echoed that of his partner. "They're already in prison. With life terms. They're not getting out. Trial's over. And you can't say it's for tainted evidence because we didn't use any of Aaron's evidence. They were sentenced based on Peter Kozlov's wife's murder, which he ordered his brother to carry out. The two turned on each other."

"Exactly," Hardwick said with a sigh. "They're saying that Natalie Kozlov's murder was your fault. Indirectly so. Or something to that effect."

"What do you mean?"

"Aaron manufactured evidence that got Peter locked up. We knew about said manufactured evidence, and instead of letting him go, we went after his wife to testify against him. So he had no choice but to silence her. It's your fault, being as Aaron's dead and no one's left to blame, and since you were his partner, how could you not have known? Regardless, it's your fault for forcing him to hire his brother to kill his wife. In a nutshell."

"You gotta be shitting me," Parks cursed.

"Wish that I was," Hardwick said with as much comfort as she could muster up. "Now, this isn't official yet. Though I did hear paperwork's being drawn up. But Adam Wolfe is about to go into trial for Katherine Norton, which is a very public trial, so I can't see him really wanting to spend a lot of time on this one. I hear it's the brothers pushing his hand, and I think he's hoping a judge will just quickly dismiss it. Regardless, he has to file on his clients' behalf. So, if this does happen, you've not heard about this before. But the department will handle it for you on your behalf, unless you wish to seek out legal representation of your own. But the department will handle this for you. Free of charge. They're not hitting the department with the lawsuit, or so I've heard, which is strange, considering they've deeper pockets than you, but maybe that's why. They don't want them involved. But don't worry about it. If this does move forward, we'll handle it. The department's got your back on this one. Okay?"

"But if this lawsuit does move forward and a judge doesn't quash it, then we get to dredge all this old bullshit back up again, correct?"

"I'm sorry," Hardwick repeated. "Again, this is just rumor for now. I don't want it to affect you, and I was considering not telling you altogether, just to see if it even would happen, but I figured you'd rather know in advance."

"Great," sighed Dave. "Well, thanks for the heads up. What's the other thing you have for me?"

"On a hopefully brighter side, I've got a case I'd like your view-point on," Hardwick said carefully. "It's one of our—it's a delicate mat-ter. To say the least. You were always good with those."

"Oh. Okay," Parks said cautiously. "Sure.

Parks was used to being asked to look at other detectives' cases from time to time, just to get a different perspective on things, though it had been a while since anyone had trusted him with that request. Truth was, even though he was still assigned cases as per their lineup, now that he no longer worked directly under Hardwick, no one asked him for special assistance of any kind anymore. True, he no longer worked for her. But they still saw each other around. It was as if she had lost respect for him, and he couldn't really blame her. She didn't know everything about what had been said in that interview room with Christopher Stone during the Knott/Davis murder case. And he knew that was where things had changed for him. But sometimes not knowing—only having one's imagination to run wild—was even worse than the truth. However, it wasn't anyone else's business. And Parks didn't feel he had to defend himself. He would get through this. He always did.

"What about Reed?"

When Parks had been moved to Robbery Homicide his supervisor had also changed, with him now reporting to the Director of Special Operations Thomas Reed. He had known the man for over a decade now and believed him to be a fair and just authority in his field, one that Parks had no issue reporting to or taking orders from.

"He's aware of the situation. Actually, he's waiting for you in my office as well. He was going to bring you to me, but I needed a minute or two alone to vet out a few bits of information before we proceed.

Before there are too many ears to silence any further gossip."

Parks stared up at his former boss, taking in her words. If Reed was aware of the situation and thought he could help, then that was what he would do.

"Always glad to help. You know that." Parks stood up and turned to Moore, who raised her eyebrows in both surprise and pride that he was finally being trusted once again. She had been assigned as his partner when their team had been dismantled back in May, and she had taken on the whisperings and glares from the other officers with no hesitation. She loved her job, and in a sort of sisterly way, loved and trusted Parks as well. She had known him since he joined the department almost two decades ago, and she had long ago learned to both trust his instincts and know that he always had everyone else's best interest at heart. Even when it usually meant putting himself on the back burner. "I'll be back shortly. Or whenever."

"Actually," Hardwick held up a hand to stop him. "You can bring her along as well. She might be just as helpful. This case...I think it concerns both of you. Somehow."

Parks made a questioning face at Moore, and the two of them followed Hardwick to the elevators.

"Any clues as to what this is about?" Parks asked. He hadn't recalled hearing about any major crimes having occurred within the last twenty-four hours. Maybe this time the LAPD had actually managed to keep a high-priority homicide under wraps.

"Parks, I need to ask you a personal question. Without getting into details, I need the honest truth. I'm not digging for gossip, but I need to know so I know how to advance on this case," Hardwick began as the three of them got onto the elevator.

Standing behind Hardwick, Parks turned to Moore, eyes slightly wide as he waited to hear what their superior had to say next. Maybe they were better off being part of the forgotten masses on the floor below.

"If I have a case I need you to work on with Jacqueline Isley, how much of a problem will that be for the two of you?"

Parks felt his entire body shift at the mention of Isley's name. No matter what he had been preparing himself for, it hadn't been that. It had become common knowledge throughout the department that both Parks and Isley had dated the year before but that things had fallen apart after the conclusion of the Palisades Poisoner case, which also included the false accusation by Parks of Jackie Isley's one and only son.

It had been a year since the two of them had talked and at least six months since he had last seen her around the department. It was hard not to hear gossip throughout the department. It was practically a high school around there. You heard things. About everyone and everything. It just happened. He had even heard whisperings of her leaving her position as a full-time forensic toxicologist to become a part-time teacher at one of the local universities.

"Honestly?" Parks asked.

"No, I want you to bullshit me, Parks," Hardwick snapped, without turning around.

"Honestly, I don't quite know," Parks admitted. "I'm not sure. But I can tell you, without fully speaking for Miss Isley, I would think that you could expect nothing less than complete professionalism from the both of us."

"Good," Hardwick said with a nod of her head. The doors chimed and opened. "That's what she said as well."

She said? So they had already talked with Isley.

"Why?" Parks asked. "What's up?"

"What do you think has happened?" Hardwick asked, trying not to sound snippy. "We called *her* and we called *you*. Someone's been poisoned."

"Okay...I'm sorry to hear that. And I understand why you called her. But why exactly are you reaching out to me about this case? I mean, no disrespect, but don't people get poisoned all the time?"

"Yes, they do, Parks," Hardwick said with a smile as she stopped at her door. "But with this one...there's more to the story than first meets the eye."

EIGHT

Parks took a deep breath and entered Hardwick's office a few seconds after her. The first person he came face to face with was one of the last people he had expected to see in Hardwick's office: Mark Wilkes. The last time the two of them had been in her (old) office, the meeting had resulted in blows being flung by Wilkes at Parks and Hardwick suspending Wilkes for a week. This too had been a year ago. A lot had happened during the Palisades Poisoner case. Things had changed during that case. Things had changed due to it. And a lot had happened since.

"Wilkes," Parks said as he offered his hand.

Wilkes accepted it, smiling quickly, knowing what needed to be said and done when around people of higher authority and in positions to change futures. He was, after all, first and always a true politico. No one knew office politics better than Mark Wilkes. Even if his feelings about bringing Parks in on *his* case were only being made crystal clear to Parks himself.

"Parks," Wilkes said, abruptly turning to Rachel to shake her hand.

As Wilkes stepped aside, Parks finally caught sight of Jackie Isley next to Amy Tanaka, the two having been on the sofa near the far wall

of Hardwick's office. The two women rose at the entrance of Hardwick and the two detectives. Jackie was just as radiant and full of life as
he remembered. Her beautiful, fire-red hair had been straightened,
now coming to just below her shoulders as it hung down around her
ivory-colored skin. Her lips were a dark crimson color, which accented
her face as opposed to appearing gaudy or out of place. She was otherwise barely touched by makeup, a light dash of green splashed above
each emerald-colored eye.

"Detective Parks," Jackie said, breaking Parks's study of her and offering a hand to him, trying her best to stay professional. There was a
look, just a flash in her eyes, as she took in the sight of him. It wasn't
the look he had expected. It was almost pity. As if the sight of him was
not what she had expected. As if he had somehow disappointed her.
He wasn't sure why, or what she had been expecting, but only knew
that the image she had kept in her head of him wasn't the image she
now saw.

"Miss Isley," Parks replied as he offered his hand. "I mean doctor.
Sorry."

Their hands touched, first fingertips to each other's palms, and
both immediately felt guilty from the electricity they could have sworn
could be seen by everyone in the room.

"Doctor, yes," Jackie said, smiling. "Miss is fine too."

Was she intentionally telling him something by adding that last
part?

"Tanaka," Parks nodded, as he looked over Jackie's shoulder. No
matter what had happened between Parks and Jackie, Tanaka was still
the go-to medical examiner that Parks preferred to work with and had
done so on dozens of cases over the last year. They still had their playful relationship, and Tanaka had all but silently voiced her enthusiasm

of Parks and Isley mending broken fences and having a baseball team's worth of children one day.

Tanaka winked and smiled at Parks but remained quiet, the excitement of what was to come beaming across her face. And just to prove how she shouldn't have felt, Director Reed stood off to the side, next to Hardwick's desk, the look on his face proving that it was not a good thing, them all meeting there.

This brought Parks back to reality. There was a homicide to consider. People had lost their lives. That was generally the only reason for them to gather.

"Well..." Parks began. "Someone going to tell us what we've been brought here for?"

Hardwick looked to Chief Reed, whose crystal, ice-blue eyes concealed too many secrets, while a knowing look flashed between the two, and Hardwick began.

"We've have a double homicide and we feel your experience would be helpful in wrapping it up," Hardwick began. "Wilkes?"

"Yeah, all right," Wilkes began as he took the floor. "Right. So we've got Mary Delancy and her thirty-seven-year-old son, Scott Delancy, found together, in bed, poisoned to death. By strychnine. Or so Isley says."

"It was," Tanaka said sharply.

"The movie star?" Parks asked. Everyone turned to him, surprised by his knowledge of the woman.

"Very good, Detective Parks," Hardwick said with a nod. "Proving me right by bringing you in on this already."

"I've met the woman. A few times. Back when I was on patrol," Parks explained, noticing the shift in the room to his words. Something was wrong. But he wasn't in on whatever it was. "She often called about stalkers and intruders on her property. Most of the time it was nonsense, but a few times they were legit. One time we caught a guy peeping in on her who killed her...friend, or someone like that."

"I vaguely remember that. Wasn't it her husband?"

"No. Her husband died years before. I think it was some guy she was seeing. Who was killed. Thomas something...Carmel. Or Cream. Or Candy. Something like that. I can't remember. Guy who killed him was one of Mary's stalkers, who snapped when he saw her with him. Nicholas Vaquier."

"Nicholas Vaquier," Hardwick whistled. "I remember him. Piece of work, if I remember correctly."

"He was. Sick twist. He's been in and out of prison a few times, but I think he's locked up permanently now."

"This changes things," Reed said from his corner near Hardwick's desk.

"We don't know that," Hardwick replied without looking at the man.

"It's too much of a coincidence that Parks knew the victim," Reed objected. "We have to take that into consideration. This could all be a set up."

"Excuse me," Parks interrupted, confused and wanting answers. "But what are you talking about? So this woman I met fifteen years ago was poisoned. Yes, I've handled poisonings before. But so what? I mean, we don't think that Lewis Hay—tell me that man isn't out?"

"No," Hardwick said, all but jumping out of her seat. "Sorry. We didn't mean to imply that. We've checked. Lewis Hayward is still locked up."

"Well, you meant to imply something," Parks said, shortly. "We have a poisoning. Everyone in this room is being cryptic. Now will someone please tell me what's going on?"

Reed and Hardwick both stayed silent, neither one sure whom should begin or take charge. Parks had a feeling that happened a lot when the two worked together.

"At first, this was thought to be a possible suicide pact," Jackie said, taking charge of the discussion. "Forgotten starlet and her only son. She has two, but one moved away and hasn't spoken to her in years. So the quick conclusion was suicide."

"But you've since changed your minds?"

"Some of us have," Wilkes interjected, letting everyone know he thought this whole meeting was horseshit.

"They were poisoned by strychnine," Jackie said matter-of-factly. "That much is true. However, unlike any strychnine poisoning I have ever witnessed, this was highly aggressive. Even by strychnine standards. The effects of the poison had manifested physically on the body twofold compared to a normal poisoning."

Jackie let her words settle in on everyone. The only words that Parks could focus on were "a normal poisoning." He almost had to laugh.

"Guess a little bit of Peter Parker rubbed off on Mary Jane after all. Got her Spidey-sense tingling as well," Wilkes quipped, everyone hearing him and knowing what he meant.

"What did you find?" Parks ignored Wilkes and focused on Jackie instead.

"I went back," Jackie continued. "You can read about everything in the murder book."

Parks nodded. He would, but he still wanted to hear the abbreviated version.

"What did you find?"

"It was behind the headboard."

"And how the hell was anyone supposed to find that?" Wilkes shot out.

Hardwick glared at Wilkes, who immediately shut his mouth. From behind Jackie, Tanaka was beaming. She was proud. Her girl was proving her worth.

"What was behind the headboard?" Parks asked.

"This," Jackie answered as she handed over a picture from the crime scene. "It wasn't visible to the naked eye, but with a black light you could see it."

Parks stared at the symbol drawn on the wall of a supposed homicide victim. A symbol so familiar, he could have drawn it himself. Yet completely different from what had been left behind at the Palisades Poisoner crime scenes.

"Kyū," Parks said silently.

The Palisades Poisoner had left behind the Japanese symbol for ten at each of his crime scenes. At least that was what the task force Parks had been in charge of the year before had come to believe. Truthfully, they had never gotten confirmation one way or another what the symbol meant. Or what it stood for or why it had been left behind at the scenes of his victims.

"It is Kyū, right?" Parks asked.

"It's the Japanese symbol for nine," Hardwick spoke up. "And it confirms what we thought about the previous symbol left behind by

Lewis Hayward."

Parks stared at the photo, taking in the information he was given. What did this all mean? Did this have anything to do with him? If so, how? Why?

"We don't know what this means. Or what the previous symbol meant. It's just Hayward playing his mind games, as far as we know. He's counting backward, perhaps?"

"Or down," Hardwick offered.

"To what? Why?" No one had an answer for him. "What substance was this written in?"

"It was a combination of substances," Jackie answered. "The victim's semen and sweat, mostly. As well as a substance that we've come to identify as Phalaenopsis orchid. We found one in the downstairs foyer of the victim's house. It's being tested now."

They were still holding out on him. Parks could feel it.

"You've got a copycat," Parks replied, handing the photo back to Jackie, but holding onto it for a second longer than necessary when she grabbed it. "Plain and simple. You'll find him—or her. That's all."

"Could be," Hardwick agreed. "But we never let the fact that Lewis Hayward left behind the Japanese symbol at the scenes of his victims be known to the public. And if it is a copycat, then why not the same symbol?"

"So what are you saying? I mean, if it's not a copycat. And it's not Lewis Hayward?"

"It's not," Hardwick repeated forcefully.

"Then it's..." Parks thought about this, not giving it a lot of focus, when it suddenly hit him. "He's got a follower. Lewis Hayward. No. Strike that. The Palisades Poisoner has a follower. Or someone he's teaching. Or taught."

"We believe so," Reed said, finally giving some input.

"So you already came to this conclusion before I just suggested it. Why? What do you know? I thought we were monitoring all of Hayward's correspondence. Both in and out. Even limiting it."

"We have been. We are," Reed confirmed. "No one besides his lawyer. Even that contact has been minimal. Lewis Hayward has been speaking with no one. That we know of."

"Well, if this is connected to him, then I'd say he's been in communication with someone," Parks disagreed.

Reed tilted his head in a way to let Parks know he was right.

"What—what do you have? What did you find?"

Reed looked to Hardwick once again.

"This is on you," Hardwick said, offended by the circumstances, having voiced her opinion about it to Reed before. "Now you get to deal with the consequences of your actions." Hardwick turned to Parks. "I told him to show you when he first got it—though Lord only knows when that even was. When he first showed me. Sorry."

"What is it?" Parks asked again.

Reed remained quiet as he picked a single, photocopied piece of paper out of the file in his hands and handed it to Parks.

"This was delivered here. To the station. We don't know how it got here or how it even got out of the prison in the first place. And before you ask, yes, we've had it tested. The original. It's him. His fingerprints are all over the letter and envelope."

"What is it?" Rachel asked from behind Parks, as he focused on the letter in his hands.

"It's a letter," Parks finally said as he let out a deep breath that he had not realized he'd been holding. "From Lewis Hayward." He finally looked up. "Addressed to me."

NINE

"What...the...*hell* is this?" Parks had the letter from Lewis Hayward in his fist, all but crumpled up as anger surged through his body, his hands shaking. "I mean: really? What the fuck?"

"It didn't concern you—"

"The hell this doesn't," Parks all but shouted. "The man I locked up in prison for poisoning people somehow manages to get a letter not only out of a state prison but practically to my doorstep—addressed to me—and you don't think this concerns *me*? Is there anything else I should know about that *doesn't* concern me?"

"We weren't sure about the validity of this letter," Reed said, stepping up and making sure to get in Parks's face. He was still in charge. He still had the final say in any decision he decided to make, no matter the reasons or outcome.

"And when you finally were? You can't tell me you just got confirmation on this letter five minutes before you called me in here?"

"We had to figure out how to handle the situation. We still don't know how. We never got full answers for Hayward's motivations or his plans. Ever since his arrest, he has been mute. We don't know anything. Hell, you visiting him back in May about the Knott/Davis murders is the only time he has spoken to someone outside his lawyer. And we're still trying to decipher what he said."

"You—" Parks bit back his tongue. "Why should I even be surprised?"

Parks could feel Rachel's presence looming behind him, and he handed her the letter without even looking at her.

"So why bring it up now? Because we have two new corpses that have been poisoned? There is no connection between those two bodies, this letter, or myself. Let alone Lewis Hayward. The symbol at the crime scene isn't even the same. We don't know what it all means."

"I think that's pretty damning evidence—"

"On the contrary. It's bullshit, and you know it. This wouldn't mean a damn thing in court. So...? What? *What?*"

"What?" Reed delayed.

"What do you want from me?"

"On the off chance that this crime is related to Lewis Hayward, we need to know. To try to get ahead of this. We have no leads as of this moment. That's what you're here for. To determine the connections—*if* any exist—between this crime and yourself and Lewis Hayward. We don't need another Palisades Poisoner terror spree in this city." Reed looked to Wilkes who looked away, more out of disgust for this whole situation than out of embarrassment about the lack of progress made on the case. "Not only is Lewis Hayward not allowed contact with the outside world, but he refuses to cooperate with us."

"There's a shocker," Parks breathed deeply.

"That's where you can help."

"What do you—? You want me to go talk to him?" The expression on Reed's face said that was exactly what he wanted. "Hell, no. Go find yourself another patsy. It won't be me."

"There is no one else," Reed said sternly. "He's engaged with you somehow. We're not sure why, but apparently he feels a connection with you. We could use that."

"He would know what you're up to. He'd only play with me to screw with you. And you should know that too."

"Look. We only want you to—"

"*No*," Parks said sharply, causing several people in the room to flinch. "I don't do that anymore. Remember? I'm not part of Homicide Special Section or Major Crimes or whatever you're calling it these days—where I'm sure this case will be handled. I don't work on any of your task forces any more. I am a simple detective. As you wanted it. So that's what I do. The simple homicides. A plus B equals C. That's it. Anything more is someone else's job. You all said I was too flashy for you. Liable to cause too many issues with the public image of the department. And I didn't fight you, did I? I did what you wanted. But I refuse to be yo-yo'd back and forth. You made your bed; now sleep in it. You thought to keep me out of this so far. So just keep doing it."

"What do you want?" Reed asked cautiously.

"To be left alone to do my job. I'm sorry if your killer of these two is somehow related to the Palisades Poisoner. But that has nothing to do with me anymore. You've got her"—Parks pointed to Jackie—"and she's one of the best when it comes to poisons. If not *the* best. Wilkes, despite his flaws, is no slouch either. He is a damn good detective. They can work this. They'll get your guy for you. You don't need me."

Parks stood up, stared down at the picture of the Japanese symbol once again, and then shook his head.

"You don't need me," Parks repeated. "We've work to do. Rachel?"

Parks turned to leave the room with Rachel at his heels.

"Parks," Reed barked.

But Parks was gone and not coming back.

"He's right, you know," Wilkes offered immediately. "Me and Mary Jane can handle this. You don't need him. We got this."

Reed stayed quiet as he stared out into space, thinking.

"You really want him on the case?" Jackie asked to no one in particular, as she wasn't sure who was in charge of the investigation.

"We *need* him," Hardwick replied, barely audible.

The two women stared at each other, eye to eye.

"Wilkes?" Hardwick said, looking beyond Jackie.

"Huh?" Wilkes replied, caught off guard.

"You finished your report for me yet?"

"Still working on it."

"Well, it's not going to get finished with you sitting in here on your ass. I want it by the end of your shift." Hardwick turned to Amy. "Thank you for your help as usual, Dr. Tanaka."

Both had been dismissed, though only Amy had the intelligence to know it and leave, grabbing Jackie's shoulder and giving it a squeeze on her way out. Wilkes continued to stay in his chair until Reed glared over at him, and he left without another word.

"You think we can get him back?" Hardwick asked Jackie.

"Oh, for crying out loud," Reed barked. "He works for us. We tell him what the hell to do, and he does it. That's all there is to it."

"And you saw how well that worked," Hardwick shot back. "You want a detective working a case against his will? You've already seen evidence of that. Just look at Parks's solve rate since you transferred him over to your division last May. Still just as impressed by him working in an environment that he doesn't feel agreeable with?"

"We've got half our men and women out there working on cases they don't like. We're the LAPD. That's what we do!"

"True. But Parks isn't like half your detectives on the force. And working a case like this? A Palisades Poisoner case? A case like this requires full devotion. And you know it. Parks is good. One of our best. But not against his will."

"So what do we do?"

"What are you willing to give him to work the case?" Jackie asked. "Of his own volition."

"The department doesn't have any more money," Reed said.

"I'm not talking about money," Jackie shot back. "But I can see how that's the first thought you'd jump to."

"Then what *are* you talking about?"

"Everyone in this room knows about Parks. His history, I mean."

Reed looked to Hardwick and then back to Jackie to signal her to continue.

"No family, so to speak. A father who killed himself when he was a boy. A mother he hasn't seen in almost the same amount of time. An aunt and uncle he sees on holidays. This department, his *team*, which you disbanded and took from him—*that* was his family. And for lack of a better term, you orphaned him. Hell, *he* might not even know it. But it's true. That team he worked with, they were his family. He's lost without them. I can guarantee you that. I saw him when he first walked in here. He doesn't look the same. Sure it's been a year, but it's been a rough year. He looks beaten. He's become a drone. Day in and day out. The same old thing. Trust me. He wants on this case. Maybe more than even he's willing to admit to himself. And you can give it to him. Easily. But you know what you have to do."

"We just...can't..." Reed sighed as he shook his head. "After everything that happened with the Knott/Davis case—"

"What exactly did happen with the Knott/Davis case?" Jackie shot out. "I know that that case is part of the reason you decided to disband his team. But why exactly?"

Reed stared at the woman and almost shrugged at her.

"My point exactly," Jackie quipped, taking charge of the conversation. "Who knows? I sure as hell don't. And neither doesn't anyone else around this department, at least from best as I've been able to determine. Oh, sure, we all know something happened. But as for what? None of us could tell you exactly. In fact, I'm sure that other than the few of you who were around to witness whatever it was that happened to cause you to take the actions you did, no one else knows why. Hell, the rumors going around the department are probably worse than what actually did happen. And you two, above all others, should know how harmful false rumors can be. People don't know what happened so they're making it up. All we do know—despite your best efforts to bury the details of the case—is that two sick men blackmailing students into preforming sexual acts of depravity for their enjoyment were stopped from harassing the student body of PSU any further. That sounds like a reason to give commendation as opposed to a slap on the wrist. Which, let's face it, in the eyes of his fellow peers, is exactly what you did. You've told them all Parks did something bad without telling them what. So they're imagining things. This, as we all know, is worse. People need answers."

Jackie stood to leave.

"Can you get him back here?" Hardwick asked without looking at Reed for confirmation. "I mean face to face."

"I can," Jackie nodded. "But this will only be a one-time deal. This isn't going to be back-and-forth negotiations. You'll only have one other chance with him. Will you play ball with him or not? How much do you really need him? Figure out what's the most you're willing to offer for this to happen. And then push yourself to go higher."

Hardwick swiveled around in her chair and caught Reed's glance. The two of them had a silent conversation without uttering a single word.

A few seconds later, Reed finally broke. "Just get him back here."

TEN

Parks was driving down Olympic Boulevard, headed home, when he pulled into a Ralph's supermarket parking lot. Minutes later he felt his body drag through the aisles, trying to figure out what exactly he was shopping for, wanting to get the essentials, though not even sure if he needed those.

He grabbed a carton of orange juice and threw it in the red basket he held with his other hand when he caught sight of his reflection in one of the freezer windows. He had loosened his tie around his neck and pulled his buttoned-down shirt out from the constraint of his belt, giving him a hung-over, disheveled look. He looked as if he were coming off an all-nighter, when in fact the only thing he had been doing the night before was reading case files and fiddling with one of his puzzles. The bags under his eyes had gotten darker since he last checked, and, for the first time in months, he realized he had been losing weight. Not an unhealthy amount per se, but for David Parks, who usually carried a little over two-hundred pounds of muscle, it was noticeable. He wondered what his co-workers thought and wanted to know why Rachel had never said anything to him.

He closed the freezer door and moved along to the next aisle, seeing a special on brownie mix and picked up a few boxes, though he himself had never before baked a single brownie.

He grabbed two dozen eggs, some bacon, and a few cans of cat food before heading to the self-checkout lane, which ended up proving damn near impossible before a checker finally came to his aid. He had to admit to himself that he was distracted and needed to get home and think about his current situation and clear his mind before he did some serious damage.

When Parks arrived at his home, the sun was still blazing, though the horizon taunted it from mere inches, something that he wasn't all that used to. He was more used to late nights at the office and barely making it home before midnight. But Rachel and he had finished their work for the day, and he had taken the few case files he needed to type up with him, seeking the comfort of his own home to carry out the remainder of his tasks as opposed to the murkiness of the downtown station. He had dry-swallowed a few blue pills that he had been recently prescribed and decided to change into a pair of gym shorts and a white tank top, sure that he would need to take a break in-between typing up reports to run or do something physical to clear his head, when his doorbell rang. Parks answered it before whoever waited for him could ring again.

"I saw you come home. Hope this isn't a bad time?" In the doorway stood Tracy Scott, one of the two neighbors who lived below him.

A children's book illustrator, Tracy Scott spent most of her time at home and so had become familiar with Parks's around-the-clock schedule after moving into the condo below his six months prior. They had first been introduced some three months before when she had a clogged-up sink and couldn't get ahold of the landlord. Parks, looking for a distraction, welcomed the challenge. Two hours later, after conversing over broken pipes, the two found that they were physically attracted to each other, and it was only natural for the situation to conclude as so many adult situations often did. Though his schedule was out of whack and she often traveled for work purposes, neither one had ever asked for more from the other than what was already being given: the occasional late-night conversation, a break from aloneness, or emotionless—if not engaging and stimulating—sex.

"Naw," Parks answered. "Just about to start some paperwork. What's up?"

"Same problem," Tracy said innocently. "Stupid sink. I swear, I'm either going to sue the landlord or move one of these days."

"Yeah," Parks chuckled. "I've been saying that for years. I'll come take a look at it."

"Are these for me?" Tracy asked as she picked up the two boxes of brownie mix that he had left out on the counter.

Parks smiled and shrugged.

"You remembered," Tracy beamed. "My hero."

"See, some men do listen. Let's go check out that sink. I bet I can get it fixed in no time."

"Good. I'll make us some sandwiches."

"You don't have to make me food for looking at your sink." Parks smiled as he followed Tracy out the door and down the wooden steps. "Really."

"I know, I know. But whenever we do the other stuff after you fix something, I feel like one of us is whoring ourselves out. And I'm still not sure which one of us that is."

"I don't mind the other stuff. No feelings of whoredom at all on my behalf. We're adults. Engaging in adult activities. It happens. I think we'll survive."

"Good," Tracy said perkily as she opened her front door. "Glad you feel that way." Tracy turned around and kissed Parks once he entered her place. "Then why don't we agree that the sink can wait a little while. And get to some of that other stuff that doesn't make us feel like whores."

"I think I can agree to that," Parks said, as he picked Tracy up in his arms and carried her down the hallway to the bedroom.

Ninety minutes later, with the sink fixed to the point that Parks swore he could have thrown a football down the drain without the sink clogging, he gathered the untouched sandwich Tracy had made for him and headed back to his place. As he headed up the wooden stairs to his place, he saw a glimpse of red hair just above the horizon of the balcony, and before he made it to the top of the landing, he knew who was waiting for him at his door. He paused at the top of the steps, and the two stared at each other, taking in the silence, neither one letting it bother them.

"Stop off somewhere for a bite to eat?" Jackie asked with a smile, her eyes glancing below her, as if she knew where Parks had gotten the food.

"Why are you here?" Parks wasn't sure whether he was irritated by her intrusion or actually comforted by her appearance, his emotions feeling particularly mixed at the moment.

He walked up to Jackie and then past her into his condo, leaving the front door open, an invitation Jackie took.

"Guess she doesn't really know you all that well, now, does she?"

"She was being friendly. That's all."

"Sure," Jackie smirked as she peeked at the sandwich. "Well, I mean, come on…turkey and Swiss on wheat with all the fixings. Most men would have finished this sandwich before they left a woman's place. But not good ol' Dave Parks. You have no intention of eating this sandwich, and you didn't want her to know that. Awww…"

For a second Parks had forgotten that Jackie knew about his weird eating particulars.

"Ever get that tic figured out?" Jackie asked, seriousness and genuine concern across her face.

"Why are you here?"

"You've had a rough year."

"We all have."

Jackie glanced around his living space, the nearly unmanageable disorder and chaos, and took it all in. There were three times as many boxes of puzzles scattered around the place. Boxes of case files were stacked all over the kitchen table, to the point that no one besides Parks could sit at the table, something he preferred. It was as if Parks had ignored his living conditions for the past year. It hurt Jackie to see him living like this.

"But apparently you more so. You don't look so good, Dave. You look…older, somehow. The man I remember took good care of himself. You seem to have overdone yourself. You seem defeated. I'm surprised ADA Beasley lets you get away with this look."

"What's he have to do with how I look? He's not my keeper."

"True. But he is in the middle of the trial of the century with the High Society Black Widow"—Jackie paused as she controlled herself from smiling or laughing at the lunacy of Katherine Norton's moniker, just as irrational as Lewis Hayward being referred to as the Palisades Poisoner—"and being as you are one of his key witnesses, I'm just surprised he hasn't made sure you aren't more appealing to the mass public watching this trial."

Parks glared at her but knew she was right. Beasley had been on him a few times to make sure he had a new suit and looked kempt and clean when presenting his evidence against Katherine Norton. There hadn't been a trial—public or otherwise—for Lewis Hayward, so the public was thirsty for this one. This would most likely result in the trial becoming a circus and both sides relentlessly ruthless in their attacks. He figured Katherine Norton's lawyer must have been having a field day as he prepared for Parks's testimony. Luckily, he still had two more weeks until it was time to shine. Maybe he would get a haircut between now and then.

"Well...I guess this really hasn't been my year. Between suspensions, a demotion, nearly losing my life several times, and then—well, it just hasn't been my year."

"Then I say it's time to change all that. You're coming back," Jackie said, looking at one of the case files opened across the table. "To work the poisoner case. Palisades Poisoner or not."

"Is that so?" Parks crossed his arms defiantly.

"You know you are," Jackie said turning back to Parks and walking up to him. "Come on. People were killed. More could be. You and I both know you could never live with yourself if innocent people were harmed and you could have done something about it."

"What makes you so sure there are innocent people left in this world?"

"Ouch." Jackie sighed. "Look. I know I may have had—"

"I don't blame you," Parks interrupted. "I mean...well...I mean, I get why what happened did. Why you and I never..."

"Do you? I mean I know what I did and said. Though, sometimes I'm not sure if I get if it was legit or not. My reasoning, that is."

"How is Ricky?"

Jackie remained quiet. Jackie's one and only son, Ricky, had never really approved of Parks, not because of the fact that there was a new man in his mother's life, as he genuinely wanted his mother to be happy, but because he saw Parks as just another in a line of men who never stayed. Who never kept their word. Much like his birth father whom he had never known. And in a way, even though it wasn't entirely his choice, Parks hadn't kept his word. He hadn't stuck by. He had left. Just as Ricky had said he would.

"Guess you and I weren't the only ones hurt by Lewis Hayward, huh?"

"No. That bastard did a lot of damage. Most of which can't be undone. But we're human. So the only thing we can do is move on. Move forward."

"How?" Parks genuinely asked.

"A day at a time?" Jackie shrugged. "I don't know. I think that works though. At least for a little while."

Parks wasn't sure what to say when he noticed Jackie staring past him. He knew what had caught her eye. There had to be at least five orange prescription bottles up on the counter next to his sink, each a different size according to the medication they contained.

"You have something to drink?" Jackie asked, breaking the silence. "Or want to get out of here? Go somewhere. It's depressing as hell in here. I mean, I get that you've had a rough couple of months, we've all heard about the Knott/Davis fiasco, but it stinks like you've got a rotting corpse in here. You should open a window and air this place out. And hire a maid or something. This isn't you, Dave Parks. You're better than this. Whatever it is that happened, you need to find a way to get past it. I don't mean to sound like a mother--though I haven't been doing enough of that lately, so maybe I do—but if what you need is a good, swift kick in the ass, then you better believe I'm sure as hell gonna be the one to do it."

Dave looked around his place, embarrassment starting to settle in.

"Give me ten minutes to shower and change real quick?" Parks held up his hands. "I mean, I *have* been digging through a clogged sink for the past hour."

"Find a razor and give yourself a shave while you're at it, and I'll give you twenty. I mean, we all know you can pull off the chiseled, gruff look, but there's some gray starting to show. Might want to nip that before the ladies catch sight of you aging. In this town. What would they all say?"

She teased him, in her own playful way. And suddenly he found himself feeling younger, more alive than he had in months.

"Yes, mom."

Jackie smiled. There was that spark.

Parks showered, shaved, and found clean clothes. Jackie drove while Parks directed her along Wilshire until they found a bar/restaurant over by the university and nestled into a booth near the back. Other than a few people playing pool, they had the place to themselves. They both ordered drinks—Jackie tequila and soda while Parks had vodka and orange juice—and Jackie ordered a breakfast wrap for Parks and a plate of seasoned fries for herself. She had already eaten the turkey and Swiss sandwich that Tracy had made for him while he took his time in the shower. She figured it was only fair after he made her wait for him.

"There's food we both know you'll actually eat," Jackie smirked.

Parks looked around the almost empty table and settled on a sugar packet to throw at her. They sat there in silence until their drinks arrived. Parks finished half of his in one swallow.

"So…" Parks began. "You think I'll come back? To work the case, I mean."

"I know what you mean. And you know I'm right. You will. You're too good a person not to. You know there's a chance—sure, we hope it's a slim one—but there's still a chance that there could be more. Poisonings, I mean. And don't tell me you're not at all interested, if not *concerned*, about what Lewis Hayward wants with you."

"Fuck Lewis Hayward."

"God damned right."

Jackie took another sip of her drink.

"So what is up with Ricky?" Parks asked.

"God, I forgot how you do that."

"Do what?"

"Jump around. You keep it all compartmentalized in your brain somehow. We'll be talking about you coming back to the case. Then Lewis Hayward. Then you jump to Ricky. Next you'll jump to the latest TV show or book, then to something happening halfway around the world, and before I even know what's what, you'll be back on the topic of work again. You always manage to circle back to close up any unfinished topics or unanswered threads."

"It's a gift." Parks grinned.

"It's damned irritating is what it is." Jackie shook her head. "Can't you just stay on one topic and finish it before moving on?"

"What fun is that?"

"I'm gonna strangle you one of these days, I swear," Jackie said, as their food was brought to their table.

Parks shrugged as he doused his wrap with Tabasco sauce. Jackie could smell the vinegar and red pepper all the way on her side of the table.

"Ricky is...Ricky. He's fine. Studying hard. He decided to stay at school this summer."

"That had to hurt," Parks said, feeling sorry for her. He knew how close she was with her son.

"It did. It does. But he's a grown man now. I need to accept that. Can't be babying him for the rest of his life. Though we both know I totally would if I could."

"Yeah, we do." Parks shook his head and took another bite.

"Hey," Jackie yelped. "You're supposed to be on my side."

"Oh, is that so?" Parks said with amusement. "I think maybe Ricky and I need to form some kind of a club. The Jacqueline Isley Survivors Club."

"Hey..." Jackie laughed as she threw a fry at Parks.

"Where did that name come from, anyway?"

"What? Isley?"

"Jacqueline. It's neither Italian nor Irish."

"No," Jackie agreed. "It's French. Female version of Jacques. Which is the French version of James, I believe. And though my mother would love to romanticize and claim she named me after Jackie O—or so she would tell everyone when I was a little girl—truth of the matter is, it was picked out of one of her Harlequin romance novels. Of that, I am sure. Woman loves her some trashy romance novels."

Parks smiled at the thought of Jackie's mother. Though he had never met the woman, he had seen pictures of her around Jackie's place near the Venice canals. She was a stubborn woman with a strong jaw and a commanding presence, with a matching full head of fire-red hair. Just as equally a looker as her daughter.

"But to stay on topic," Jackie said, eyeing Parks to let him know he'd jumped topic again. "Ricky's good. I believe. I know he's had nightmares since…but I think he's seeing a school therapist. He may not be talking to me, but at least he's talking to someone, right?"

"And how are you?"

Jackie thought about that question, not sure how to answer it. "He left me with so much doubt. Lewis Hayward. Like there was something more I could have done. Maybe less people could have died."

"I understand that. It's bull, but I understand it. Can't deny I haven't had the same thoughts myself."

"Maybe everything that happened…maybe it could have all been prevented."

"Doubtful. But it's good to hope."

"Maybe we could have had a different outcome as well. You know?"

Parks thought about what she said. "Still can. Neither one of us is dead yet, you know?"

"There's the optimist Detective David Parks that I know." Jackie smiled. "Speaking of which…?"

"Why?" Parks asked as he raised his palms to his eyes, elbows raised above his head as he leaned back. "Why? Why should I come back to that? That case? That time in my life?"

"Closure?" Jackie asked. "Because it's what you do? Because you are damn good at your job. A hell of a lot better than Wilkes. You help people. You're damn good at it, and you actually care. You don't always let it show, which is good workwise. But for the few of us who have gotten glimpses into that David Parks psyche, we know. You care. About all of them. Every case, every body that comes across your desk. You care about them. You want justice for them."

"He's not that bad. He might be an asshole. But he's not a bad detective."

"Who? Wilkes? He's crap compared to you, and you know it. This case needs you. Just like you need it. You hate Lewis Hayward? Then beat him at his own game. He's threatening you? Screw him. He's in there. You're out here. He can't get you. Not like before. You can beat him."

"I can't," Parks said. "I don't know how."

"Alone...maybe you can't," Jackie said as she reached across the table and placed a hand over one of Parks's. "But you won't be. You weren't before, and you sure as hell won't be this time. That man's affected too many people for you to do this on your own."

Parks looked up at her.

"This case," Jackie continued. "Lewis Hayward. The Palisades Poisoner. This is your ace in your hand. Up your sleeve. Wherever you want it. But this is it. What do you want? What do you need, and what do you want? To work this case? Beyond this case. This is your chance to secure your future. Maybe not all of it. But part of it. So again, what do you want?"

The two stared silently at each other, both knowing immediately what he was thinking about, of whom he was thinking.

"Exactly." Jackie smiled. "So go get them back."

WEDNESDAY

ELEVEN

"Detective Parks, thank you for agreeing to meet with us again," welcomed Director Reed with a firm handshake that Parks had temporarily forgotten was usually quite stiff and firm. Not unlike the man's all-business demeanor, which fit perfectly with his ability to run a tight ship at the LAPD.

"Because I had a choice?"

Reed smiled and sat behind his desk with Hardwick opposite him, next to Parks.

"Before you begin, either by flatly refusing us again or by trying to negotiate, may I initiate these proceedings?"

"It's your office," Parks nodded.

"I know we've talked briefly in the past, but I want to make sure you're aware that the dissolution of your team was not taken lightly. And not everyone felt that the disbursement of its members was for the best of the department. Particularly when dealing with the high-profile cases. This is L.A., after all, and high profile cases come with the territory. And back when you were still part of a team, you and your team had their fair share of them. Let's take the Palisades Poisoner case. Hell of a lot of bad publicity on that one. Member of the LAPD poisoning the citizens of L.A."

"Yes, sir."

"But for as bad as it was, your *team* managed to keep most of it under wraps during the actual investigation," Reed said. "Then, when it was over, you somehow also managed to come out of it without making the LAPD look bad, despite the Poisoner being one of our own."

"Yes, sir."

"We managed to show that while a movie star and famous baseball player had been murdered by this guy, the public was more interested in bringing that man to justice for what he had done, as opposed to the number of people he killed due to us not being able to stop him." Parks wasn't sure whether this was a backhanded compliment and kept quiet. "Luckily, Lewis Hayward wasn't killed during his apprehension, and that gave us a face to put to the deaths and all without the showmanship of a trial."

"I didn't expect any special treatment, nor did I desire any. My team was ready for their reassignments just as everyone else in the division had been given."

"Glad you saw it that way." Reed looked to Hardwick who raised her eyebrows as if to say 'I told you so,' obviously referring to a conversation they'd had before Parks joined them. "It's like you said: This is Los Angeles. Hollywood. Beverly Hills. Bel Air. The Palisades. The entire southern California area is somewhat *elite*. At least parts of it. But the parts that are, they're elite. They like their privacy. Sure, they want help from the police when they need it, but they want to make sure their problems don't end up all over TMZ or whatever. They have that right too, as far as I'm concerned. Movie stars. Sports players. Industry people in one way or the other. Doctors. Plastic surgeons. Computer geniuses. Politicians. We got them all down here. We're next to the ocean, have beautiful scenery and easy access to the rest of the world. We're a desirable location."

Reed took a breath and collected his thoughts.

"I'm with you so far, sir," Parks said encouraging Reed to continue.

"It's difficult dispatching officers to help these so-called well-to-dos when their business will be plastered all over the news. They become paranoid. Closed in. Withdrawn. Testy. Difficult to work with."

"I know the type."

"Yet you have a way of getting around that. And without the entire case being spelled out play by play on the nightly news. Your team is good publicity for the department. People feel safe with the team who stopped the Palisades Poisoner out working cases."

"Yes, sir. I'm still not sure what you're saying exactly, though."

"He's offering you the opportunity to re-form your team," Hardwick chimed in.

Parks looked from Hardwick to Reed, who nodded. He knew this. He simply wanted to see if Reed would say it.

"I am. You're right about several things. This *is* a popularity contest. The image of the department is key on several levels. Now, none of this is permanent. Everything's on a temporary, twelve-month trial basis, including the current two-man detective teams. Things are still being figured out. Budgets. Groupings. Results. There's a lot revolving around this entire process, most of which you are not privy to. And won't be."

"So you want to put us back together to solve your next little publicity-problem poisoning case just to tear us apart again in a year's time? No thanks."

Reed stared at Parks, both men in a mental game of chicken. This was negotiation time. And both men knew it.

"Thirty-six month contracts. Nonnegotiable depending on a higher percentage of case solves."

"I can accept that."

"There are some conditions to this offer."

"Such as?"

"Robbery Homicide is being divided into sections. Robbery. Assault. Cold cases. And what you used to be a part of, Homicide Special Section. I'd like you back in it. Your objective—*our* objective—if you agree to re-form your team is to keep the high-profile cases private. Now, I don't expect this to work a hundred percent of the time, as we'd desire, but I hope that your team will be able to help keep a tighter grip on the leaks coming from this department. At least as far as your cases are concerned. We are using you because of your ability to keep a lid on things. Your team will also help and assist with other homicides and high profile cases as needed. You will report directly to Jane, as you did before. I know you two have a good rapport." Reed paused and shuffled through some paperwork, and Parks glanced over at Hardwick, who smiled briefly. "This gives your team four full-time members. We are also making allocations for you to add two more members on a full-time basis as well as one part-time specialist when allotted for certain cases. I'm sure these numbers could, and probably will, fluctuate depending on staff, budget, and case requirements."

"What does that mean?"

Parks stared at Reed. He was sure Reed wished he would just say "Yes, I'll take whatever you're giving me," but Parks wouldn't be the detective that they needed if he did. It was a double-edged sword, a fine line, and one that had to be played just right without offending anyone and backing himself into a trap. This could backfire on the department in ways he didn't even understand yet, and Parks knew that if it ever came to that, he would be the one to take the fall. Alone.

"We'll be adding two more full-time detectives to your team," Reed finally continued. "We have a fresh batch of detectives that just graduated. AC Hardwick is vetting the files to find you several viable options."

Reed looked to Hardwick, who nodded in agreement.

"You haven't steered our group wrong." Parks nodded to Hardwick as he brought himself back into the conversation. "What about Wilkes? We both know he won't like this, and he'll throw a fit as far up the chain as can be heard. Considering his connections, I take it he's being promoted in some way. What exactly are the lines between him and me?"

"For starters, if you desire, you can add him to your team. But since you and I both know it's unlikely he'll take the position, he will be promoted," Reed confirmed. "He'll be a Grade Three detective like you. However, I see you moving on up to lieutenant, captain, maybe even commander one day. But all in due time. You keep working the cases you do the way you do and I don't see why that's not possible. But due to the fact that this Delancy poisoning case was originally Wilkes's, he will be temporarily assigned to work with your group until the completion of this case."

Parks realized what was being asked of him and knew it was best if he played along at that point in time.

"I understand, sir," Parks nodded.

"Good," Reed said, standing behind his desk and offering his hand. "Just to let you know, there will be some more hobnobbing required of you upon accepting this position. More late dinners and meetings with the mayor and myself. Checkups, if you please. To see how this transition within the department goes. We're trying to make this work as smoothly as possible, and I will expect you to be both the voice and reason of the department when called upon."

Parks thought about this but saw no reason around it. He wasn't much for kissing ass, though he did know the game well enough to survive it. That was more Wilkes' specialty, and he wondered if it might not reflect better on the department if Wilkes was allowed more one-on-one time with the higher-ups. That might just be a good topic of conversation and the beginning of a bridge between the two men.

"I take it then you accept this position?" Reed asked, interrupting Parks's train of thought.

"My team and I are fully appreciative of your assessment of our capabilities and look forward to helping serve the city to the best of our abilities," Parks answered, taking Reed's hand and shaking it firmly.

"Glad to hear it. Now about those other members of your team..."

TWELVE

Former Detective Jake Fairmont snapped photos of a man and woman, both scantily clad, save for some faux (or so Jake hoped) animal furs and strategically placed hands and legs, in his studio on La Brea near Melrose, when Parks walked in and settled himself near the front door without interrupting. Jake's studio was spacious with brick walls and great lighting from all angles. Parks wasn't sure what Jake paid for rent, but figured the head shots and fashion shoots more than paid off for him if he could afford this space. Parks observed his former detective for ten minutes before his cell began to ring and one of the models looked over at him, sidetracking Jake's attention and causing him to stop taking pictures. A short, balding man in his late forties immediately rushed to Parks from over on the side, where he'd gone unnoticed until then.

"This is a closed set," the balding man practically stammered with authority. "You're not allowed in here."

Parks took out his badge and flashed it at the man, not caring if he liked him being there or not as he answered his phone.

"Hello?" Parks said into his phone. "Hello?"

"It's all right, Sal," Jake said quickly upon seeing who was visiting.

"We can all take ten. Why don't you have your models go eat—well...absorb something." Jake set his camera down and made his way over to Parks.

Parks checked the caller ID and saw that it was the same unlisted number with an Arizona area code. Joshua Levinson.

"Josh, is that you?" Parks asked quickly. "I wish you would talk to me. I really d—"

The line went dead before Parks could say anything more.

"Detective David Parks, LAPD," said Jake as he reached Parks and shook his hand. "What's up?"

"You tell me," Parks asked, eying the studio.

"This? Well...gotta make ends meet somehow," Jake shrugged. "When they split up the team, they decided they needed me taking pictures of crime scenes instead and moved me back to SID." Parks had momentarily forgotten that Jake had started off in the Scientific Investigation Division. It made sense that they would put him back where he had begun before joining Parks's team. "Now that's even been reduced to part-time, and I needed to do something to supplement my income. Basically"—Jake pulled out his cell and showed it to Parks—"I wait for this thing to go off with a text message with an address on it, and I show up to snap some photos of a dead guy."

"You haven't talked to Rachel?" He knew about the relationship between Detective Rachel Moore and Jake Fairmont, but it had never been within his jurisdiction to do or say anything about it.

"She mentioned something about you possibly stopping by. She didn't say why. What's up?"

"There was a double homicide. Up in the hills."

"That happens," Jake smirked as he turned to his camera and began fiddling with it. "Or so I recall. Maybe my mind's a little rusty."

"They were poisoned. And a symbol was left painted on the wall above the bodies."

"A Japanese ten?" Jake asked, showing more interest than he had hoped. "Is Lewis Hayward free?"

"No. He isn't. And no, it wasn't a Japanese ten. It was Kyū. Japanese nine."

"So those were tens Hayward left behind at the scenes of his victims." Jake beamed.

"We don't know what those were. Or what they mean. Or meant. Maybe something. Maybe nothing. Regardless, we just need to work this case. The one currently open and unsolved."

"We?" Jake paused and faced Parks.

"We. Us. The team. They want us back."

"All of us? Rachel too?"

"She's on board."

"But..." Jake mulled over his relationship with Rachel and what Parks's offer would mean for the future of it.

"Look," Parks said. "You two don't currently work together. Hell, I don't even know what your working status with the department is. So whatever relationships that were formed during your time *apart* from the department...well, that's just life."

"Dave...You know we started seeing each other—"

"Once you two no longer worked together," Parks interrupted. "I know. So what? I'm willing to accept you both on my team knowing your current relationship status. We're all adults. It doesn't bother me. So long as the two of you don't mind working together."

Jake's face lit up with a smile.

"So, can I take that as a yes?" Dave asked, extending his hand.

"Mr. Fairmont, will we continue this session sometime today?"

called out the little man with the whiney voice that just grated on Jake's ears.

"When do we begin?"

"Where's Milo?" Jake asked as he leaned back in the chair at his newly assigned desk up on the Homicide Special Section floor of the LAPD's downtown station. He had sat around for thirty minutes before Parks showed up and brought him up to where they would conduct business.

The area of the floor where they would do business was carved out mostly on the northern side of the floor, with six desks set aside for Parks and his team as well as all the necessary white-board space for current cases.

"Milo's...he was a little more difficult in cutting the red tape with," Parks sighed. "Not sure if he's joining us."

"Well, isn't he just Hardwick's personal bit—I mean, doesn't he do stuff for her?"

"He's been reassigned to the Cyber Crimes Online division with Computer Forensics," Parks answered. "And they made it clear they don't want to give him up."

"No shit, they don't," Jake huffed. "He's the freaking best. But tough shit. Did you tell them to go eff themselves; he's ours?"

Parks glared at Jake, relaying his disinterest in his side commentary, despite that he may have felt the same way.

"I was allowed to make requests for my team. In no way was I given any guarantees. The higher-ups have assured me they will do what they can but made no promises."

"But—"

"It is what it is," Parks cut him off. "We'll get him back if we get him back. There's only so much I can do."

"But the little squirt will be lost without us. Imagine little Nemo out in the ocean, all alone. That's what it's like for Milo out in the...what's he out in again? I mean, at least Nemo had Dory. Who's Milo got? A computer?"

"If memory serves me, Milo Tippin can do a hell of a lot more damage with a simple computer than all you men could with your so-called guns," came a female voice from behind Jake, startling him but not enough to cause him to fall from his chair as Jackie Isley walked onto the floor.

"Ohhhh, sheeee-iiiiit," Jake said snidely for comic relief. "Everyone hide all sharp objects and firearms. Lovers' spat about to take place."

"Jake—" Jackie looked to Parks for approval, which he gave with a slight nod and she slapped the back of his head and walked on. "Mind your manners. There are ladies present on the floor."

"Oh?" Jake laughed. "Where? I don't see any—"

"Do you plan on talking the 10 home or the 101?" Rachel interrupted, by listing the two different freeways Jake could take after work and thereby giving him the ultimatum of coming home with her or going home alone.

"Speaking of lovers' spat," Jackie almost whispered. "Or, oops, was I not supposed to know about you two?"

She winked at Jake and he immediately shut up and sank back in his seat. He was just hopped up on adrenaline, excited for their first day back as a team. Parks could understand. He looked at the mug next to him and found it empty. He grabbed it and before he could stand from his position on the edge of his desk, a fully filled mug of fresh coffee was motioned in front of his face. He turned to see Milo Tippin holding it out for him as he had often done so many times before.

"Figured you'd need one of these already," Milo smiled. "Welcome back, boss."

"Yeah, that's my boy," Jake howled as he jumped up and grabbed Milo, giving the boy a hug. He still looked barely twenty years old, though he was now twenty-three. His hair was slightly shorter, and his clothes just as tight fitting on his near skeleton-thin body. There was something to the kid's eyes; Parks wasn't sure what it was, an edge, possibly even a darkness to them, but he brushed the thought away, just happy to have his whole team back.

He was, after all, part of the family.

"All right, all right," Parks said as he ruffled Milo's hair and gave Jake a push. "You two take your seats. We have a lot to go over. And I'm sure I don't even want to know how you got released to join me here."

"Just a temporary suspension." Milo smiled innocently. "I swear, I totally didn't mean to leak the contents of Rush Skylar's phone to the media. I mean, if only he hadn't taken those pictures..."

"Enough," Parks said with a roll of his eyes. "I don't want to know. Besides, we need to get serious here. There are two dead bodies out there that we need to work on."

"Man," Jake whined. "Stupid dead people always getting in the way of our fun."

Parks cleared his throat and put on a serious face as Hardwick entered the floor with Mark Wilkes next to her. "Chief. Good morning."

"Good to see you all settling in and playing nice once again," Hardwick said with a brief smile as she walked to the front and settled in next to Parks, Wilkes still at her heels. "You all know each other. You all know what strings were pulled to get you all back here. And, especially with Dr. Isley here, you all know the stakes at hand. Hopefully this won't be anything like our last rodeo with Lewis Hayward. But just in case, everyone stay sharp and do your jobs, and we should all come out of this smelling like roses. Now you all know Detective Wilkes. This was originally his case, so he's here to go over what we've got already on this ongoing investigation." Hardwick took a deep breath as she paused and then continued. "We all know this case has certain similarities and connections to the Palisades Poisoner case. That's what we're here to go over. To see just what's going on here. Parks, this is your show."

"Thanks," Parks said as he stepped forward once again. "What we have here are two victims of homicidal poisoning. What we also have is another mysterious symbol. One that might possibly link our two homicides to the previous victims of Lewis Hayward, in some way we don't yet know. The whys and hows...well, that's what we need to figure out. So...what do we got so far?"

THIRTEEN

For the next hour, Detective Wilkes brought Parks's team up to date with the information he had on the double homicide. Their leads were limited, and due to the Delancys exclusion from society for the past several decades, new and current information was at a minimum. Wilkes had convinced the sole surviving heir to the Delancy legacy—Mary's oldest son Benjamin—to fly in the following day from San Francisco to help bring their thin files to a fuller understanding. They also pulled all calls that Mary Delancy had made to 911 over the years. This also included the one previous homicide that had been committed at the Delancy residence: that of Thomas Cream, Mary's lover who was attacked one night by one of Mary's stalkers, Nicholas Vaquier. Each member of the team had seen the report from that night as well as the numerous crime photos that were also making their way around the table. Dave let the facts sink in with the team and then dismissed them for a ten-minute coffee break.

Next, Jackie took the floor, relaying all pertinent information on the poison used on Mary Delancy and her son Scott. Though she had ruled the poison as strychnine, she had not yet been able to determine whether it had been altered in any way, as she was still waiting for test results that would take several more days to get back.

"So we've got what? A Frankenstein-like poison we're dealing with?" Fairmont asked as he went over the files in his hands.

"Possibly," Jackie confirmed.

"Sounds like Lewis Hayward's hand at work, doesn't it? I mean, besides this Japanese nine on the wall. Then again…those two facts are circumstantial. Not a real connection. The Lewis Hayward factor in this case could be merely coincidental. He may have nothing to do with this case at all. We need something more to connect it to him."

Jackie looked to Parks. This was it. Now or never. Time to spread all the facts out and let them fall where they fall.

"Speaking of Lewis Hayward." Parks cleared his throat. "We believe and are acting as though this person, whoever they are, that killed Mary and Scott Delancy could somehow be connected to Lewis Hayward. We don't know how or why—only that they possibly are. A copycat? Possibly. Though a student or protégé is more likely. Or so I think." Parks paused and collected his thoughts. "There is also one other reason why we feel this case may be connected to Lewis Hayward. There's also this." He passed around copies of the letter addressed to him from Lewis Hayward.

"What the—?" Fairmont spat as he looked up at Parks. "Are you kidding us with this shit?"

"When did you get this?" Milo asked, worry plastered across his face.

"Apparently it was delivered to the station a few weeks ago. There's been tests run on it to confirm its authenticity. It was written by Lewis Hayward. How it got out and here is another question that's being investigated. This letter was brought to my attention when I was brought onto this case," Parks answered.

THE BLUE CONDITION | 105

"So, what? If you wouldn't have taken this case they never would have shown you this letter?" Fairmont asked, getting riled up. "That's jacked up."

"Let's not worry about what might have been and worry about what is. These are the facts. As we know them."

"Not counting whatever else we might not know," Fairmont quipped.

"Drop it," Parks ordered. "We have what we have. Let's work with that. We've done it before and with less to go on. Our main priority right now isn't Lewis Hayward. It's whoever our killer of Mary and Scott Delancy is. Yes, there may be a connection between their murders and Lewis Hayward. He may very well have ordered them killed. But Lewis Hayward is locked up. At this very minute. So he did not physically carry out these murders. Someone else did."

"You don't think a threat being made against your life, from Lewis Hayward no less, is something you should take seriously? What if that's the connection between Hayward and this case? What if it's through Lewis Hayward that we'll be able to identify who our killer is? What if it's all just a ruse to get you on the case and playing one of his games again?"

"Those possibilities are all being considered," Parks said, feeling the weight of the case already bearing down on his shoulders. "They are. And while I appreciate your concern, I do, our priority right now is this case. I think if we solve one, the other will be dealt with as a result. Okay?"

"But how do you—"

"Jake," Rachel said from behind him as she squeezed his shoulder.

He turned around and saw the look on her face that told him to drop it. Now wasn't the time. He turned around and nodded his head for Parks to continue. He would drop it. For now.

"We're rusty, but we're good." Parks threw on a smile and took control again. "We need practice, and I think this is just the case for us. Now, I appreciate all your concern, and trust me, we will deal with this"—Parks held up the letter in his hand—"but right now we've bigger, more-immediate fish to fry. Okay? Mary and Scott Delancy. They are our main priority."

"Got it, boss," Fairmont replied on instinct.

This was good. This was what they needed. A purpose. They worked well with perimeters.

"Are you going to see the crime scene first hand?" Rachel asked.

"I will. Just not now. I'll stop by the crime scene tonight on my way home to get a feel for it. Okay, everyone, Milo especially..."

"Sir?" Milo said, pepping up, his stance at attention and his eyes alert.

"I want you to go over Mary and Scott's history. Personal and otherwise. The works. Their financials. Backgrounds. Schooling. Her professional career. Everything."

"Got it, sir." Milo nodded as he typed away on the iPad in front of him.

"I also...I also want all of the Palisades Poisoner files pulled. We cannot ignore that the facts of this case are too similar to that one. We're going to need to go back over the details from a year ago."

"Will do."

"Jackie...Wilkes...not sure what I can do with you two—"

"I'm at your disposal with this case," Jackie interrupted. "Last thing we need is another serial poisoner. Whatever you need from me or my department, you need only ask. We're running all tests we currently can; I'll be at my lab overseeing that everything's going according to plan."

"Good to hear," Parks continued. "You said there was something off about the flowers at the crime scene?"

"They're called a blue Phalaenopsis orchid. The moth orchid. They're rare. They can be ordered from flower shops, but they're not common. They come blue, but when they die off and re-bloom, they are white. So no matter what the flowers mean, whether they were brought or delivered by the killer or not, they were put there recently. Blooms were still blue. But something felt off about them. Could be nothing."

"Could be nothing. Could be something. Could be everything. We check it out. Work with Milo on it. When the son arrives from San Francisco, I want you to sit in on the interview with me. I would like a woman's perspective, et cetera, et cetera. Okay?"

Rachel nodded agreeably.

Parks turned to Wilkes but remained quiet, not sure what to say, how to give the man an assignment without making it look like he was ordering the man around.

"Lewis Hayward took out my whole team," Wilkes said quietly. "Not to mention he made a fool of me and the department. That sick fuck has anything to do with this case, then I'm going to be there to take his ass down. Just tell me what you need."

"Mary Delancy made numerous 911 calls over the years. I know old records are hard to come by, but they're out there. And not all on computer. So we need to dig through old files. I need all 911 calls made by Mary or her son Scott and the results from them. Gather information. Talk to someone from TMU and see what they have on record, if anything, pertaining to Mary Delancy." Parks noticed Milo make a face at the acronym. "TMU is the Threat Management Unit.

They handle most of the stalking cases. If we need to, we'll divvy up and talk to whomever we need about those calls. Witnesses. Neighbors. Old officers. On a side note, part of the reason I want you to work this angle is I was a responding officer on several of her 911 calls." Parks paused as everyone's focus became more alert. "I know, I know. Another connection to the victims, Lewis Hayward, and myself. We'll explore it when we get to it. Everything in its proper order and in its proper place. Okay? But I need someone who isn't going to be biased against getting the facts, even if they have to come from me. I need you to do this. Use Jake to help you research if you need it. Okay?"

"Like I said," Wilkes said, sounding irritated by the amount of physical paperwork he was going to have to dig through but seeing the possibility of busting Parks's chops as an upside, "consider it done."

"I want all threats made against her to be categorized, and we'll take them based on their level of intensity. We have stalking, love obsession, erotomania, and false victimization syndrome. Classify each threat. I want to know where they fall into these categories."

"Sounds like you know enough about the subject already," Milo commented.

"One of the joys of working in this city is we get a lot of stalkers," Parks said, nodding to Rachel and Wilkes as they too had been through the same situations. "They've got classes for us where they hit up stalking as a subject at least once a year. There's always something new to learn about the topic. Stalking is serious business, people. Stalking is a serial crime—in that it continues to happen. These usually aren't one-time deals. Stalking is repetition. Some of these calls may fall under the false accusation threats. But we need to examine each and every threat made to her to know for sure. Our killer could be someone on this list."

"What are you doing?" Jackie asked, wondering but not lecturing.

"I have a meeting and...I'm going to check out the possibility of visiting Lewis Hayward. It's been a while, but he and I need to have a little chat. Okay, you all know what to do. Let's get on it. Time is precious here, people. We all know it."

As all the team members gathered their notes and files and began to go about their just-assigned duties, Parks motioned for Milo to follow him.

"What's up, boss?" Milo asked.

Parks tilted his head toward the door and the two left the room and headed for the elevators. Both men remained quiet until they were outside the building and away, near the grassy knoll. Milo sat down on the edge of a cement seat near some recently planted flowers.

"So right off the bat, I'm aware I'm an asshole for even bringing this up. Worse still for bringing you into this. But I wouldn't be doing my job if I didn't. Even though everyone would throw a shit storm if they knew, in the long run they'd all feel safer knowing it had been done."

"Done what, exactly, sir?"

"Lewis Hayward was a cop. He had inside information that always kept him a step ahead of us. We can *not* ignore that fact. And if this case does have any direct relation to him, then that factor needs to be taken into account."

"And do what, exactly, sir?" Milo asked again.

"I need you to investigate members of the LAPD. Starting with the people directly involved with this case and working your way out. Now, I'll be honest, I'm not expecting the same mistake to be made again. And I doubt it has been or would be. But again, I wouldn't be doing my job if I didn't double-check. So I need you to do this for me."

"Double-check, sir?"

"Off the record…"

"Yes, sir."

"This entire conversation never happened. Like Mission: Impossible never happened. However—again, and this is also off the record, I have it on good authority that ever since Lewis Hayward's attack, Internal Affairs has taken a closer look at the members of the LAPD. We all have active open case files with IAD. Not that we didn't before, we're all members of the LAPD after all, but this is different. Now, I'm not asking you to spend every waking moment going over every detail of our lives. But if you could somehow access IA's files and check on them—see if there are any immediate red flags—that would be helpful. I'm not expecting there to be. After all, I would expect IA to take anyone raising any doubt immediately out of service. Again, this is IA we're talking about, and who knows what games they're playing. I just…I don't want to be caught off guard again. Not on something like this. You read me?"

"I read you, sir."

"Just access their files. Check them out. Give them to me to check out if you want. If there are any holes or access to anything you may have that they may not have been able to check…"

Parks didn't finish the sentence, nor did he need to. Milo knew what was being asked of him.

"Hopefully, we'll have this case solved and filed away before any further damage can be done like last time. But on the off chance that it isn't wrapped up, and we do have a mole once again…"

"I hear you, sir. But if anyone was to ever find out—"

"No one, and I mean no one, is to ever know about this," Parks interrupted. "Like I said, IA's already working on their own investigation. Hardwick knows about this. I'm not supposed to, but I've got my own sources. You are under no circumstances to let anyone know about this investigation. Either yours or IA's. But if for some reason, somehow, someone does find out about what you're doing, it's IA's investigation. You were just snooping around on them to find out what they know. At my request. You blame it all on me. You understand?"

Milo nodded silently as he took this in. Parks had captured his attention, and he knew the kid was already working in his mind how to go about his investigation. This would work. This could work. Hopefully there was nothing to work.

"You really want me to start with you, sir? And work my way down. I mean, come on. Really? You, sir?"

"In case any of this ever catches the light of day, I can't be seen as having ever ordered you to not investigate any one member of the LAPD over another. Including myself. But whether you see fit to spend more of your time on any one member over another—or *less* time—that's entirely up to you. Hell, as far as I know, you could tell me you're doing all this investigating, not actually do anything, and really, how would I even know?"

"True."

"I hate to put you in this position. But this needs to be done. We have to be sure. In case this gets out of hand. Like last time. So what happened last time doesn't happen again."

"Sir, what are the chances...?"

"Next to none, I'd say," Parks said, sounding sure and almost believing it himself. "But we have to be sure."

"I understand. I'll let you know what I find."

"Thank you, Milo. Oh, and Milo? Good having you back."

"We'll see about that, sir. But yeah, it's good to be back too."

FOURTEEN

Parks leaned back in his chair opposite Doctor Lucas Black, the department's self- and often court-appointed shrink for officers in need of counseling. Most every member of the LAPD saw Doctor Black, or one of the other dozen psychologists at the Behavioral Sciences building, at some point or other in their careers as a law enforcement officer. Though some tried to fight it, Parks just saw it as another fork in the game of life that came with the territory. He had learned in the past that it was often more exhausting trying to fight seeing one of the shrinks than simply going along for the ride. And every now and again, they even managed to help. Being the head shrink for the department, Doctor Black even helped look over cases for the department from time to time.

"So, what do you think?"

Dr. Black had been helpful to Parks during the Palisades Poisoner case, though their history went back further, to the case preceding the Palisades Poisoner: the Peter Kozlov case.

Parks had never shown or voiced any objection to his meetings with Black; instead, he found them useful, someone to bounce ideas off. He also knew Black had been ordered to keep an eye on him.

Though Black kept their sessions confidential, he still had to answer to the higher-ups.

"Well, ahem." Dr. Black cleared his throat and readjusted his glasses on his nose. "What do *you* think?"

Parks glared at the man, hating it when he answered a question with a question. Why couldn't he ever just give an honest answer?

"What did you tell Hardwick and Reed?"

"What makes you think I told them anything?"

"Come on. I know they had to ask your opinion about this. About handing me back my team. About me tackling Lewis Hayward. This case. Come on...let's not BS each other here. Just tell me the Hollywood standard: no comment, and move on. But don't lie to me."

"Honestly?" Dr. Black asked with a slight lift in his voice. "I told them I was concerned." Parks looked over at the man, surprised he had said so. To him. "But not about you taking on this case. Or you finding out about the letter from Lewis Hayward. Not about you getting your team back. But more so about what would happen to you if you didn't face any of these things head on. We've been having our sessions for over a year now, Dave. And you've had some ups and downs. However, you've been on a downward spiral since the Knott/Davis case. And I don't like what I see. Ever since your team was dismantled and you were reassigned, you've lost that passion within you to carry out your job in a way I know you can."

Parks thought about this. What the man said was true.

"And how's that?"

"Effectively and efficiently."

The two men stared at each other. That was the truth. Parks had taken a step back professionally, and he had let it spill into the other aspects of his life. Not only that, but he had also become a second-rate detective and found himself satisfied with being just that. It wasn't something he had set out to do. It was just something that happened. Like the social drinker who turned into a full-blown alcoholic. Or the Super Bowl better who turned into a full-blown gambler and was soon out of a house. It just happened. Without the person even being aware of it.

"You're so much more than what you currently are," Dr. Black continued. "And you know it as well. Unfortunately, we've all accepted it, and we shouldn't have. Not you. Not me. Not your superiors or peers. We've all pitied you, and it's selfish. Not on our behalf. But yours. You've been selfish, and the only person it affects is the victims you're supposed to take care of out there. You don't matter. You want to throw your life away, then that's your choice. It's your life. Your call. But you mean so much more to so many people. People count on you. So yes, I told them I had concerns. Not about your ability to take on this case. About what would continue to happen if you didn't. They asked me, and I told them that if it was within my power, I would insist you be assigned this case and this new standing within the department. Because people depend on you.

"Now, will I have new concerns with you taking on these new assignments and challenges? Of course I will. But that's my job. My worry. Not yours. You don't need to concern yourself with that. Just as much as you don't need to concern yourself with my opinion. The only one that matters is yours. You can do this. I know it. So do you. The question is: Do you want this? Do you want the change? Or are you satisfied with your life as it is? Only you can make the necessary changes. Unfortunately, it's not up to this case or this department to make those changes. They can only come from within."

Parks thought about this as he stared out the window once more.

"Still taking your medication?" Dr. Black asked as he looked down at his notebook.

"You mean the anti-psychotics that were prescribed to me?"

"I'm talking about the anti-*depressants*, yes."

"I think the ones I took as a teenager had more of an effect on me. These just seem to make me..." Parks shrugged and gave up on the answer, proving his point about the medication prescribed to him several months earlier.

"Should we up the dosage? Or change them altogether?"

"Whatever you see fit, Doc. It's your call."

"No, it really isn't," Dr. Black corrected. "Dave, I don't think you're getting all you can out of this. These medications are here to help you. You've managed to manage your depression for years without medication, and I've applauded that effort. However, this past year you've been through a lot. You appeared to need a helping hand. That was why you were prescribed these. Not as an excuse for your behavior, but to help manage it and get you back on the right path. Do you understand? Your reasons for taking them as a child are different than why you take them now."

"My father killed himself and my mother left me. I was abandoned. You don't think that was a good enough reason to be sad in life?"

"There's a difference between being sad about something and being depressed."

"I get out of bed every day, same as everyone else."

"And thoughts of suicide?"

"Never once crossed my mind," Parks said comfortably. "I'm serious. Never once. It's not that bad. I'm just in a funk. I'll get out of it. You'll see. These drugs usually take a while to truly kick in. Give 'em another couple of weeks. I'll be fine."

"Since you brought them up, do you want to talk about your mother? Or father?"

"What's to talk about? He checked out so long ago I don't even remember the man. And I haven't seen her since I was a child. Maybe ten or so was the last time. I don't remember her any more either. Could barely tell you what she looks like. Or if she's even still alive. She could have died years ago for all I know."

"Really?" Dr. Black asked, his tone giving away his doubt. "You're a cop who has the means of tracking down people, and you've never once located your mother in all your years on the force?"

"Why? What for? She left me. She didn't want me or to be around. So why should I go looking for her? She made her choice. I don't need to change her mind. Make her believe she made the wrong choice. Whatever reason it was. The past is the past. Life goes on."

"It's not like you were an orphan. You did have a family growing up."

Parks thought about his aunt and uncle, his mother's sister and her family who raised him after his father took his own life and his mother abandoned him. He was grateful for them. To them. Always had been and always would be. They were his family. He held no resentments against them. They truly did love him, and he loved them back.

"They're still not the reason you're on the medication now. We both know that."

"Can't just fix me with pills, Doc. Or talking. Or time."

"You really believe that?"

Parks wasn't sure how to respond.

"Well, I think this has been a good session," Dr. Black continued. "I think we've made progress. Don't you?"

Dr. Black didn't need to say anything else any more than Parks needed to reply. They both knew the answer to all of Black's questions and concerns.

FIFTEEN

The patrol officer guiding Benjamin Delancy and an unknown female, who held onto Benjamin's arm with possibly a little too much force, onto the main floor of the Homicide Special Section division paused near the doorway, not entirely sure where to take the two. Parks motioned to the young man who turned and said something to the couple before leaving their side, neither of the two moving to follow him.

"Benjamin Delancy?" Parks said when the patrol officer got to him.

"Yeah," the patrol officer said as he looked around the room in awe, soaking in his surroundings, obviously having aspirations beyond patrol duty. The kid was young, barely out of his twenties, with sandy-blond perfectly parted hair and a name tag that read "Hardy."

"Who's the woman with him?"

"Girlfriend," Hardy replied, as if Parks should have known that. "Don't remember her name. Dammit. That's something I should have known. Or remembered. Or written down for you."

"It's okay," Parks reassured. "I'll handle it from here. Thank you for showing them in."

"Yes, sir," Hardy said with a nod.

"Benjamin Delancy?" Parks asked as he offered his hand to the man who was Mary Delancy's only surviving lineage.

Benjamin Delancy's hair was a brownish-orange shade of spoiled peach, slicked back though every now and again a few strands found their way into his eyes, which were large and bark-colored, without any of the life that Parks had remembered sparking his mother's eyes. He was on the heavier side, though he managed to hide it well, his weight barely showing in his stomach and chin areas. He was well-groomed, with equally impeccable clothing choices, even if they were on the duller side of attractive.

"I'm Benjamin Delancy," Ben confirmed as he offered a firm hand to shake. His voice was an odd mixture of nasal and raspy.

"And this is?"

"My fiancée, Katrina Thompson," Benjamin introduced, as he placed a hand on his fiancée's waist and guided her up from behind him to his side. She, on the other hand, was far more attractive, with short-trimmed, midnight-black hair and large, becoming eyes. Parks guessed her to be in her late thirties. Though she was somewhat thicker through the hips and chest area, she appeared to take good care of her body and enjoyed showing it off with slender, more form-fitting attire. Her skin was paler than that of Benjamin's, and for a split second the image that came to Parks's mind was that of Snow White.

"Though everyone calls me Kat." Kat smiled, as she too offered her hand. She held onto Parks's hand, and for a second he could have sworn she wasn't going to let him go when she did. As she stared at him, he recognized the look she gave, having seen it before. That of attraction. "Kat Thompson."

Something was off about her voice. Her accent. The fact was she had none, no discernable one at least, that Parks could tell. Like when a foreign actor in a movie tried to pull off an American accent by overdoing the nothingness to his words. None of the words she spoke stood out as different except for her name. When she spoke the two words of her name, there was a flair in them, as if by mentioning her name one should feel seduced. Perhaps it was just the way she said her name to him. As if she wanted to seduce him. Or perhaps he simply imagined things. No sooner had all these thoughts entered his mind did he notice that she was at Benjamin's side, hugging his arm as if in need of protection from the world.

"Yes, well, thank you for coming in," Parks said, as he showed the couple the way to a nearby room where they could talk privately. As they walked, Parks mouthed the word "Rachel" to Milo, signaling for him to find her and send her in. "We just have a few questions we'd like to go over about your mother and brother at this time. Clear a few things up, if we can."

"And you are?" Benjamin Delancy asked as he and his fiancée sat down on one side of the table.

"Oh, sorry," Parks said. "I'm Detective Dave Parks. I'm the one handling your mother and brother's case." Just then, Jackie Isley walked in, eyed Parks with wonder, and sat down next to him.

"Rachel's occupied at the moment. Figured I could help?"

"And this," Parks said, turning back to Benjamin and his fiancée, "is Dr. Isley. She'll be assisting me with various aspects of this case."

"Nice to meet you," Benjamin Delancy said by way of greeting as he offered his hand to Jackie. She shook it and then nodded toward Kat Thompson, who appeared cold but shook her hand as well.

"What is it you'd like to know?" Benjamin Delancy asked, starting the conversation. "I'm really not sure what all you expect me to tell you about my mother and brother. What—what is it you'd like to know?"

"For starters, when was the last time you saw them? Spoke to them? Just the general stuff like that," Parks asked as he scribbled a few notes in his pad.

"I spoke to my brother about six months ago. My mother—my mother I can't remember. Sometime last year. I saw them both two Christmases ago. We didn't exactly get along. We weren't the picture-perfect, happy family I'm sure America would like to paint us as. Between the *True Hollywood* stories and the tabloids, I'm sure we were the Partridge Family. But I'm here to tell you, detective, we weren't. My mother was—we weren't."

Delancy appeared as if he could keep going when Kat placed a soft yet firm hand on his forearm, signaling for him to both watch what he said and to remind him that she was there.

Parks remained quiet as he stared at Benjamin Delancy. Everyone was well aware that they had just opened Pandora's Box. The question was about how far Parks could push the subject. How far he could push Delancy without a lawyer present. And how much the man wanted to be considered a suspect.

"Mr. Delancy, where were—"

"I was up north in San Francisco. I have other people who can vouch for me being there as well. I was at work. My office. Other people will confirm that. I was at work. I was there until almost three in the morning. And I—I was in San Francisco."

"And, Miss Thompson, where were—"

"What reason could Kat possibly have for murdering my mother and brother? She'd never met them before. Either one of them. I doubt she even knows what they look like. Unless she just happened to jump a plane down here that night and randomly kill the two remaining survivors of my bloodline by mere coincidence. Huh?"

Parks thought about that. "And how long exactly have you two been together?"

When Benjamin paused for a moment, Kat answered for him, "A year back in August."

They were going on fourteen months. And the woman had never seen a single picture of the members of her fiancé's family, let alone met any of them? Parks couldn't help but be suspicious.

"And your fiancée has never seen a picture of your family?"

"No," Benjamin answered flatly. "Why would—no."

"And you didn't think that was odd?"

Kat Thompson simply shrugged. "It is what it is. I don't pry."

"Never talked about his family? No stories. Of growing up? Of birthdays? Good memories? Bad? Anything?"

"We didn't have that kind of a relationship," Benjamin snapped, as if that answered every question Parks had thrown at them.

"What? You don't like to talk about your family? Or you just wished they had never existed?"

"I simply didn't talk about them. I don't care to focus on the past. I'm more interested in the future. The past means nothing to me. Who cares about it? Who cares what cereal I ate as a child or what present I didn't get for Christmas that made me upset with my mother for a week or so? The past is in the past. Who cares? One needs to just let it go. I have."

Let it go?

Benjamin Delancy continued to squirm in his seat but remained silent while his fiancée stared Parks down.

"You want to know where I was when my mother and brother were murdered. No problem. I'll gladly give you every last detail you

desire. I have nothing to hide. I didn't murder them. My mother and—
I didn't murder them. But I'm not going to sit here for the next few
hours and dredge up every last memory of my childhood. It serves no
purpose. Okay?"

"Mr. Delancy, I'm going to be honest with you. You haven't in-
voked the right to a lawyer yet. And in my opinion, I don't see you or
Miss Thompson as my prime suspects. But you're beginning to make
the hair on the back of my neck stand on end, and I'm not entirely sure
why. Now, you may not have physically carried out the deed of murdering your family, but something's off. And *even* if you *didn't* hire
someone"—Benjamin appeared as if he was about to laugh at the
speculation when Parks sat straighter in his seat, taking command of
the conversation and continued—"even if you didn't, I think we all
know there's more to your story. So why don't you save us all a lot of
time and aggravation and let me in on your little secret. Now, none of
this is on the record. And if you need it to stay that way"—Parks set
down the pad of paper and pen he had been scratching away at—"I can
keep it that way. For now. But this is a one-time offer. One time only.
Do you understand me?"

"You have no right—*no right*—to put my family through the ringer
like this. Forget my mother. I don't care what you know or what people say about her. But Kat has no reas—"

Kat squeezed Benjamin's forearm and he turned to his fiancée and
the two relayed information that was relevant only to the other. They
had a language all their own, known to one another with nothing
more than simple looks.

Benjamin cleared his throat, composing himself as he fiddled with
his hands and then placed them flat on the table before him.

"Truth of the matter is, I ran away from home at sixteen and haven't been back since. I've seen my brother on a few occasions, but never at *that* house and never with *her* around. Not that she would ever leave that house anymore. My mother was a bit...eccentric. I was lucky when I could get Scott out of the house. And that wasn't until he was well into his twenties. Before that...perish the thought. Mommy dearest wouldn't dare let her baby out of her sight. And especially not to be free out in the real world where her wild, rebellious son could possibly influence him into turning against her." Benjamin stopped, his face shaking as rage swam through his body. Not rage at Parks and his questions, but rather at the past as it began to overwhelm him; memories long forgotten begin to swim to the surface of consciousness. "She and Scott had a bond that went a little further beyond the typical mother-son relationship. If you get what I mean?"

Parks stayed quiet. This was Benjamin Delancy's story to tell. At his own pace in his own words. Even though he didn't find the situation all that shocking. He had heard it before, and knew he would hear it again many more times before he retired. This was the world they lived in. The world he dug his way through looking for light at the end of a never-ending tunnel.

"She'd tried with me at first, of course. But I was older—grew up faster than Scott. Though it wasn't about age. Not to my mother. I don't mean what I say like that. She wasn't a pedophile. She didn't like little boys. Not even me. She just liked Scott. Scott was—Scott. In some ways—in some ways I fear Scott was stunted by her. Physically. Emotionally. Mentally. She spent less time with me because father was around when I was a child. But after she had Scott, and after father had died, she became possessive. She changed. She never left. Her heart broke. Almost literally, I would say. She never trusted after father's death. She blamed him, you know? For dying. Claimed he betrayed her. Tricked her. Lied to her. By dying. Naturally. Mother, she—she blamed him."

Ben paused and looked around. He needed something to parch his thirst, and Parks looked to Jackie, who understood and immediately got up to fetch a glass of water from one of the neighboring break rooms. She came back less than a minute later and handed two bottles over to Ben and Kat.

"Thank you," Benjamin said as he downed half the bottle and gasped. "After father's death, mom changed. She kind of…well, I guess you could say it was like she had turned Scott into a living doll. She babied him. Dressed him in weird clothes. Girls' clothes. Gowns. Frilly dresses and the sort. Claimed that since father abandoned her and she would never have a daughter that she would have to make do. It was wrong, what she did. I knew that. But I was only a child myself. There was only so much I could do."

"And how old were you when your father passed on?"

"Father passed in '82. I was ten. Scott was only five. For six long years I put up with that woman's crazy. But I had to. For Scott's sake. What kind of a brother—what kind of brother would I be if I hadn't stood up for him? Then finally, I couldn't take it anymore. I tried to take Scott with me. But two children? Out on their own? We'd never survive. They would have sent us back in a heartbeat. To live with that woman. Whom everyone loved so much. She was still somewhat known back then." Benjamin took another swallow of water and wiped his brow with the back of his hand. "Besides, Scott didn't want to leave. She'd poisoned him by then. His mind. His way of thinking. Living. Existing. He loved her. Unconditionally. Knew of no other way to live. Or love. Still doesn't. Didn't. Whatever. At least up to the last time I had seen him. He never knew any better."

Benjamin wiped a tear from his face. His cheeks were blanching, his breathing labored, the fear of the words of his story getting to him. "I tried to rescue him. Several times. Over the years. But I mean, he's a grown man. How can you save a grown man who doesn't want to be saved? Who doesn't know he *should* be saved? Huh? How do you do that? Tell me how? What I should have done? What could I have done? I don't know. I just...I never knew."

Benjamin finally broke down, sobbing as he threw his hands to his face and looked to the ground, his head between his knees.

"My fiancé had nothing to do with his mother's murder. Though God only knows he'd be justified if he had." Kat Thompson said her words in a way that let everyone know the interrogation was over. "That woman...that woman had no right having children. Had no right being a mother. No right."

SIXTEEN

Despite his fiancée's objections, David Parks and Jackie Isley questioned Benjamin Delancy for another hour, asking more questions about his childhood, dates, places, and other information that might have meant nothing to the man being questioned but could have meant the world to Parks. Benjamin Delancy looked as if he had not slept in a year, his eyes red and runny, barely able to stay open, his shoulders slouched, and his demeanor spent. Parks finally suggested they finish for the evening, as long as Benjamin would be around for the next few days in case he had more questions to ask. Benjamin said that he would be at the Stay On Main hotel downtown for the next week until he wrapped up all of his mother and brother's affairs. Benjamin gave them all the appropriate information and ways to contact him, and then he and his fiancée went on their way.

Parks and Isley stood in the hallway outside the interrogation room for a few moments, soaking in the information they had just received, putting it all together. The case was moving forward. This was what they wanted.

"So, what do you think?" Parks asked.

"I don't know. I mean, I'm sure there's some truth to what he said.

Hell, it's probably all true in this day and age. But there was something rehearsed about what he told us. Like he'd been preparing a speech or a monologue. I don't know. He just kind of rubbed me the wrong way. But that doesn't make him a killer. And there's something off about her as well..."

"I thought the same thing," Parks agreed.

"Sure you did." Jackie smiled. "You were too busy checking her out to notice anything *off* about her."

"I was not," Parks protested as he made it to his desk and sat down.

Jackie winked at him to let him know she was playing with him. "So now what?"

"You tell me?" Parks asked, quizzing her.

"You need to type up that interview. Go over it again, at least once. Do some more paperwork. Research Mr. Benjamin Delancy. Check him out. See if there isn't some ulterior motive to his story. Go visit the crime scene still. You need to see it for yourself."

"I do," Parks said as he leaned back in his chair, thinking. "Care to join?"

"I've already seen it," Jackie shrugged. Parks knew this. "But it never hurts to see something twice. And through the eyes of a master."

"That all sounds like a plan," Parks agreed. "But first, why don't we go have a visit with Amy?"

Parks let Jackie drive the two of them over to the L.A. county coroner's office while he called ahead to inform Amy Tanaka that they were on their way.

With the aid of her *diener*, Amy Tanaka assembled the bodies of Mary and Scott Delancy for Parks and Jackie to observe. Parks noted the room, from the smell of the bodies to the looks and sound of everything inside, all coming together to form the very definition of morbid. There was a cold, impersonal feel to the room. It was clinical, like any other medical professional's examining room. Florescent fixtures hummed from all around, giving a background soundtrack to the tasks at hand. Though the entire department was receiving a physical facelift, Parks knew that in the end it would still be the same place.

The two bodies had already been examined by Tanaka—all forms of trace evidence bagged and tagged, the head and pubic hairs combed and packaged, and victim's mouths swabbed—all under Wilkes's and his partner's watchful eyes. The results that Amy had sent away for were just getting back, and Parks wanted to be able to look at the bodies and see if anything stuck out at him.

"You were right. Someone's been reading up on their Agatha Christie," Amy began as she put on a pair of latex gloves. "Strychnine poisoning. Both of them. Best I can tell, they drank it."

"Painful way to go?" Parks asked.

"Very," both women said at the same time.

Amy looked to Jackie, the two women getting the full extent of the damage the poison had done to its victims, both having seen the effects first hand.

"There's more," Amy said referring to her notes and looking down at the two bodies. "The bluish tint to the victim's finger and toenails, around the eyes and mouth—"

"Those aren't normal?" Parks asked.

After seeing Allison Tisdale's blood turn purple from cyanide during the Palisades Poisoner case, Parks figured nothing was unimaginable when it came to poisons.

"Not to this degree. At least never that I have seen before. And not from what I could find online from anyone else. Either." Amy looked to Jackie for confirmation.

"Agreed," Jackie nodded. "I'd say our killer had played with the poison. Added a compound to up its half-life or the effects. No idea what they could have mixed with it to make it work like that. We have to do more testing to figure it out. Nothing comes to mind. I've never seen someone do this before."

"Yes, we have," Parks corrected. When both women looked up at him, he added, "Lewis Hayward. He used a few compound poisons on his victims."

Both women remained quiet as they thought this over.

"Anything else you can tell me—us—about the murders?" Parks asked.

"Nothing you haven't already read in the reports," Amy sighed. "Both died between 10 p.m. and 1 a.m. The son first, then the mother."

"How can you tell?"

"Defensive wounds on the son," Amy explained as she walked around each body laid out on their respective cold metal tables and pointed out what she described. "I'm hypothesizing that he began convulsing first and the mother tried to aid him, accidentally scratching him as she tried to restrain him. As you can see here and here."

"How did they...did they drink it? Eat—"

"It was in both glasses according to the tests we ran," Amy said, walking around the bodies and picking back up her file. "Lethal amount, yet not strong enough to stop either one from drinking more than a swallow."

"How can you tell?"

"Other than they're dead?" Amy asked with a smirk.

"We don't know for sure," Jackie explained. "But the son's glass was less than two millimeters full, while the mother's was half full. So, going with the *assumption*—yes, I know I used *that* word—but I'm going on an assumption they each poured the same amount or at least the son a full glass..."

"I get you," Parks finished. "So we've got all we're gonna get."

"We'll run more tests," Jackie said, hoping to give Parks a spark of light at the end of a dark tunnel.

"Hey. We have a cause of death. That's more than some cases ever get. What about this strychnine stuff? Can we trace it?"

"Shockingly enough, I don't think you can just order it up on Amazon or at your local hardware store," Jackie said gleefully. "I mean, you can get rodent killer and other forms, but not with the concentration that we're talking about. This is pure strychnine. Mixed in with whatever our killer came up with. I'm sure there are a few chemists who have access to it with the proper credentials and papers...so we should start there. Of course, back at Pacific State University would be a good guess, since that's where Lewis Hayward got most of his poisons before."

"I've already got Hardwick filing the proper paperwork to get PSU's records," Parks agreed. "And with Bill Norton no longer in charge and around to run things there and with Elizabeth Norton's trial about to get underway, I'm sure there won't be as much red tape to cut through to get what we want out of them."

"Good." Jackie smiled. Parks didn't appear to be as down as he had been when she saw him at the start of this case. His spirits were already picking up—and his physical well-being was improving as well. She was glad. He needed a good case to get him back into the swing of things.

"You'll send over all the paperwork?" Parks asked.

"It will be in your office first thing in the morning," Amy said with confidence. She meant it, too. She would stay through the night and into the following morning if that's what it took to get this case moving forward. Though none of them said it aloud, everyone was already worried about how closely this case would mirror the Palisades Poisoner. And more particularly, that killer's timeline of turning up a new victim every five days.

"So now what?" Jackie asked.

"Now? Now we do some good old-fashioned detective work. We dig through piles of paperwork and online files and start to put the pieces of the puzzle together."

"Oh," Jackie winked. "Your specialty."

THURSDAY

SEVENTEEN

Today was game day. Parks leaned back in his chair and stared up at the few facts they had about the Delancy case, written up on the white murder board. Taped to the murder board were pictures of Mary and Scott Delancy, with a few known facts about each person scribbled below them in Parks's rather legible handwriting.

Everyone was nervous—no, anxious—to begin. To prove themselves. To prove that their second chance was not a wasted time or effort on the department's behalf.

"So?" Parks said, swiveling around in his chair. "What do we have? Let's start with the beginning. How did our killer or killers do their job? Rach? Jake?"

"Okay..." Fairmont began, as he and Rachel walked to the board and laid out a blueprint of the Delancy house and grounds. "Here is the Delancy house. Well secured. Private home security system. Top of the line. Everything intact. Bars over every window. Each door has numerous locks—this woman was paranoid. But you had to wonder—was she keeping someone out...or someone in?"

"Why?" Wilkes asked.

"Alarm was never triggered the night of the murders, and there is nothing on record with the alarm company to show that there was ever anything out of line. No accidental tripping of any of the alarms or anything like that. Add to that the grounds are surrounded by a ten-foot-tall brick-and-iron fence, and the front gate is and was locked and secured. No evidence of any tampering. As far as we know, or can tell, no one broke onto the Delancy grounds or into the Delancy house."

"So then our intruder was invited in?"

"That's the scenario we're going with," Rachel agreed. "Unless the perpetrator happened to be the world's most advanced cat burglar, in which case, why wasn't anything stolen from the house? From best we can tell, nothing was. This wasn't a burglary. This was a murder. Our intruder—whoever he was—was there for one purpose. To kill the Delancys."

"According to their records, the alarm was turned off at 9:17 that night and was reset at 9:43."

"So the Delancys did have a visitor?" Wilkes interjected.

"We think so. Which would mean either the Delancys were alive when their visitor left or the visitor knew the code to reset the alarm," Rachel surmised.

"What about trace evidence?" Parks asked.

"Well, they died in the bedroom," Rachel began as she flipped through some pages of notes. "Amy concurred with that." Parks nodded, and she continued. "So the bedroom was our main focal point. And that room was trashed. Hair and fibers were hard to determine, but from all that we could gather and collect, it all points to the victims. They died a painful death. They made a mess of that room. Urine. Sweat. Other human secretions were all from the victims. Nothing out of the ordinary with them dying the way they died."

"Got it," Parks said. "Nothing out of the ordinary. Anything else?"

"Actually," Rachel turned to Jake who shrugged for her to continue. "We're not sure about this next piece of evidence. It seems a little...circumspect."

"What's that?"

"Prints."

"Prints? As in fingerprints?"

"The one and only."

"Why don't you appear thrilled about this fact?"

"*She* isn't thrilled," Fairmont interrupted. "*I'm* over the moon about them. Especially when you take into account who they lead to."

"It's just odd, is all," Rachel explained. "The entire room shows evidence that Mary and Scott Delancy were the victims of a violent poisoning. The room is trashed, but nothing out of the ordinary. There's nothing to suggest that anyone purposely trashed the room to hide evidence of anyone's presence. Then we find prints. Clear, precise, unquestionable, easy-to-scan-and-identify prints. Every set of prints in that room, all belonging to the two victims, are smeared and almost unidentifiable, except for the fact that they came from the victims. I mean, Dave, you know how rare it is that we actually get a good, identifiable set of prints. That almost never happens. And at this crime scene we happen to get a good set of prints on one of the two glasses that the Delancys drank out of?"

"They were on the glasses they drank out of?" Wilkes asked.

"Right? That's a good thing!" Fairmont said with glee.

"You think they were left there on purpose?" Parks asked Rachel.

"I think this has Lewis Hayward and his twisted mind games written all over it. It's like we've been put on a scavenger hunt, and these prints are the next step to whatever the next phase of this so-called game is," Rachel stated matter-of-factly. "I feel like we're being toyed with, and it's bullshit."

Parks took this information in. He had expected something like this, if this case truly was related to Lewis Hayward in some way or another. The man loved his mind games. Parks's last visit with him up in San Quentin had proved that.

"Did we get anywhere with the prints?"

"IAFIS gave me a list that was narrowed down to about ten people."

"And of those ten you were able to narrow it down to one?"

"I think our best shot is one Mr. Henry Townes," Rachel answered without resorting to her notes.

Parks focused on her, but out of the corner of his eye he saw Detective Wilkes make a jerk reaction to the name.

"What's up?" Parks asked.

"You had me investigating Mary Delancy's so-called stalkers," Wilkes began, as if everyone else needed reminding. "Out of the dozen or so calls into 911 over the years, only three of them turned out to be somewhat legit. Which is three more than any of us probably need, considering the intensity of these fellows. A Mr. Nicholas Vaquier, who is currently serving time up in San Quentin, on and off since '99. First for a B&E charge against Mary Delancy. He got out in '03 and then got locked back up again the following year for another B&E charge. Out in three and then he hit his third strike in '08 for another B&E *and* manslaughter charge. He liked to send Miss Delancy letters with erotic situations of what he'd like to do to her described in them, along with what were described as 'tokens of his love.' Fingernail clippings. Hairs. Shavings of his skin. Once, he sent a package with a towel that he had…discharged into, if you catch my drift."

"Nice," Parks said shaking his head. "Go on."

"The second suspect is dead. Mr. Fountaine. Died three years now thanks to a drug OD. Thank God. Mr. Fountaine had actually managed to get his way onto both movie sets and Miss Delancy's home property on numerous occasions. Liked to dress up and pull cons. And I swear, according to the file, these were detailed lies. This man created entire personas to find ways to work his way onto a movie lot. Usually he was stopped because he had knives or other such weapons on his body. But there were two times in the three years he stalked Miss Delancy that he still managed to get onto the set. And twice he managed to make it onto her personal property and once even into her home. Broke in, moved stuff around, jerked off on her bed, and was caught when a neighbor called the police."

"Celebrity sure has its price," Fairmont sighed.

"Screw them," Wilkes snapped. "They get paid the big bucks so they can handle shit like this. Comes with the territory. They don't like it, then find another job."

Parks stared down at Wilkes. "But he's dead. So we move on. Who's the third?"

"The third is one Mr. Henry Townes." Wilkes leaned back in his chair. "Of course, this could simply be a coincidence. But I mean, how many Henry Townes could there be out there?"

"What do we know about him?" Parks asked.

"Not much. Other than what's in his file, which is longer than my dick," Wilkes shot out, catching a slight bit of stifled laughter-turned-coughing from Fairmont. "Guy's a career B&E boy. Had two restraining orders put out against him by ex-wives and three by celebrities, the latest by Mary Delancy, though that was almost a decade ago. Been in and out of jail his whole life. Done some time up in Folsom. Three years for burglary, though he was out in twenty months for good behavior. Likes to send letters. Flowers. Presents. Stuff like that."

"That all?"

"The guy's your typical creep," Wilkes added. "He's a Grade-A sleazeball with an IQ that would make a third-grader look like a college graduate. He's horny and feels an immediate connection to anything shiny and pretty. Is he our killer? Doubtful. He just doesn't understand the meaning of boundaries. But he is out 'n' about in the world and currently living in Los Angeles."

"You have a location on him?"

Wilkes held up a file, signaling that he was ahead of the game.

"His prints were found at the crime scene. Get a warrant. Then find him. Get him in here. I want to talk to him. Take Jake with you."

"You really think some stalker is our killer?" Rachel asked.

"Without having met the man, I can't say. But stalkers—the good ones—are by nature patient creatures. That is until they reach the boiling point and need something more than an affair from afar. Maybe our stalker had been hunting Mary Delancy, and he finally reached his boiling point and snapped. Maybe not. Maybe it is just coincidence. But his prints are at the scene of a homicide, and intentional or not, I want him in here to answer some questions. If they were left there intentionally, I want to know why."

"Then again, maybe he simply broke in to sniff the old lady's panties and get off, and just so happened to do it on the same day that she was murdered," Wilkes added with a gleeful smile.

"And we all know how I feel about coincidences."

"We'll have him in here," Wilkes said, managing to make the promise sound like a pain-in-the-ass, off-the-wall request.

"What about Vaquier?" Jackie asked.

"What about him? He's locked up. Kinda doubt he broke out of prison and came down here just to do this."

"True. But he is up in San Quentin right now. And so is Lewis Hayward. You can't tell me that's not something worth looking into."

"Unfortunately, prisons are prisons, and while we have quite a few of them, they are still limited. This probably is just a coincidence. But you're right. We should still check into whether the two men have ever crossed paths or spoken to each other. When I visit Hayward, I will check out Vaquier as well. Probably won't happen until Monday. But I'll try." Parks turned back to Rachel and Jake. "All right. What else have we got?"

"I've got the flowers," Jackie said, sticking a hand up. "Though, before I begin, and I know you're going to hate me for saying this, but can I just point out the obvious similarities between this homicide and Allison Tisdale's? She was found holding that bouquet of purple flowers that we had to do this same search for. And then there was what's-his-name who was found surrounded by the passion flower?"

"Kyle Oni," Fairmont shot out.

"Yes, him!"

"I'm sure by now we've all done connect-the-dots with the similarities between this case and all the homicides attributed to Lewis Hayward," Parks replied. "We'll get to all that. What do you have on the blue flowers found at the Delancy home?"

"Well, like I said, the flower is a Phalaenopsis orchid. They are rare. The flowers are white but are often dyed blue when they first bloom and come from the flower shops. And from what research we did into the Delancy's finances—both Mary's and Scott's—we can concretely tell you that neither one of them ordered the flowers."

"So who did?" Parks asked. "I mean, if it wasn't either of them, there can't be a long list of people having ordered that flower from any shops, either locally or online?"

"There isn't," Jackie said excitedly. "In fact, we actually found the order that was placed for the flowers delivered to the Delancys."

"Oh?"

"The order was placed online via a credit card belonging to a Denise Jones of right here in Los Angeles," Milo offered up, finally speaking to the group. "We're still trying to pull her records to see who she is or where she is and what her connection to the Delancys is. Was. Whatever. As soon as we get the proper information, I'll let you know more."

"Okay. Good. What about financials?"

"Nothing out of the ordinary at all. Mary Delancy has money from her acting days, and her royalties are still pouring in. She brings in about 1.9 million a year. She has a few charities in her name that money gets automatically donated to. Nothing worthy of noting though. Her son...well, this is where it gets weird. Scott Delancy doesn't work. And from what we can determine, he never has. Never filed any taxes. No work history or financial income to prove he ever has. Apparently, he lives off his mother's wealth. But this family is somewhat strange. They had everything delivered. Groceries. Clothes were ordered online. Necessities around the house. A gardener came once a week to keep up the landscaping around the house. Jake?"

Milo turned to Fairmont, who took over.

"The gardener was a Jose Sanchez, legal citizen of our country going on thirty years now. He maintained the outside property for over twenty years. Always paid on time. No complaints. No witnessing of anything strange or out of the ordinary, but he admitted he was only there during the days and never at night when Mary's stalkers usually showed up and did their...stalking. Though..." Jake paused a moment as he looked up from his notes. "He did confirm that there was evidence from time to time that people had been on the property. Unless, that is, Mary or Scott had been out trampling through their own bushes to leave footprints in the lawn, etcetera, etcetera—and with them you never know, they could have been." Jake shrugged. "But other than him, there was only his wife, Maria, who stopped by twice a week along with him to help clean up around the house. She would also bring whatever other necessities were required by Mary or Scott."

"What about the relationship between Mary and Scott? Did either Jose or Maria have anything to say about that?" Parks asked.

Jake shrugged and tilted his head back and forth, not exactly sure how to word it.

"They admitted they never *saw* anything," Rachel began. "But there was something about the way they behaved. They said it was a little less mother and son and a little more...Mister and Misses of the house. If you catch my drift? But they were adamant, that though the two may be dead, they wouldn't speak ill of them. They never saw anything inappropriate, as they put it."

"Anyway, back to the beginning," Jake said jumping up from his chair and throwing an empty coffee cup in a nearby trash can. "They had no outstanding debts or anything like that. Didn't owe anyone any money. They had enough to live comfortably. Nothing out of the ordinary. As we said."

"So now what?" Wilkes asked, unfolding his arms.

"Now?" Parks glanced at the board and then back to his team. "Now I put all of this information together while Milo finishes finding out who this Denise Jones is so we can talk to her. And you"—Parks stared at Wilkes as he continued—"and Detective Fairmont go find me this Henry Townes so we can have a chat with him."

EIGHTEEN

"Henry Townes, open up, this is the police!"

Detective Wilkes had been reluctant to go with Detective Fairmont to pick up Henry Townes, let alone get out of the car and go up the three flights to the man's apartment, but knew better than to argue with Parks.

Wilkes drove, and once he found an illegal parking spot blocking several tenants' parking spaces near the apartment, put on his emergency flashers and turned off the car. When the two men reached the run-down and rather neglected-looking apartment complex, they discovered that Henry Townes lived on the third floor, which prompted an endless parade of groans, eye rolling, and swearing from Wilkes. Fairmont glared at the older detective and considered leaving the man behind, not wanting to put up with Wilkes's bullshit simply because he had seniority.

Nearly five minutes after they arrived at Henry Townes's residence, the two men finally knocked on his red-painted, chipped front door.

"Henry Townes, open up! This is the LAPD!" Wilkes shouted with authority as he slammed a fist up against the door. "We have a warrant for your arrest, please open up now."

Fairmont sighed heavily as the two men mentally decided what to do next, when they both heard the sound of glass breaking from within the apartment.

"Mister Townes?" Fairmont shouted as both men retrieved their guns and prepared to break through the front door. "Mister Townes, this is your last warning. Open up!"

One of the neighbors opened her door to see what the commotion was all about, and Wilkes waved the overweight woman back into her apartment and instructed her not to come out again.

"Screw this. Break it down," Wilkes ordered as he motioned at Fairmont.

Fairmont gave Wilkes a face that told him to get lost.

"What? We have a warrant. Get in there."

Fairmont sighed but was about to comply when Wilkes pushed him aside and kicked at the door. The door was weak, not much more than cardboard, but a lock was still a lock, and despite the way the movies portrayed it, rarely did a door actually break down on a first try. Having loosened the entire door in its frame, Wilkes then backed up and slammed his shoulder into the door, leaning most of his weight closer to the lock. After a second attempt, the door finally broke through, splinters of wood flying everywhere as slivers made their way all up and down Wilkes's suit and hair.

"Mister Townes?" Fairmont asked as he made his way into the dark apartment behind his partner, both men immediately taking out their flashlights as they surveyed their surroundings.

The two men surveyed the front entrance, tiny hallway that it was, and worked their way into the neighboring living room. The room was empty. The carpet was a dingy color of off-green toothpaste, while the walls were a yellowed color left over from the seventies. There were sounds of creatures scurrying away from the light coming through the front door as Fairmont noted blankets nailed into the walls over each of the windows. The place had a stale smell to it, as if none of the windows or doors had been opened in a long while, despite a human being living there.

"Check the kitchen," Wilkes whispered as he kept his flashlight and gun aimed and ready for any unwanted business.

Fairmont put his gun down as he made it into the kitchen with just as little to see as the living room, save for the scurrying cockroaches.

"We heard something from in here," Wilkes said as he kept his gun aimed at the hallway. "The bedroom."

Fairmont waved Wilkes on, to which Wilkes replied, "Beauty before age."

Fairmont sighed, aimed his gun, and made it down the hallway. They checked the bathroom on the way, just as abandoned as the previous two rooms, and found themselves at the bedroom with its door shut.

Wilkes knocked on it.

"Mister Townes?" Wilkes asked as he knocked again. "LAPD. We're coming in."

Fairmont turned the knob and pushed the door open as Wilkes braced himself in a stance with his gun aimed. The room appeared to be just as empty, as the shades were drawn and the lights were out.

"Nothing here ei—" Wilkes silenced Fairmont with a gesture of his hand as he kept his gun aimed. "What is it?"

"Someone's in here," Wilkes whispered. "In the bed. Under the covers. Look."

Fairmont looked into the room, not able to see a thing when his flashlight began to flicker.

"Where's the damn light switch?" Fairmont complained. "Turn on the lights already, why don't you?"

"Fine. Quit your bit—Oww! Son of a bitch!" Wilkes flinched back from turning on the light switch to find his hand cut open along each of the fingers where he flipped the switch. "Son of a bitch." Wilkes stuck his fingers in his mouth as the two men peered down at the broken light switch. The cover plate was off and above the switch stuck a nail out of the wall.

"So you'll have to get a tetanus shot," Fairmont said, shaking his head. "Quit your whining. Could be worse."

"How?" Wilkes snapped back.

"You could be like that guy over there," Fairmont answered as he pointed to the body half-sitting up in the bed, his neck cricked back against the headboard while his head lopped off to the side.

"Son of a bitch!" Wilkes hissed as he jumped back.

The man was dead; his neck positioned in a way no one living could stand, while the color of his skin had a morbidly yellowish tint to it. Upon closer inspection, both men also saw that the areas around the man's lips, nose, and eyes were a darkened blue hue. The two men stood there for close to a full minute, inspecting the entire scene, taking in every minute detail laid out before them until Fairmont finally said, "You want to call Parks or Tanaka?"

"Why don't you call them both while I fix up my hand," Wilkes snapped back as he held up his bleeding hand and stormed out of the bedroom.

Fairmont shook his head as he got out his cellphone and dialed up Amy Tanaka first. He relayed where he was and what she had to look forward to once she arrived. When he hung up, he looked out into the hallway, not bothering to move.

"You find the medicine cabinet okay?" Fairmont called out as he dialed Parks. He could hear a stifled reply and some grunting as the man bandaged up his hand. Fairmont rolled his eyes as Parks answered. "Hey, Parks. So, yeah, that stalker guy you had me and Wilkes go check out? Turns out, he's already clocked out. Yeah...uh-huh. Sure. Oh, and according to his skin color, I'd say he bit it the same way Mary Delancy and her son did. Yup. Same poison, I'd say. But I'm no expert, so you may want to bring that little poison doctor of yours on down here too. Yeah, don't worry, we will...no, we're not. Okay. Oh, Wilkes is—"

A loud crashing noise from another room almost caused Fairmont to drop his phone.

"Hold on a sec, Dave."

Fairmont retrieved his gun and walked out of the bedroom and down the hallway.

"Wilkes?" Fairmont asked as he looked around, waiting for a reply.

When he didn't receive one, he started down the hallway and stopped when he saw Wilkes lying on the bathroom floor, blood smeared across the counter and floor, leaking from a wound on his head as his body slowly jerked back and forth.

"Oh, shit," Fairmont exclaimed as he ran for Wilkes's side, putting his gun away while he set his cell down on the counter. "Wilkes? Wilkes?"

Wilkes was unconscious, breathing, though even that appeared to be labored and tough, a sharp wheezing sound barely exiting through the man's locked teeth. His hands were clenched, spasming in and out of a fist, Wilkes not appearing to have any control over his actions.

"Wilkes? Wilkes, can you hear me?" Fairmont asked as he checked

Wilkes's vital signs.

Had he just slipped and hit his head on the counter? Or...or was it worse? What if...what if the scratch wasn't accidental? What if it was intentional? By whatever crazed loon was out there committing these murders? Following in the steps of the Palisades Poisoner...

Fairmont immediately backed up and away from Mark Wilkes's body, grabbing his cellphone as he exited the bathroom.

"Parks," Detective Fairmont choked out as he tried to collect himself.

What if he was too late? What if it wasn't from the scratch? What if it was from something as simple as touching a doorknob? Or being close to the body in the bedroom? What if whatever affected them was airborne? Was it too late for him already?

"Parks," Fairmont repeated, not remembering whether he had started talking to Parks or not. "Parks, call for an ambulance. And the CDC. And you better make it quick."

NINETEEN

Detective Fairmont stood guard outside Henry Townes's apartment, even after the CDC okayed an ambulance to take Wilkes off to the nearest hospital for treatment. Once Parks had arrived, Fairmont assured him that he had secured the perimeter and that only Amy Tanaka and members of the C.D.C. had been in to see the body at that point, each promising to leave the crime scene relatively untouched.

"How are you?" Parks asked. "*Jake*, you okay?"

"I'm okay," Fairmont replied, forcing a smile to his face. "I've seen worse scenes than that before. But if it's all the same to you, I think I'll just stay out here with the fresh air and check everyone who goes in and out."

"Whatever you want," Parks nodded. "You sure you don't need to be checked out? Physically, I mean. Whatever got Wilkes—"

"The EMTs aren't sure what got him, but he cut his hand on a nail by the light switch and the CDC and Amy are checking it out. They think it was laced with something. They're not sure what yet, but they don't think it's airborne. They cleared the apartment and they took blood samples from me, but all appears fine for now. Further tests are being run but there's nothing really I can do until they get the results back. They said they'll let me know as soon as they do. Seriously. I am fine. I feel fine. Just go take care of your crime scene."

Parks accepted Jake's words and found his way through the apartment until he arrived at the bedroom. Amy looked up at him for a brief moment before turning back to the corpse before her.

"Where's Jackie?" Amy asked.

"She went to the hospital to check out Wilkes," Parks answered.

"Bet Wilkes will get a kick out of that." That was all Amy seemed to muster up as she went back to her duties.

Parks began making mental notes of the room: the light switch—

The position it had been in before it was touched by Wilkes.

—the door to the room—

Open or closed?

—the closet door—

Open or closed again?

—the position of the bed and all the other furniture around it; the victim's cellphone and wallet; a few magazines on a stand next to the bed; the television that was turned off—

Was the victim in here watching television when his visitor interrupted him? Or did the visitor turn the television off? Or was it never on?

—the shades that were drawn shut (and still remained so); the dirtiness of the carpet and the bed—

The victim had obviously eaten in bed on numerous occasions.

He finally backed out of the room and did the same to the hallway and every other room in the apartment until he was outside the front door next to Jake. As he continued to write down his observations in his notepad for another twenty minutes, he noticed Jake moving from foot to foot with agitation and worry.

"So there's no evidence of a break in," Parks said looking back over his notes. "Our killer, whoever he or she is, either talked his way in or was invited in. Doubt the door was left unlocked in this neighborhood."

"Agreed," Fairmont said, subconsciously nodding in agreement. "And the door was locked when Wilkes and I first arrived here."

"So our killer locked up behind himself? He would need a key to do that."

"Yes," Fairmont confirmed, having already checked the lock. "I mean, I doubt it's really that hard to pick. For a pro. But there is a deadbolt."

"No evidence of foul play. No defensive wounds, from what I could see. No evidence of a fight. Throughout the apartment that is. No blood. No immediate weapons found anywhere."

"Same killer?"

"As Mary and Scott Delancy?" Parks asked, putting his notebook away. "Very possible. I guess only a toxicology screen can tell us that though."

"Oh, come on," Fairmont quietly hissed. "You saw that body. Looked just like the other two. Same bluish tint. Same traumatized look to his face. Same bent-over, curled-up condition to the back and legs. You telling me you honestly don't think it was the same stuff?"

Parks stared at Fairmont, the two men considered their options, when Parks's name was called from the back of the apartment. Parks walked back in without saying another word.

"What do we have?" Parks asked when he entered the bedroom.

"Our Mr. Townes here has been dead approximately twelve hours," Amy Tanaka began, as she took off her gloves and motioned for her assistant Robert to take care of the body. "Victim of poison, or so I can best tell without a full toxicology screen just yet."

"How?"

"He inhaled it."

"Inhaled it?"

"Yes. He breathed it in. Or maybe the powder form was blown into his face. The most damage was done to his mouth, nose, and eye areas. I'm pretty sure a dust-form of cyanide was blown into this man's face. There's still some dust around his mouth and nose areas of which I've collected samples. Again…we'll just have to wait for the results."

"So then our killer was close to him."

"Close enough to kill him. Yeah. I'd say so."

"Thanks, Amy. What about Wilkes?"

"What about him?"

"Same poison? As what got Mr. Townes here."

"No idea. They'll have to run tests either way to know for sure."

"What—?" Parks looked to Robert, who was conducting his business within earshot, and decided on some privacy as he led Tanaka out of the room. "What are his chances…?"

"Honestly, Dave? I don't know. For all I know, Mark Wilkes could be dead already."

Jackie was pacing near the nurse's station at the Good Samaritan Hospital on Wilshire, just blocks from Henry Townes's home, when her cell phone rang, startling her into almost dropping it.

"Shit!" Jackie looked down at the screen to see Parks calling her. The one person she didn't want to talk to at the moment. The one person she dreaded talking to the most. "Dave—"

"Jackie, what is it? How's…how's Mark?"

"Not sure," Jackie answered quickly. "They're still in with him."

"Jackie? What is it? Jackie...?"

"It's not looking good, Dave," Jackie said. She looked over and noticed one of the nurses staring at her, and she turned and headed out of the hospital for the privacy of the open outdoors.

"What do you mean? Is that what happened? Was he poisoned?"

"Yes," Jackie confirmed. "They believe so. Still no idea what, though. They think it was through the cut on his hand. So it wasn't too much, which is a good thing. They seem to think he has a chance. That and how quickly they got him here. But it really depends on what he was poisoned with."

"So he'll be okay, then?"

"They don't know, Dave!" Jackie all but yelled the words at him. She knew she couldn't blame him. He wasn't used to this. Despite that they had all been through it the year before, they were still all new to this. They didn't see this day in and day out like she did.

But she also knew what else he was thinking. It could have been any one of them. Anyone else. He could have sent anyone to go after the names on that list. That was the point. Much like poison itself, whoever set up this trap didn't care who the target was, just so much as there was one.

That was the point. Anyone. At any time. They could all be taken.

Even with a task so simple, they did it dozens of times every day. Something like simply flipping on or off a light switch. Wilkes could possibly die now and all due to a stupid light—

"So what's going on now?" Parks's voice interrupted her train of thought.

"Right now they're treating him with diazepam for the seizures and morphine for the pain. They've got him sequestered away in a darkened room—"

"What? Why?"

"Because any sudden loud noises or lights could increase the intensity of the spasms. They're keeping an around-the-clock watch on him. They're checking his vitals. Even the diazepam and the morphine could have a counter-reaction with his system and shut him down. They just don't know, Dave. They don't know yet."

Both were quiet for a moment.

"I'm sorry," Parks finally answered her back.

"What? What for?"

"I know you're doing your best. I'm sorry I snapped. I didn't mean...I'm just..."

"I know," Jackie said calmly. "It's okay. We're all under a lot of pressure here. There's nothing else we can do at this point but wait."

"Wait," Parks sighed. "And get this killer off the streets before he has the chance to do this again."

TWENTY

Jackie startled awake and looked up to find that she had been rest-ing—no, *sleeping*—against Dave Parks's shoulder. She looked around, slightly confused as she tried to place her surroundings and remembered that she was still at the Good Samaritan Hospital, waiting to hear any new updates on Mark Wilkes's condition. She hadn't re-membered falling asleep. Or Dave stopping by, for that matter.

"Wha...? When did you get here?" She asked as she stretched her back and looked around, rubbing her eyes.

"Around midnight," Parks smiled as he closed the file he had been reading. "I knew you'd still be here. Waiting. So once we finished pro-cessing the crime scene and I got everything settled back at the sta-tion—and sent everyone home—I came here to check on you. You were out. I had to rescue you from the creepy hospital body thief. He was about to take you."

"Oh, was he now?" Jackie smiled, almost laughed, and playfully smacked his shoulder.

"What? You don't think I've ever seen an episode of *Criminal Minds?* They do that, you know? Only reason I'm aware of it is because of that show. They should make it mandatory viewing so people know who to be on the lookout for."

"How about people with vans with blacked-out windows for starters? What time is it, anyway?"

"Almost two."

Jackie stood and looked down the hallway one way and then in the other direction. "What, did a zombie apocalypse happen while I was out? This place is deserted."

"Trust me, you don't want a zombie apocalypse to happen." Parks smiled.

"If it means I get Brad Pitt to come rescue me, then I say bring it on," Jackie said, getting some of her feisty bounce back. That was when Jackie noticed several empty cups on the seat next to him. "What do you think the chances are they have an open cafeteria in this place?"

"At this time of night?"

"So what other options do we have?"

They found the Blue Anchor pub that also served food at all hours of the night. Parks satisfied himself with a drink while Jackie ordered a fish-and-chips special. Neither was sure if the food would be all that pleasurable coming from a bar, but since the place's specialty was seafood, they figured it was better than no nourishment at all.

"Must be tough with Ricky out of the house permanently now," Parks said in-between bites of French fries.

Jackie stared at Parks and wondered if he was at all conscious of the fact that he was eating—nibbling away at, at least—something that she didn't consider to be a breakfast-type food and not getting nauseous.

"He's still got a bedroom if he ever wants it. But the house has its lonely moments," Jackie agreed. "But it's not like I didn't see this coming. I mean, in the big picture. He is an adult after all. It was just that I thought I was going to have a little more time to transition him out is all."

Parks stared at her, and she looked up from her beer-battered fish and caught him, neither one looking away.

"Truth is, he blames himself," Jackie continued, almost too softly. "I know that's what bothers him the most about this whole ordeal. Hayward's words to him. That bastard. Poisoning my son's mind is far worse than any of those toxins he used on people."

"What do you mean?"

"Hayward's daughter. Julie. When she took her life, Ricky took it hard. He blamed himself for that. But he was getting over it. When Lewis attacked him in our house, he blamed Ricky for Julie's death. Ricky just spiraled after that. Blamed himself for everything. Julie's suicide. Her father's rage. All of the people he poisoned because of her. He blames himself. He refuses to seek help. He started taking pills to help him sleep at night, so he wouldn't have nightmares—so he wouldn't *remember* the nightmares. I was worried. That's the real reason he moved out." Jackie paused and Parks noticed tears building on the edges of her eyes. "At home there was someone who cared for him. Someone who could see the pain in him and tried to help him. He didn't want help though. He wanted to suffer. Felt he deserved to suffer."

"Did he ever attempt to..." Parks wasn't sure how to word this.

"No," Jackie sniffled as she wiped her eyes with the back of her hand and grabbed a napkin to blow her nose. "No. He never tried to take his own life. And I never truly feared he would. I think he wants to suffer. He felt that was his punishment. That he isn't allowed to take his own life. The easy way out. So instead he's away from me. Away from the love he doesn't feel he deserves. At school. Every day. Suffering through his own darkness for the light at the end of a tunnel he doesn't know how to escape from yet."

"That must be hard. As a mother."

"I love him. But I don't know what to do. Short of having him kidnapped and forced into therapy. What can I do? Just wait? That's what I hate most of all. I understand what he's thinking. Even if I don't agree with it, I understand it. I accept that. That he needs to go through this to get better. Like hitting the lowest low before you can bounce back and be fulfilled again. I understand that. And I do think he'll get there. One day. I just hate the sitting back and watching him suffer through all this until he does."

They both sat there enjoying one another's company in the silence, both noticing that in her speech Jackie had grabbed Parks's hand. She dozed off as she stared at his hand under hers, staring off into space as she thought about past mistakes.

"I miss you," Jackie said. "You know that? I don't know if I have any right to say that, but I just felt like I should. I mean, after all I said to you. The way I treated you after everything. I know it wasn't your fault. I've seen the murder book. The news reports. I'm just...I'm sorry."

"You have nothing to be sorry for," Parks said solemnly.

The two stared at each other for a minute before Jackie broke the spell.

"It's getting late," Jackie said, looking around. "And we do have to work tomorrow. Take me back to the hospital to get my car?"

"No, I thought I'd make you wait for the bus," Parks quipped. "Would serve you right for the way you treated me."

Parks mimicked a broken heart as he said the last words in an almost childish tone before winking at her.

"You know, I don't think I ever stopped loving you," Parks said as he stared at her. She looked up suddenly at him, at first slightly alarmed, then filled with the same feelings. "I may have forgotten that I felt that way, but the second I saw you in Hardwick's office earlier this week, it all just came flooding back to me. I couldn't help it. Not sure I'll ever be able to. You're just so..."

"Shhh," Jackie said as she placed a finger over his lips. "When it comes to interrogating a suspect or getting a confession out of a killer, you're a pro. You know just the right words to say. But when it comes to the real life, *your* life, you're a mess. And right now you're just too damn cute for me to let you mess up this moment with your words."

Parks cocked his head, not sure how to take her comment.

"Come on," Jackie said as she stood.

"Back to the hospital," Parks said as he stood up and followed Jackie out of the café.

"Forget about the hospital. I'm beat and need a lot of sleep," Jackie replied. "We can just pick up my car in the morning on the way to the station."

Parks was about to say something when he shut his mouth, the meaning behind her words hitting him.

And realizing he had no problem with them.

FRIDAY

TWENTY-ONE

"Henry Townes," Parks said as he pointed at the mug shot of the man plastered up on the white murder board in front of the room. "What do we know about him?"

"Uh, sir," Fairmont interrupted as he stuck a hand up. "I don't want to make it appear that I actually have any great concern for the man...but, uh, do we have any kind of an, um, update on Wilkes?"

Parks turned to Jackie, who tilted her head to the side and slightly nodded at him. She looked good, refreshed and energized for the day ahead. By the time the two had made it back to Parks's place the night before they simply fell asleep in each other's arms, the comfort of familiarity easing them into a blissful sleep. They both awoke with a vigor and excitement to face the day. Parks dropped Jackie off at the hospital to get her car, with which she took herself back to her own office to shower and change before heading over to the downtown station.

Now it was nine o'clock, and his team was assembled to review their findings.

"We don't have any official word on Wilkes just yet," Parks admitted. "But Hardwick is keeping an eye on the situation and has promised to let us know of any changes in his status. The doctors believe they have him under control, but again, they're not 100 percent sure what all he's been poisoned with, so right now our best bet is to find this guy and see if he can help ID what he's poisoning people with." Parks paused for a moment to let his words soak in. "So...? Henry Townes?"

"Guy was a class-A stalker-creep," Jake said from his desk, staring up at the picture of the man whom he blamed for Wilkes's current condition. "I grabbed the files Wilkes had on him. Up until his death, he had been stalking Mary Delancy for close to two decades. Mailed letters. Personal effects. Stuff like that. Had restraining orders placed against him. The usual. He'd been brought in several times for questioning."

"We're aware of all this," Rachel Moore offered. "We get his connection to Mary Delancy. But why was he killed? What does his murder have to do with the rest of this?"

"Maybe he's a link to our killer?" Parks suggested as he looked around to each member of his team. "Maybe he could have identified him?"

"All I can definitively say is the clear print that was left at Mary's crime scene wasn't taken from the man willingly or when he was alive."

"Oh?"

Rachel stood up and started posting several glossy photos to the board.

"Henry Townes's right index finger was severed, from what Amy is able to deduce, while the man was still alive. In addition, according to the injury on the man's body, he didn't die once the finger was removed. He was still alive for at least another seventy-two hours."

"So our killer...what?" Fairmont begins. "Kidnaps Townes, cuts off his finger, places the print from it at the Delancy crime scene to incriminate him, and then goes back and kills Townes after the fact? Why?"

"Did Henry Townes's body show signs of his finger having been taken forcefully? Against his will?" Parks asked.

"There were no obvious signs of a struggle. No defensive wounds. It was a clean cut. One single snip. Why?"

"Henry Townes is a stalker. He's obsessed. What if our killer offered him something in exchange for a finger? Something he would be willing to part with a finger for."

"Okay...what?" Fairmont asked.

"Something related to Mary Delancy," Parks admitted as he started writing the info on the murder board.

"Maybe the simple fact it was *for* Mary Delancy?" Jackie suggested.

"What's that?"

"Townes probably wouldn't offer his finger so that it could be found at her murder scene to incriminate himself in a crime he didn't commit. Especially Mary Delancy's murder. If she is truly his ultimate obsession. But maybe he thought that somehow the finger itself was going to be delivered to Mary herself. As a present?"

"Manipulation of the facts. I buy that," Parks agreed. "Okay, what else? The flowers? We ID this Denise Jones yet?"

"Yes," Milo offered. "But only because her credit card was used. Did a quick background check on her, and guess her relationship in all of this mess?"

"Who is she?"

"Mary Delancy's former publicist."

"When did she quit being Mary's publicist?" Parks asked, as he scanned over the timeline of events up on the murder board.

"Back in..." Milo flipped through several pages of notes. "Ninety-seven."

"And the reason why she quit?"

"None that I could find. Other than Mary had retired by then. From all forms of acting. For the ten years before that she had been doing only TV appearances and game show spots and stuff like that. Her flame was dying out anyway. Maybe Denise Jones wanted to move onto bigger names?" Parks was silent a moment as he thought about this. Milo continued, "The only other things were her husband's death, but that was in '83...and then this Thomas Cream, who was killed at her place. That happened just before Denise Jones quit as her publicist."

"Just a coincidence?" Jake wondered. "Or connected?"

"Dave?" Rachel prodded. "What you thinking?"

"Denise Jones was Mary's publicist. She would know something about her stalkers. What was true and what was simply publicity. Find her. Bring her in. We need to have a chat with her. Find out why she's sending flowers to her former client. Take Jake with you."

"Will do," Milo said, closing his file.

"Now, what do we—" Parks stopped when Hardwick walked onto the floor, and stepped to the side to allow her full command of the group.

"Just thought you all should know that Detective Wilkes has woken up and appears to be in rather...elated spirits," Hardwick said immediately, knocking all suspense out of the way.

"Well, someone's getting the good drugs," Fairmont quipped.

"He's going to remain at the hospital for the next forty-eight hours for observation, after which he will be dispatched home for a two-week leave of absence. I think it would help brighten his mood to know we've caught this son of a bitch. All right?"

There were nods and murmurs of agreement from the group all around.

"Good," Hardwick said. "Anything you guys need from me? Any red tape cut or pulled or whatever?"

"All good here," Parks replied. "But there is one thing you could help with."

"Shoot."

"Lewis Hayward."

"What about him?"

"Whether we like it or not, or want to admit it or not, that man's involved in this somehow. We don't fully know how just yet, but he is. It would be helpful if we could talk with him. Can you get that cleared?"

"I'll see what I can do. Anything else?"

"Nicholas Vaquier."

"Who's that?"

"Another name on the list of Mary Delancy's former stalkers. He's currently locked up. Guess which prison?"

"Don't tell me he's roomies with Lewis Hayward?"

"The one and only. Not sure if the two know each other, but they are currently at the same prison. It's too much of a coincidence. I'd like the two to be separated, if possible, and then made available for me to question them."

"Oh? You want them brought down here first class or—"

"I'll fly up there on my own dime if I need to. Or have them shipped down here. I don't care. Whatever's easier and quickest. They may not have anything to do with this case, but I'm finding that to be more and more doubtful. I just need to question them both."

"I'll set it up," Hardwick promised him. "I'll let you know the details. But you need to be ready to drop everything and move if I tell you to. Make sure your team can handle things here without you for a day or so if need be."

"They can handle themselves just fine," Parks assured her.

"Good," Hardwick said as she left the floor.

"Okay," Parks said turning back to his team. "Who did the preliminary background check on Benjamin Delancy?"

"I got it," Fairmont offered. "Benjamin Delancy flew the coop at age sixteen, bounced around, not in the foster system, FYI. However, he did do some schooling. Got his associates degree. Did some more business classes and ended up where he is today."

"Which is...?"

"Not a hundred percent sure," Fairmont admitted.

"Come again?"

"Well, it's a little murky. Which is what I think Benjamin Delancy wants. I think he is in the wine business. Officially. Though he doesn't own any vineyards"—Fairmont dug through some files until he found what he was looking for—"he does more distribution. I believe. Again, it's hard to tell. I had Milo pull his tax records and whatnot, and even he can't determine anything for sure. I have them all here for you to look at though. Maybe you can decipher his steps."

"Though there is one thing we were able to determine," Milo offered from behind Jake.

"What's that?"

"Benjamin Delancy is 100 percent broke," Fairmont answered with an even larger smile. He loved it when suspects just handed a motive over to them.

"Oh?"

"Completely," Milo agreed with a nod. "Been living off credit cards for the past year. Has acquired quite a debt."

"How much?"

"Close to a hundred thousand."

"Which boggles my mind," Fairmont interjected. "How the hell does someone acquire almost a hundred thousand in debt? Who's forking over that much money? And how do I get in that line?"

"In fact," Milo continued, "the only reason he's still surviving in any sort of way is through his girlfriend, or fiancée or whatever she is. She's keeping them both afloat."

"She's got money?"

"Yeah. Not a lot, but she has enough to live on. From what I can tell. Not sure where from though. Probably work of some sort. Or family. She's more of a dead end. Though I haven't dug into her as deeply as Benjamin Delancy. But I can?"

"Sure. Do it. But while you're at it, can we get an amount on how much Mary Delancy is worth? Or what she's left behind? Or to whom?"

"Close to seventeen million," Rachel Moore answered.

"What?" Fairmont whistled from his desk. "You're kidding me?"

"The woman was a highly paid actress," Rachel Moore explained. "She brought in the money back in the day. And she's been living the last twenty-something years as a hermit. She doesn't go anywhere, doesn't spend any of her money other than to have things delivered to her house. Her house is worth more than anything else in her name. The improvements she's done on it have increased its value. And she's still collecting residuals. She's got it coming in."

"Where's it all going to?"

174 | TYLER COMPTON

"She had a will done up thirty years ago," Rachel Moore continued. "And since she's never left the house to see a lawyer, and rarely had hers visit the house, it stands the same today as back then. All goes to her children. Every last dime."

"And with not only the mother gone...but his brother and only other surviving heir also deceased..." Fairmont let the words hang in the air.

"Someone just became a major suspect again," Parks said confidently.

"What about his alibi?" Milo asked.

"Seventeen million can buy a pretty solid alibi."

"Do we pick him up?" Fairmont asked with glee.

"Not just yet," Parks answered. "He had an alibi. Shaky, but we bought it. We need to do more digging into him. His background. His debts. Financials. Etcetera. We need to be ready to pounce on him when we bring him in. We'll let him sit for now. He's not going anywhere."

"Okay," Milo said, taking the cue to begin his online research into the life of Benjamin Delancy.

"Okay. So then, Rachel and Jake? You two think you can handle the publicist?"

"Old biddy should be a piece of cake," Fairmont said, standing up and grabbing his coat. "Especially after the last person you sent me to interview." Fairmont paused, then turned to Rachel and smiled. "But just to be safe, you might want to avoid touching any light switches."

TWENTY-TWO

Once everyone disbursed with their assigned duties, Milo pulled Parks into his office, closing the door behind them to make sure they had privacy.

"Sorry," Milo apologized. "But I think the assignment you gave me you wanted for me to keep on the down-low."

"Thanks," Parks said. "I appreciate that."

There was a quick knock on the door, and Jackie poked her head in.

"Oh, sorry," she said when she saw the two were about to get into a serious discussion. "This can wait."

"Thanks," Parks said, turning back to Milo.

"Actually," Milo shot out, addressing Jackie and then turning back to Parks. "You may want her in here for this. She might be able to give a different viewpoint on certain aspects, and she has been a part of this from the beginning."

"But what about…?"

"She's clear," Milo said. "At least as best as I could determine. That's not to say she isn't involved, but…well, that's your call really."

Parks weighed his options. "Come on in and close the door."

"What's all this secrecy about?" Jackie asked as she pulled up a seat. "Do I get the secret password? Or is it a handshake?"

"You're not going to like this. In fact you may be pissed at me again after you hear what I'm about to tell you," Parks began, ignoring her questions as he got right into the facts. "But after what happened with Lewis Hayward, I couldn't risk the alternative. I've asked Milo to check into everyone remotely associated with this current ongoing case."

"You mean you had Milo do some work on the DL into members of the LAPD to see if anyone looked suspicious?" Jackie clarified as if she already knew this. "It's smart is what it is. I mean, I personally doubt anyone one would be, simply because you're suspecting it already and having Milo check up on it. So Lewis Hayward—if he is involved in this case—would already know you would suspect this as well. He wouldn't pull the same trick twice. Not with you. But you have to cross your t's and dot your i's. I get it. It's smart. I would have hoped I'd have been smart enough to do the same thing. Or had the balls to pull it off. So what did we find out?"

"Milo?" Parks asked, surprised by Jackie's enthusiasm and positivity concerning his sneaking around.

"For starters, though I can't confirm anything 100 percent when it comes to the Palisades Poisoner, I think I can with all certainty say that no one within the LAPD or working on this case from this end has anything to do with Lewis Hayward or the murders. At least as best as I can determine. Financially or computer-wise or anything. No one's hacking in and accessing our records. No one's receiving or has received any suspicious amounts of financial wealth. No one's had any contact with Lewis Hayward of any sort. So that's where I am with that angle."

"Good to know," Parks said with a breath of relief. "So what *do* you have?"

"Well, to be honest I wasn't sure what or where to investigate," Milo began. "So I looked up Lewis Hayward. Or so I tried. That man has more blocks and dead ends than a person in witness protection. There's nothing. Or next to nothing before coming here to Los Angeles to work for the LAPD. And everything before that appears to be minimal. We know he worked on the east coast for NY and Philly departments. Other than that, nothing. It's like he's erased most of his past. But why?"

"I'm aware of what's out there in the way of Hayward's past. And what's not."

Jackie turned to him, surprise across her face.

"What? Just because the LAPD considers the case closed, I'm supposed to move on?"

Jackie turned from Parks, and both looked to Milo.

"What have you got?" Parks continued.

"Well, I started thinking. Why do we even consider this case to be related to Lewis Hayward? Other than the poison?"

"Well..." Parks began. "We have the letter. From him. To me. Saying he was ...going to do whatever he was going to do. Come after me or something. Who knows. But we know he's up to something."

"True. I forgot about that."

"Kyū," Jackie blurted out. "The symbol written behind Mary and Scott's headboard."

"Yes," Milo agreed. "The Japanese nine. I think we need to admit that the symbol is what links this case to Lewis Hayward. He may not be physically carrying out these murders, because he is currently locked away—and I've checked. Personally. He is still locked up. But he is still connected to all of this."

"How did you—" Parks stopped himself. He figured the less they each knew about what the other was up to and how they went about it might just prove their savior if at any time in the future this case came back to bite them in their professional asses. "You know what? Never mind. I don't think I want to know. Continue."

"This is someone who is either copycatting the Palisades Poisoner's work or, more likely since they've connected this case to the Palisades Poisoner case through details never released to the public, is somehow connected with Lewis Hayward. Like Hayward is feeding our killer information. Though I don't know how, as I have personally checked every line of communication that man has made in the last year, and I don't see anything that stands out. Or that even gives me an inkling of suspicion."

"So we're at a dead end," Jackie said. "Where does that leave us?"

"We're dealing with a follower," Parks said mostly to himself. "Someone who knows the very details of Lewis Hayward's previous crimes—was possibly even around Lewis Hayward while he committed them."

"A follower," Jackie agreed. "Okay. I buy that. But how do we find this so-called devotee? I mean, someone dedicating their entire existence to emulate another person—even to the point of murder—well, that's not someone who I would think could completely fly under the radar. I get how Lewis Hayward was able to do so. He's insane but brilliant. Smart enough to carry out his own plans without the aid of another. But a follower...? That's someone who wants to do the damage but doesn't have what it takes to carry it out on his own. He needs that little extra push."

"I've gone through every last inch of communication that Lewis Hayward has made with any living, breathing soul over the last year,"

Milo professed. "I got nothing."

"Go back further," Parks said, thinking through his ideas.

"What?"

"What Lewis Hayward carried out last year as the Palisades Poisoner wasn't done overnight. It took time. Planning. Years, even. Maybe. We know he...he's a stalker too." Parks paused as he thought about this new connection to the men in Mary Delancy's life. "Hayward was with the LAPD for two years before the 'Palisades Poisoner' reared his ugly little head. Not only did he use that time to locate his wife and daughter, he also planned during that time. Every minute here he gathered information, putting plans into motion and possibly even gathering followers. Believers. In his cause."

"The Council of the Ten?" Milo asked.

Parks looked to Milo as he mulled over the information laid out before him.

"Go back two years. To the time Hayward first started with the LAPD. Check everything in his personal and professional communications. I know it's a lot of work, but if he had contact with our killer, it would be during that time. At least initial contact. Our killer...our person is devoted. Especially if he kills in the name of or for Lewis Hayward. So if we're right, then all this time Lewis Hayward's been locked up, they haven't been in contact. That means this was all set in motion before Lewis Hayward went to prison. Which means he planned on being locked up."

"No one can foresee all that," Jackie objected.

"Overall, I would agree. But I've thought about this for a while now. Truth is Hayward could have had several options for multiple outcomes. And because this is the path that was taken, the murders of Mary and Scott Delancy were set in motion. Perhaps if Hayward had gotten away and fled, then a different set of peoples' lives would have been taken. Maybe not. Maybe he still would have killed Mary and Scott Delancy, only he would have done it himself. It's a stretch, but who knows? I've seen stranger things. Then again, maybe it's all BS."

"What about the devotee?" Milo asked.

"What?"

"You were starting in on the devotee of Lewis Hayward. I think you had an idea about them being separated all this time?"

"Oh, yes. Our follower has a sort of love for Lewis Hayward. I believe. And if so, then this separation would be killing him or her. They would need something to get through this period of silence."

"Like what? A memento?" Jackie asked.

"Exactly." Parks smiled and faced Milo. "Milo, I need you to do some deep undercover stuff. Maybe even go back to your friends at the Cyber Terror blah blah whatever they are and call in a favor or two."

Milo looked uncomfortable at having to go back and ask for help from his former colleagues but asked, "What do you need me to do?"

"Online black market stuff. I know eBay has legalities about selling contraband and other various illegal substances, but I also know there are places online where people can get things."

"What kind of things?" Jackie asked.

"Mementos. From crime scenes. From victims. From killers. A cast Ted Bundy once used. Crime-scene tape from one of the Green River Killer's crime scenes. A watch the last victim of Richard Ramirez wore. A court document from Jeffery Dahmer's trial. That sort of stuff. I need you to search for anything remotely associated with the Palisades Poisonings. Stuff the victims wore or owned. Stuff from the places where people were killed. Stuff Lewis Hayward may have touched or owned. Anything like that. See who's out there buying up this type of stuff. Our devotee will have bought something. More than one thing, if I'm right. It wouldn't be the first time this person has bought something like this. But once he had one-on-one contact with Lewis Hayward, then stuff relating to the Palisades Poisoner case is all he will have bought from then on out. Look for a change in someone's online browsing habits. That sort of thing."

"Isn't owning or *selling* this stuff illegal?" Jackie asked, surprised she even had to ask the question.

"Because being illegal has always stopped people from doing a particular activity?"

Jackie knew he wasn't being snide, simply trying to educate her in the ways of the world that they worked in. She understood that, just as he understood her reason behind needing to ask the question.

"Not in every state," Parks finally shrugged. "Think you can do it?"

"I'll try my best," Milo replied.

"Good. Because we may never find our killer any other way. if Lewis Hayward is the one who chose Mary Delancy to die, then there will be no connection between her and her killer. It will be between her and Lewis Hayward. So we should start checking for that as well. My partner and I often made house calls to the Delancy house. We should check to see if maybe Hayward ever made an official visit out to the Delancy home as well."

"Sounds good," Milo said, as he went to leave the room.

"Parks? Who was your old partner?" Jackie asked. "When you worked patrol?"

"Ryan Ballard. Why do you ask?" Parks answered and asked.

"Well, that was back when you had first started on the force. Everything was new to you. You were still learning. But your partner should have been more experienced than you. Maybe he's got a different viewpoint of the whole Delancy house calls than you do?"

"Not a bad idea," Parks agreed. "I've still got his number. It's been a while since I've talked to him. It would be good to catch up. You never know."

TWENTY-THREE

"I don't know what to tell you," Denise Jones said as she sat behind her desk, the view of the Hollywood Hills nestled behind her glass-walled office on the fifteenth-floor of her mid-Wilshire-area office. "But I haven't had anything to do with Mary Delancy in seventeen years."

"So you're telling us you didn't just send her some flowers last week?" Detective Moore asked.

"What flowers?" The woman laughed. She was a narrow woman, except for her hips, appearing to have taken on the form of a human pear, with the top of her head covered in a recently dyed haircut of short red spikes. She wore dark red rimmed glasses, with a chain attached to keep them on her at all times, no doubt due to her constant movement forward. She had a sharp nose and a small, if not equally sharp, mouth, both thanks to years of repetitive plastic surgery. Her voice squawked, like that of a parrot or cartoon character, every time she talked at the two detectives. "What are you talking about? Flowers? From me? To that woman? Ha. I don't think so."

Moore looked to Fairmont, the two mentally exchanging thoughts and ideas before turning back to the woman to continue their line of

184 | TYLER COMPTON

questioning.

"But you are familiar with Miss Delancy?" Moore asked.

"Mary? Yes. Of course I am. I was her publicist for twenty years. We go way back."

"Yet you haven't had contact with her in what...? How long did you say?"

Denise shuffled in her seat, appearing uncomfortable. The two detectives remained silent as they let Denise Jones think about her answer. "We had a falling out nineteen years ago. I haven't seen or spoken to her in about seventeen."

"You are aware of her untimely passing though, correct?"

"I heard about it on the news, yes," Denise answered, playing the part of being upset over the old friend's death, as she dabbed a tissue at the corner of her dry eyes for effect. "But like I said, we hadn't talked in years. And I don't know who sent her any flowers, but it sure wasn't me."

"Are you aware of any purchases that have been made with your credit cards over the past few weeks?" Denise began shaking her head in the negative. "Any credit cards stolen? Ever out of your possession?"

"Not that I'm aware of," Denise replied. "I have strict control over all of my credit cards. They are on my personal being at all times."

"Do you have most of your credit card information stored online at various e-stores to make purchasing quicker?" Fairmont asked, trying to find a way past this woman's defenses.

Denise Jones shrugged, but everyone knew Fairmont was right.

"So anyone who knows what they're doing would be able to access your account information through various online retailers," Fairmont sighed.

Denise shrugged again and nodded when her assistant entered the room, holding a pile of mail and other papers and setting them down on the corner of her desk.

"Thank you, Carol. That's all for now," Denise smiled quickly as her assistant left the room without saying a word. Both detectives studied the woman, immediately hit with the impression that the smile intended for her assistant was not an action the woman was used to performing; she was obviously putting on a show for the detectives.

The detectives stared at the rather large pile of mail, piecing together what they had been told with what was the truth.

"Truth of the matter is I've been out of town the last week. Doing damage control for Rush Skylar in New York. Someone got a hold of his cell phone and leaked some damaging photos. Luckily"—Denise Jones smiled, every line in her face becoming exaggerated—"he has me on his team, and I know just how to handle such an incident."

"All is fine with the actor, then?" Fairmont asked, less concerned over the actor's well-being than that of Milo, who had leaked the photos in order to be reassigned back onto Parks's team.

"Perfectly," Denise Jones beamed as she sliced open a letter with a gold-plated letter opener. "If anything, it's made him more of a star. I mean, after all, if that's what you're hiding, then why not show off what God gifted to you? Know what I mean?"

"We get you," Moore said.

"Though we will be looking into whoever leaked the photos and pressing charges," Denise Jones assured the two as she tossed the letter into a shredder at the end of her desk before going through the several catalogs she had been handed, ripping her personal information page off the back of each magazine and shredding said page.

"What's this have to do with why we're here?"

"Oh, yes, right," Denise Jones smiled as she continued with another catalog. "So I haven't been in town the last week. I was across the country."

"And you haven't gone over your online statements yet so you wouldn't know if something was off?" Fairmont finished for the woman. "Do you have access to these accounts now?"

"Sure," Denise said slightly hesitant.

She pulled a wireless keyboard out from a sliding drawer on her desk and began to type away on the computer screen to her left. After a few minutes she turned the screen around to face the two detectives.

"I'm not sure what transaction it is you're looking for, but here's my account, starting today and going back..."

Denise handed the keyboard over to Fairmont who started scrolling down the pages while she went back to sorting through her unopened mail for the week.

Fairmont took out his cell and dialed Milo as he scrolled through another page.

"Hey, Milo...yeah...what day am I looking at for the Denise Jones transaction? Which credit card is...okay. Got it. When? Okay...hold on, I'm searching..."

Denise Jones tried to ignore her guests when Carol reentered the office with a USPS Priority mail envelope in her hand.

"I just had to sign for this," Carol said as a way to explain her interruption. "Figured it might be important."

Denise Jones dismissed the girl without a word as she ripped open the seal on the cardboard envelope and withdrew a pristine, blinding-white envelope with her name beautifully written in blue-inked calligraphy on the front. There was no return address on either the USPS envelope or the smaller one within, and she immediately opened it up with her golden letter opener, no doubt an invitation to yet another soirée she could not attend. Inside was a single white card with a blue-inked symbol on the front, a symbol she did not recognize nor could claim to have ever seen before. She turned the card over, saw nothing on the back side, and finally opened it and read what was written inside.

She jerked her head back, not from fright, but from confusion at what was written inside. She then brought the card up to her nose and smelled it, the scent familiar to her, though she couldn't place what it was or where she had previously experienced the aroma. She then rubbed her finger over the symbol on the front and noticed that it smudged under her finger, a blue chalky substance rubbing along the paper and coming off on her finger. She then rubbed her thumb and forefinger together, and looked closer at the blue powder on her fingers.

Denise Jones put the card down and searched in one of the desk drawers for a tissue when Fairmont addressed her, turning the computer screen around to face her as he pointed out the transaction in her purchasing history for the blue Phalaenopsis orchids delivered to Mary Delancy.

"I've no idea what those are, but I can assure you I never made that purchase," Denise Jones protested. "Never. That wasn't me. I'm sorry. Some sort of sick joke. Someone must have hacked into my account. Though why they would do that simply to send some flowers is beyond me. I think this is just sick. Though I guess that saves me from having to send any condolence flowers now, right?"

"Do these particular flowers mean anything to you? Or to Mary Delancy, as far as you know?"

"Orchids? No. Not as far as I'm—" Denise Jones stopped, thoughts flashing past her eyes, as she brought her hand up to her chin, appearing to be thinking hard. "Orchids."

"Yes, orchids…" Fairmont nudged.

"They were her favorite flower. She loved orchids."

"Mary Delancy?"

"Yes. She loved them. Always had them around the house. Maybe even growing outside. Aren't they a delicate flower? Don't know how they could grow outside. I don't remember. Maybe I'm wrong. But she did love that flower. Always had them delivered to whatever hotel she stayed at."

"So she received them all the time? As presents?"

"Yes. Her husband always gave them to her. Purple ones. Or white. I don't remember. One of those two colors. I do remember always seeing those two colors around her. A lot."

"But never a blue orchid?"

"Blue?" Denise chuckled. "I didn't even know they came in blue. No, I never—"

Denise Jones stopped so suddenly it was hard for the two detectives not to notice as the woman's face went pale and her eyes widened in horror. She had a look, not one of having been caught trying to hide something but rather one of having just admitted to herself something she had tried long and hard to forget—that was, until the detectives came knocking at her door.

"Yes, Mrs. Jones? A blue orchid. You have seen them before. How?"

"*He* gave her blue orchids," Denise Jones answered in a barely audible voice.

"He?" Moore asked. "Her husband?"

She jerked her head from side to side, as if shaking it back and forth wasn't enough to express the feelings bottled up inside her.

"No?" Fairmont asked. "Who? One of her stalkers? Henry Townes?"

Denise Jones continued to shake her head from side to side as she spaced out, appearing to recall several events from yesteryear, not really hearing what the detectives asked.

"No? None of them? Not Henry Townes? Nicholas Vaquier—"

Denise Jones jerked her head toward Fairmont so suddenly he stopped and leaned forward. The name meant something to her.

"Vaquier? Nicholas Vaquier sent her blue orchids?"

Denise Jones stared at the two detectives, all sixty-two years of her age finally showing on her face, no matter how much she had spent on surgery to hide the wrinkles. She then stood up, walked across the office to a small counter bar, and poured herself a drink.

"No. Not Nicholas Vaquier."

"But you're familiar with the name?" Rachel Moore asked.

"Oh, I'm familiar with the name. As well as Henry Townes and all the other men who were...yes, I know the names. But no. They weren't the ones who sent the blue orchids."

She made her way back to the desk and sat down, the tumbler filled to the top with chilled vodka, no ice.

"Mary loved orchids. So *he* sent her orchids. As she requested. Demanded. As always. But he wanted her to know they were from him. To set himself apart from everyone else who sent her thankless gifts. He wanted her to know that his were special. Rare. Hard to procure. So they were blue. Funny...there are several meanings to them being blue. She never knew that. Simply thought they were different. She would. Stupid, simple woman. Someone like her. So unappreciative." Denise Jones paused and took several swallows, draining half the glass. "But I knew. *They* had a meaning."

"From someone else? Not her husband? Or her stalkers? She had a lover? An affair?"

Denise barked a laugh and took another swallow.

"She had several of those. Lovers. They never stayed long. But this one was different. He was more possessive. But she liked that about him. Felt safe with him around. Protected. From Townes and Vaq— and the like. I think she was using him. For that reason. To protect herself against men like Townes. Not that they were all creeps like Townes and Vaquier. Some were...nice. Regardless, he saw it as more. Saw it as eternal love. Would do anything for her. And did. That should have been a clue to her. What he was willing to do for her. To cover up for her." Denise took another swallow. "Her husband. Vaquier. That poor...I mean, don't get me wrong. Vaquier wasn't an innocent. But what they did to that man...and that other one who was killed at her place."

"Who? Mary's lover? The one that Vaquier killed? Thomas Whatshisname?"

"Cream," Denise Jones replied, barely audible as if recalling a horrific memory from the past. "Thomas Cream. Nicholas Vaquier was no angel, I'll give you that. He may not have done what—but he was no angel. I don't pity that man at all. But Thomas Cream...what they did to that man...he was a boy, really. Barely into his twenties. Small town boy in love with a movie star. I told him not to. To get away and be done with her. But she had poisoned his mind and confused him. Used him really. His only crime was being too gullible and simply being caught in the wrong place at the wrong time."

"Thomas Cream was killed by a psychotic stalker who was jealous of Mary Delancy's affections going to someone else," Fairmont said confused.

Denise Jones's face gave a look that told him he knew nothing about what really happened.

"What? What did they do? Who are they?" Fairmont demanded to know. "Who sent her the blue orchids?"

"She never told me his name. Everyone else she was with—yes. It was part of my job to know. For publicity's sake. But never his. And I tried so hard to find it out, believe you me. But she never broke." Denise Jones stopped as her face froze and her chin dropped to her neck, giving her the appearance of being strained and petrified. Then she looked up at the two detectives, as if having been in a trance and not knowing where she was.

"Mrs. Jones?" Fairmont asked as he looked to Moore, who studied the woman.

"Yes? Wha...?" Denise Jones looked around her desk and picked up the glass with her left hand and threw back another two swallows. She set the glass back down, then rubbed her hands over her face and looked up at the two detectives, blue smears appearing across her cheeks.

"Mrs. Jones, you have some smudges on your face from something," Moore said politely.

"Wha...?" Denise Jones looked down at her hands and smiled as she held them up for the two to see. To them it looked as if a pen had broken in her hands and the ink had leaked all over. "Stupid card. Don't know who sent it."

She picked up the white card with the foreign blue symbol on the front and waved it around before tossing it back onto her desk and picking back up her drink.

"Mrs. Jones, what is that?" Rachel Moore asked.

"This?" Denise Jones asked as she nodded toward the card. "No idea. I just got it in the mail. I thought it was an invitation to something, but it's not. I've no idea what it is."

"Who cares about her damn mail?" Fairmont asked. "Just ask her—"

"Look," Rachel Moore said pointing to the card and standing up, neither moving closer to Denise Jones nor further away from her. "Look at it."

"What about it? It's just—" Fairmont noticed the smudged symbol across the front of the card. Kyū. The Japanese nine. He too stood up, too petrified to move any more, not sure what he *should* do.

"What is this?" Denise Jones asked, as she stood. "Is this some sort of weird prank? I don't even get what it means." She opened the card and faced it so the detectives could read it.

```
     Just like when you were a child,
              scratch and smell.
            Once you go wild,
        tell Parks to ring my bell.
```

"Who the hell is Parks?" Denise Jones demanded to know.

"Shit," Rachel Moore spat as she stepped back and away from the woman and quickly got out her cell phone, dialing Parks. "Where the hell did that come from?"

"I don't know," Denise Jones said about to stand. "My assistant just brought it in."

"Don't move," ordered Fairmont, as he held his hands up at the woman. "Don't touch anything. Just set the letter and the glass down and don't touch anything."

"Parks!" Rachel yelled into her cellphone. "We're with Denise Jones, and I think she's just been poisoned. Not sure how or with what, but she was delivered a letter with the Japanese symbol for nine on it and it has your name written on the inside of it. Yes. You're with Jackie?" Rachel looked up at Jake. "They're calling the CDC now. No, we didn't touch anything, but she did. I think we're okay. No idea. She's...yeah, I think she's been infected somehow."

"Yeah, she has." Fairmont stared bug-eyed at the woman.

Denise Jones's face stiffened up again, her chin jerking down to her chest as her face twitched from side to side. Her hands flexed, her fingers straightening out, the glass falling out of her hand and shattering on the floor below as her arms spasmed and the muscles constricted.

"Parks, I think we're too late. What do we do?" Rachel shouted into the phone as she felt her entire body break out in sweat, fearing that what affected the woman was possibly going to happen to them as well. "What do we do? What can we do?"

"Wha..." Denise Jones's speech became restricted as her jaw tightened.

Her head started jerking upward, as her back curved, her breasts sticking up to the sky as her neck began to curve back, a guttural sound emitting from her mouth as if the woman wanted to throw up. Her arms pointed straight down at her sides, every muscle in them pulsating, her veins carrying the poison throughout her body. Her neck and face appeared heavily strained, the look of tension throughout her body simply exhausting the two detectives who stared on at her, knowing they could do nothing for the woman.

Denise fell back into her chair, her torso curving to the side as it wrapped around the back of the chair while she remained seated in it. Her legs curved up under the seat, wrapping themselves up along the legs of the chair, while her arms refused to move and her hands stayed splayed out, every bony finger pointed away from her body.

"They're on their way," Rachel relayed to Jake.

"Heeellphh," Denise Jones was barely able to get out through her clenched teeth as she continued to wrap around her chair, her back bending backward as the poison attacked her spinal column.

Without thinking, Fairmont took a step forward when Rachel stuck her hand out against his chest and stopped him.

"Sorry," Fairmont breathed deeply. "Just instinct, I guess I—"

"There's nothing we can do for her now," Rachel Moore said. "It's too late."

"We can't—?"

"There's nothing we can do."

"Should we look away? I mean, out of respect?"

"No," Rachel Moore shot out sternly. "She needs to know that we're still here for her. That we won't forget this. That we won't forget her. That we will make sure the people responsible for this are punished. You need to see this. To remember this. And if ever for one second during this case you have a moment's doubt about continuing on, you just remember this. You let this feed you. To remind you why we're doing what we're doing. To drive us efficiently and as forcefully as needed so as to make sure this never happens again."

"No one should ever die like this," Fairmont said as he wiped a tear away.

"I may not agree with much about your generation," Rachel Moore said turning from Fairmont back to the dying Denise Jones. "But I couldn't agree with you more right now about anything else in the world. Nothing more."

Five minutes later the ambulance arrived.

Five minutes after that the CDC.

Ten minutes after that Denise Jones succumbed to death.

TWENTY-FOUR

Though official testing was needed, both Jackie Isley and Amy Tanaka believed Denise Jones had been poisoned. How it had gotten into the woman's system, through touching the card or smelling it, they had not yet been able to determine. Due to the rapid speed at which Denise Jones had shown symptoms—not to mention the onset of death—the homicide was deemed a high priority.

Due to the fact that the victim had died before their eyes, both Detectives Moore and Fairmont had been separated and questioned about the events before Parks sent them along with the CDC to be checked out and eventually—hopefully—sent home.

Parks had also interviewed Denise's assistant Carol, and upon determining she had nothing new to add to the situation besides the delivery service that had dropped off the package, had sent the somewhat distraught woman home. That was why he was surprised when she interrupted him some twenty minutes later during his review with Jackie and Amy.

"You know you are allowed to leave?" Parks questioned.

"I know. I know. I just had to finish up a few last-minute things here at the office…not sure what's going to happen next. But anyways, the reason I stopped you was I noticed something strange in Miss Jones's calendar."

"Her calendar?"

"Yes. I have total control over it. Actually, Miss Jones never alters it in any way. She doesn't have access to it. I'm the only one. So I know every name and every appointment in it."

"And?"

"Except one. This is a new one. I don't know where it came from or who put it in there because I know Denise doesn't even know how to open the program, let alone put entries into it. Trust me. This woman has me—had me do every last thing I could for her."

"What is it?"

"It's an appointment for tonight. Which I know I didn't put in there because she just got back from New York and she had her evening cleared so she could catch up with everything she was behind on. She had no new appointments until tomorrow morning."

"When's the appointment?"

"Eight o'clock tonight."

"Where?"

"It doesn't say. Only with whom."

"And? Who is it?"

"Someone named Benjamin Delancy?"

Parks pulled up to the Stay on Main Hotel in downtown Los Angeles and parked behind a taxi loading up a young couple. Parks walked past two marble statues of what he assumed to be Greek goddesses, or some variation on the theme, his shoes echoing as they marched along the polished floor. He marched past a flight of stairs on his right and an elevator on his left up to the front desk where he flashed his badge and asked for Benjamin Delancy's room. The man at the front desk was about to call Benjamin's room when Parks heard his name called out from behind him, and he turned around to find Katrina Thompson walking into the lobby with a bag of takeout food.

"Miss Thompson," Parks greeted. "Have you been out?"

"Benjamin wanted me to pick up some dinner while he finished with some work stuff," Katrina said. She looked tired as she stood there before him, in jeans and a button-up blouse, her hair pulled back in a band, up out of her face. She wore no makeup, but didn't need any as she had spent the day digging through her fiancé's mother's house for whatever items they may have deemed salvageable. "Do you need to speak with him? I'm going up. Come."

Parks nodded politely to the desk clerk and followed Katrina to the elevator.

"How is the case coming along?" Katrina asked as they got on the elevator. "Or am I not supposed to ask about that?"

"We're following up on several leads at this time," Parks answered without looking at the woman.

She nodded, shrugged her shoulders, and faced the elevator doors.

"We really are in love, you know?"

"Personal relationships aren't part of my jurisdiction," Parks replied. "Unless it relates to the case I'm working. I don't judge."

"But you did," Katrina said, tartly. "I could tell. That first day when you met Benji and me. I could tell. The look on your face. You wanted to know something, and you never asked. What was it?"

"I don't remember. Though I'm sure at the time it was important."

"Yes, you do. If I had to make a bet, I would say you still remember. Mind like a steel trap. That's you. I can tell."

"You'd been dating the man for over a year and yet knew next to nothing about his personal life. You had never even seen a picture of his mother or brother?"

"First of all, detective, let's not beat around the bush. I knew who Benji was. I knew who his mother was. I knew her movies. So I didn't need to see a picture of them up in his apartment. It wasn't important. They were part of his past. And his past hurt him. I could tell. Why force the issue?"

Parks looked like he was about to say something and then stopped, not sure what to say.

"We are about each other, detective. Not each other's families. I..." Kat paused for a moment, and Parks turned toward her, the look of hurt etched across her face.

"You lost someone close to you. I can tell that much as well."

The elevator stopped and the doors chimed open. The two of them stood there, both facing the hallway.

"We all have pasts, Detective Parks. That's what makes us human. Some people's are just more painful than others. Maybe that's what drew Benji and myself to each other. Yes, I too have a past I don't care to dwell on. My sister was murdered a year ago. She was so young. And beautiful. Unfortunately, God has a bigger plan for all of us, and for reasons beyond my comprehension, He saw fit to take her from us early. Mine is not one to question. If it is His will, then so it must be done." Kat looked up at Parks, all looks of sentimentality erased from her face. "This way. Just down here."

Kat stepped off the elevator and led Parks down the hallway. She juggled her dinner with one hand as she dug through her purse for the key to the room. Parks stayed two steps behind the woman, taking in her appearance: her short, raven-black hair; her thin yet muscular neck and shoulders. She was a woman used to posture, used to posing a certain way, to maintaining a particular look while in public. Perhaps she had learned such mannerisms in a private school as a child.

She opened the door, and before Parks could comprehend the scene before him, Kat let out a blood-curdling scream as she dropped the food and her purse and ran into the room.

Parks quickly withdrew his gun and slammed through the door just in time to see Kat reach Benjamin Delancy's body, lying on the bed. The man's throat was ripped open, sliced from ear to ear, almost to the point of decapitating him. Blood soaked through the sheets of the bed, as if the body had been purposefully pumped of blood to make sure he wasn't staying around to accuse the person who had done this to him.

Kat screamed and cried, a mess of mixed emotions, as she knelt next to Benjamin and immediately threw her hands over his throat, as if expecting to be able to stop the bleeding, the fact that he was already dead beyond her comprehension. Parks tried to get the woman off of and away from Benjamin's body, but she violently swung her elbow back at his gut as she continued to hold her lover's body, pulling him in closer to her as she scooted herself in closer to the man until his head rested on her lap. The fact that she was contaminating the crime scene, and thereby making it that much more difficult to do his job, made little difference to the devastated woman.

Parks backed up a step and took out his cellphone, dialing for assistance. As he relayed the information to his team, he noticed the Japanese symbol for nine had been written in the victim's blood on the wall above the bed. Parks didn't for one second believe that Benjamin Delancy had written the symbol himself, instead having been used as a pawn to leave behind one more taunting message as the killer laughed in Parks's face.

TWENTY-FIVE

"I've made it mandatory for both Detectives Moore and Fairmont to take the weekend to recover and relax and for both of them to see Dr. Black first thing Monday morning, before even reporting to you." The look on Hardwick's face more than relayed to Parks for him to agree and not even think of putting up an argument.

"I figured just as much," Parks agreed.

"I might even recommend a week off for Detective Fairmont, pending Black's evaluation Monday morning."

"Is that really necessary? I mean, we are in the middle of a case." Parks took the chair opposite Hardwick's desk, and the two locked eyes without saying a word for almost a minute. "You think he's suffering from PTSD."

"In this week your entire team has not only had the excitement of coming back to a full-time and highly stressful job, but they know they're on probation, so to speak. They wish to prove themselves, and I think the level of stress is high. Not to mention we're dealing with Lewis Hayward once again, and he more than has everyone on edge dealing with his unstable poisons. Your team is on edge. Which I'm not necessarily saying is a bad thing. It just is what it is. Then Fair-

202 | TYLER COMPTON

mont also had to deal with the *near* death of Wilkes and *the* death of
Denise Jones earlier today. Both attacks, might I add, were carried out
with uncontrollable substances. Substances that just as easily could
have taken his own life. He's had two near-death experiences this
week. You don't agree that he might be getting overworked?"

"I'll agree with whatever you and Dr. Black deem will be the best
for him. Or any other member of my team. Just so long as you know,
due to this so-called probation, each and every one of them will fight
you on any sort of stress leave."

Hardwick was about to say something when Parks stopped her.

"Now, you don't need worry about that. That's my job. If they need
a break, I'll make sure they get it. Just so long as you're being fair to
them. And trust them. And me. I don't want to see anything happen to
any one of them. Or anyone else who could be harmed due to the
competency of the members of my team. Trust me to be able to make
that judgment call?" Hardwick nodded. "If it is seen fit that Jake or
anyone else needs time off, then let me make that decision one-on-one
with them. It will come easier from me. Right now that is."

"Agreed," Hardwick nodded. Parks stood and prepared to exit. "Just
so long as you know, Detective Parks, that both your team and you
work for me, and any final calls I see fit will be the final word and will
be carried out. Regardless of whether we see eye to eye. Understand?"

With his back still to her, Parks nodded once and left the office.

Katrina Thompson stood in front of the LAPD station downtown, the
night air finally getting a chill to it, but refusing to let it bother her as
she inhaled her third cigarette since the officers had brought her back
to the station. Her hands shook, how she managed to hold the flame to
light a cigarette, let alone the cigarette to smoke, was beyond Parks's

comprehension.

While he did not yet know the killer's true intentions or the motivation behind his or her killing spree just yet, Parks did know that said killer had just wiped out the entire Delancy bloodline in less than a week.

"Is there someone you'd like me to call?" Parks asked gently.

"Who?" Katrina replied. "I don't know anyone in this city. This stupid cursed city." She took another drag off her cigarette. "Nothing good ever happens in this damn city. My sister used to live here. Did you know that?"

Parks was about to answer but remained quiet. An initial background check into Katrina Thompson had raised no red flags, and they had moved on. Most of the personal information they had drudged up on her already forgotten.

"She moved here with her husband five years ago to start a family. They didn't have any children, though they wanted them. Fortunately she was blessed with a little boy. A little boy who, due to accidental circumstances, was taken from this earth all too soon. No one did anything. The universe wasn't out to get him. He simply died. These things *do* happen. Some people just aren't meant for this world all that long. They come, fulfill their part in the circle of life, and move on. As much as I hate to say it, maybe it was good my sister passed when she did, so shortly after her son. She didn't have to suffer a broken heart like I have. All because of this stupid city. City of big dreams. Everyone wants to come to Hollywood. That's why my sister picked this place. Out of everywhere in all of—she just wanted out and away from home. So they came here. And look what it brought her?"

Katrina took another drag of her cigarette and stared at it, studying it as she blew smoke out into the night air.

"We were almost free, you know? Of this place. Everything here. He was finally free. Going to be. Be able to move on from the hold this place had on him all these years. You know...he would have denied it, but he had never truly moved on. He still loved her. His mother. Even after all she did to him, she was still his mother. Sick, isn't it?"

Parks wasn't sure what to say.

"Then we got the call about his mother and I thought to myself, yes, finally, he's free. Maybe now we can have a life of our own. So I agreed to come with him here to this godforsaken place and help him pack up his former life so he could move on. And look at what it brought us? He never should have come back."

"Maybe he needed to," Parks offered. "Maybe he needed to come back to this place—to his own personal haunted house—and say one final goodbye."

"God damn that house," Katrina spat. "That stupid, cursed hellhole. Nothing but boxes of a life expired. To *her* glory days. So many rooms, each of them a shrine to *her*. Even that stupid bird of hers—every time it squawked, I swear it said her name. Everyone—every*thing*—in that house idolized that woman. Her the most. She loved herself like no one else."

Katrina finished the cigarette and threw the butt out, then lit up another one, tears beginning to flow from her eyes once again.

"When I saw him lying there, all that blood...I couldn't think of anything but the life he missed out on because of that woman. I wanted to save him. To give him what he couldn't give himself. I wanted him to move on. I loved him so much, but I just couldn't..."

Katrina finally broke down in tears, the cigarette falling from her hands as she began to collapse, Parks barely catching the woman in time. Parks sat there on the cold concrete, holding the grieving woman as he let her continue to cry, hoping to excise every shred of pain and loss from her very being. He knew how she felt. Sometimes that's all you could do. Just cry the pain away and hope it never found its way back.

Parks knew that was a lie. It always found a way back. That's what it did. That's how it survived. By latching on and making sure you were never free from its grasp.

He had known this only all too well.

SATURDAY

TWENTY-SIX

Parks was exhausted from the night before, staying at the station until well after midnight. After filling out extensive amounts of paperwork, he then relayed to Hardwick and Reed the events of the entire week before that had led up to the deaths of Denise Jones and Benjamin Delancy. Luckily, with Moore and Fairmont taking the next two days off and Milo more than aware of what his duties were, he was able to take the morning off. By the time Parks made it back to work, he was glad that it would just be him and Milo at the station for the day. It would allow them time to go over the various aspects to the case that he had assigned to just the kid.

"What have you got?"

"I'm not totally sure, but I think this is what you were looking for," Milo began as he handed over a few files and other assorted of papers that further detailed his findings. "I wasn't able to find any one particular person who had or has been purchasing any sort of Lewis Hayward or Palisades Poisoner...merchandise? Souvenirs? Not sure what to call them. Anyway, there hasn't appeared to be any one person more interested in his stuff than anyone else out there. And you'd be surprised at the number of people out there who are interested in this sort of stuff."

"Not really," Parks said, as he began to dig through Milo's paper-work. "That was part of the reason why I thought to have you look. I'm more than aware of what's out there and who all is looking for it. So that's it?"

"Well…I think I found something else that might work for what we're trying to find," Milo continued. "I wasn't able to find anyone who's buying a lot of this stuff, but I was able to find someone who *sells* a lot of it. I thought that maybe we might be able to get something from them. Or, rather, her."

"Smart thinking. Who is she?"

"She goes by the name Ana," Milo admitted. "She's managed to keep her real identity hidden, and trust me, I dug hard to try and find it. However, I think I know how to find her. Despite the large number of people out there in the world who are interested in this type of stuff, belongings of victims of crimes and serial killers and whatnot, they're still overall smart enough to know to keep their proclivities on the down-low."

"At least they're smart enough to know that."

"But I think I still found her, and it's kinda brilliant."

"Do tell?"

"Well, everyone at one of these things or online looking for this stuff has a pseudonym. No one online uses his or her real name. So…if you see someone's name online, you automatically assume it's a moni-ker. Most of which can be easily traced back to their source, despite the fact that those involved in illegal activities do more to hide their identity. But what's more hidden than what's in plain sight?"

"You think she's using her real name as her 'fake' profile name thinking everyone will automatically assume it's a fake, because that's what everyone else does?"

"Exactly."

"And?"

"There's a group out there called P.S. or P.V. depending on who you ask or what branch of their…club you're talking about or to," Milo continued to explain. "Kind of a play on the post script thing, as in they're adding a post script to people's lives by handling these types of items. Or something along those lines."

"P.S. is this Post Script group. And P.V.?"

"Post Vitae," Milo clarified. "Post being the Latin for after, and vitae being the Latin for lives. They're mostly groups that are interested in the macabre. Death, serial killers, true crime-type stuff. They visit crime scenes, have get-togethers, the works. If you catch my drift. P.S., I think, is the more public front to the group. They have get-togethers. Visit crime scenes. Talk. Spout conspiracy theories. Blame the cops. Or was it all a cover-up? Is the real killer still out there. Stuff like that. Nothing illegal."

"But they're just a front for this Post Vitae group, who are more hard-core?"

"I think you get what I'm saying."

"I'm aware of these types of groups," Parks admitted. "So this woman we're looking for who sells Palisades Poisoner materials belongs to one of these two groups?"

"I think so. Now, if this was some deep undercover job where I had months to develop an online persona, I could probably learn something and get myself into the group. But since I've had only a few days, most of my work has been done through hacking—which, let me tell you, has not been easy. These people are paranoid. But still—I'm not without my merits."

"So we're not a hundred percent sure what we have or who's done what with whom, but this is as good as we're going to get under our time constraint and we're going to have to make a move and hope it's the right one?"

"More or less. I also reached out to a few of the people I thought I could still get a helping hand with from the Cyber Crimes division and they were able to help speed some of my ingestion up as well. FYI, we owe them one. Regardless, getting a face-to-face meeting with these people will be tough," Milo admitted. "And without too much evidence, it's going to be hard to pressure her, or anyone for that matter, into spilling to us what we want. After all, most of them think we're the enemy trying to cover up the truth."

"So how did you find this Ana...?"

"Bernal. I found several packages of Palisades Poisoner souvenirs shipped out over the last year, and I was able to determine where they originated, based on the shipping and tracking information that was available online. Even though what these people buy is illegal, they're still paranoid as hell that they'll lose it and not get their money's worth, so they usually ask for tracking numbers to their packages and have them emailed to them. I back tracked it from the recipient to the sender, thank you very much UPS and FedEx, to find out who's paying for what and when, and we have our patient zero."

"Good job. So if she's selling items from crime scenes, who is she? I mean does she have a connection to anyone on the force?"

"None whatsoever," Milo admitted. "She's not related to anyone on the force, not married to anyone on the force. Never worked full or part time on the force. She's not currently or, best as I could dig up, has never in the past even dated, or been married to, anyone connected to the LAPD either. As far as I can tell, she's got no connection to anyone in any way with any connections to the Palisades Poisoner crime scenes. Which might make sense."

"Oh?"

"Here..."—Milo handed over a printout with pictures, prices, and other details of various objects on them—"...is a copy of every item she's sold over the past year in connection to the Palisades Poisoner case." Parks looked up at Milo. "I figured it might be easier to coerce particular information out of her if we can prove that she's actually selling these illegal items. Though, I have to be honest..."

Parks looked closer at the sheet of paper.

"These aren't illegal," Parks said, shaking his head. "People are allowed to sell whatever they want so long as they are the legal owner of said property. Most of these items are throwaway junk. It's not like they came from an official evidence bag or sealed documents. These are just senseless items that desperate people will pay money for."

"Correction. Pay *good* money for."

"You've gotta be kidding me," Parks all but gasped. "They paid five thousand for that? What would they have paid if I had given them a real item from one of the actual crime scenes?"

"Right?"

Both men looked at each other, making sure the other was simply joking, then continued.

"Half of these items are BS," Parks continued. "You can't prove anything with them. They aren't actual pieces of evidence. A bottle of wine that Kyle Oni drank before he died. But you can't actually prove it."

"Although for that one they swear they have a certificate proving that it's Kyle Oni's fingerprints on the bottle."

Parks stared over the paper at Milo, who simply shrugged.

"And exactly who out there is authenticating these pieces of crime history? Pictures that Ian Harris took himself. The fork that Christina Maddox ate her last meal off of. That *should* be locked up in evidence. Although, now that I think of it, it was probably thrown out with the salad. I honestly don't know. If it was bagged and tagged at the scene, then it is illegal to possess."

"Not only is the fork not sealed in evidence, but there is no proof that it was ever gathered, bagged, and tagged."

"You've got to be kidding me."

"Don't know if the fork's legit or not, but given how meticulous these people are, I'd say it would have to be a damn good fake if it wasn't legit. These people do their homework. They don't settle for anything less than originality. Plus, they're not doing this for the money. They're doing it for the prestige of owning what they say they own."

"Evan and Wesley Cosway's transfer papers?"

"Missing," Milo admitted. "Not in the murder book. I've checked."

"And she sold them? To a buyer who paid for them? That is illegal."

"And shipped them out."

"And that makes this a federal crime. This is enough. We got her." Parks looked up at Milo. "I'll call for a warrant. Now, where is this woman?"

TWENTY-SEVEN

Detectives Dave Parks and Milo Tippin made the forty-five-minute drive from downtown Los Angeles up the 101, past Warner Bros. studios, deep into the heart of Burbank. Parks kept his car running while they sat in park, across the street from Ana Bernal's house, taking in the layout of the middle-class, suburban neighborhood. Everything was perfect. Nothing appeared off. Most likely, no one would have any idea one of his or her neighbors bought and sold crime scene memorabilia.

Parks wondered whether the woman herself would surprise him just as much as this entire situation.

They approached the door and, after a few knocks, could hear children playing somewhere throughout the house as a woman approached the door.

"Sorry to disturb you," was all the more Parks got out when the woman who answered the door threw her hands to her mouth, eyes bugging out, as she tried to catch her breath as if she had just been offered a million dollars. "Are you all right?"

"You're...you're...you..."

The woman was short, barely reaching five-foot-five with long burnt-coffee-colored hair with the occasional blonde streak through it. She appeared healthy, if not somewhat thick, as if a former athlete of yesteryear who had succumbed to years of motherhood. She was in her late thirties, with signs around her eyes and mouth that gave her the appearance of being slightly older. She was dressed in plain khaki slacks and a bluish-green blouse with the arms folded up to the elbows. She had several rings on both hands and two plain-looking gold loops through her ears. To Parks she was the perfect woman next door, the every neighbor that no one would turn to look at twice yet everyone would gather around and gossip about the second the police dragged her in, each one proclaiming to have known all along that there was something "off" about the woman.

Parks grew concerned as the woman tried to regain her focus, her hands waving rapidly in front of her face as if having been terribly surprised. She reminded Parks of those videos of unsuspecting mothers who are caught off-guard by sons just returning from years overseas at war. He was neither sure why he received this reaction nor what to do about it when he glanced at Milo, who had a guilty look on his face as if he had expected this to happen.

"I'm sorry, but could—"

"You're David Parks!" the woman all but shouted in his face, taking him aback for a moment. How could she possibly know—"I'm sorry. I meant Detective. Detective Parks."

That's when it hit him. The true crime memorabilia. Particularly the reason they were there: the Palisades Poisoner case. To her, and others like her, *he* was the superstar. He was the Tom or Brad or Julia or Meryl. Or Channing or Bieber or whoever the hell people went gaga over that year (to Parks it always seemed to be changing so quickly and so often that he could barely keep it straight). He was the superstar people stopped what they were doing for and immediately tweeted about when they caught sight of him in line at Starbucks. How had he not even considered this reaction upon his introduction to this woman? If he had thought this through, he would have realized that he needn't have been worried about having to strong-arm her or even possibly threaten her with legal action to get anything out of her. Suddenly, he had to rethink his entire approach to this situation.

"Yes, yes I am." Parks flashed a smile. "And I'm sorry to disturb you at this time—"

Ana Bernal immediately broke out into a fit of giggles and threw up a hand to cover her face in embarrassment.

"Oh, my God. Oh, my God. If you only knew. David Parks! At my house! At my house! If only they—"

She stopped talking as she got out her cellphone and began to type away on it when Parks put up a hand over the screen to stop her and direct her attention away from her mobile device and toward him. He gazed hard into her eyes, hoping to somewhat hypnotize her as he tried to keep her attention diverted from her previous task.

"I don't suppose my partner and I could come in for a few minutes and talk to you about something important? Could we?"

"Oh, my God—is this about a case?" She threw a hand to her chest and looked as if she might faint.

"It is." Parks smiled. "We need some help with something. Do you think…?"

"Oh, my God—*yes!* Where are my manners! For Heaven's sake, come on *innnn*," Ana said as she stepped aside and threw an arm up to welcome Parks into her home. "You'd think I was raised in a barn. What you must think of me. Come on in. Both of you. Come on—*oh!* I know you. You must be Milo Tippin!"

Milo blushed a dark shade of scarlet.

"Come. Come. Come. Come," Ana said as she closed the front door and led the two men to the neighboring front room. There were toys scattered all over the house, not necessarily giving the place a disheveled dirty look, but rather the look of a house filled with people who used the space and loved being there. "Sit. Sit. Sit."

She found a space on a flower-patterned sofa while Parks and Milo each took two chairs on the opposite side of the coffee table. Parks glanced at Milo and then smiled at the woman once more, trying to figure out the best way to approach the purpose for their visit without offending her, knowing that, despite Ana being honored that they were there in her house, she could also turn on them in a flash.

"Actually...this is about some of your recent activities..."

"What do you mean? What activities?" She beamed with a blank look of ignorance across her face.

Parks knew if he had the time he could possibly convince this woman to assist them without taking any offense, but they were on a deadline, and he could always threaten her with legal action if need be.

"This is about the merchandise you've been selling and trading online," Parks said flatly.

"I'm sorry, but I don't know what you are referring to," Ana Bernal replied sincerely. If she hadn't been so wide-eyed and off-putting to Parks, he might almost think they had it wrong. But when had Milo's information ever come up wrong?

"I don't—" Ana's words were forced and Parks cut her off.

"Post Vitae. Mrs. Bernal, I'm going to be frank and to the point here, because I don't have a lot of time, and I don't need a line of bull thrown at me. We're aware of what you sell and trade. Through this Post Vitae group. Technically, what you buy, sell, and trade online is your business. I could care less. That's not my jurisdiction, and you know it. I work homicide. All I need is a name. That's what I need help with. So we can play this two ways. One, I haul you downtown, in front of your children if that's who I hear playing upstairs in their rooms. You get to call your husband to bail you out, and your neighbors and everyone else with a TV tuned into the evening news gets to find out who exactly it is they live next to. Do we understand each other so far?"

Ana Bernal didn't reply, a smile still plastered to her face as her eyes continued to bug out. Parks noticed the veins in the woman's temples beginning to throb as a light sheen of perspiration began to form at her hairline across her forehead.

"Simply nod if you understand what I'm saying so far."

Ana Bernal nodded.

"Good. Or there's option two. You've been selling...*items* pertaining to the Palisades Poisoner case. In particular, I want to know if any one person has shown more interest in items belonging or pertaining to Lewis Hayward himself. Especially in the last year."

There was a slight twitch to the woman's body, as if a frame from film had been removed and she had jutted an inch to the side and back without anyone being any the wiser. She already had a name in mind. She knew whom he meant.

"And if you give me said person's name, three things will immediately happen. One: I will leave here without enforcing any legal action. Two: you will have personally assisted me in an ongoing investigation. And three: I'll leave you with this."

Parks reached into his pocket and removed a sealed evidence bag. It was small, no larger than six-by-four inches, but whatever was inside was enough to get Ana Bernal salivating.

220 | TYLER COMPTON

"What...? What is it?"

Milo looked to Parks, concern and question on his face before turning his attention back to Ana Bernal.

"The key card to the room Kyle Oni was found in," Parks replied.

Ana jumped off the sofa at Parks when he pulled the evidence bag back and began to tuck it away into his coat. Ana immediately sat back down and whimpered, looking longingly at where Parks's hand had disappeared.

"A name, Ana," Parks said, still trying to play the gentle friend card. "I know you have one for me."

"But there isn't one," Ana confessed.

"Ana, I know there is—"

"No," Ana spat. "I know what you mean. I'm telling you, there isn't one name. I think, who you're looking for, well, they're using multiple aliases."

Parks had already figured on that. The list of names they did have on people purchasing and trading in illegal merchandise was rarely ever that simple. And most people were hidden online by fake monikers and numeric and lettered ID codes. What he hoped for was an address he could cross-reference for actual people residing at said residences. But he didn't need to get into that with Ana Bernal.

"That's for us to worry about," Parks replied. "I simply need the names you think this person is using."

"Caleb Denny. Clayton Dects. And Lacy Yardmen. Can I have it now? The key card? Please?"

Parks looked to Milo, who took down the names and searched through a program on his iPad.

"Would you like their address?" Ana Bernal, said standing. "I can get it for you."

Parks stared at the woman, weighing his options. They already had the names. And he didn't exactly want to let her out of his sight just then.

"Got it," Milo interrupted. "Address is in Marin County."

"That's it!" Ana squealed with joy. "See, normally you'd never realize that three different names were using the same address. But the program I use for mailing out packages asks for an address first and a name last. So when I put the second person's address in, it already popped up in my browser history. It didn't take much to figure it out then. And then after the third one...well, I figured out something was going on. But they always paid on time and without any complaints about the pricing or shipping charges. And they always wanted everything shipped overnight. No matter what the cost was."

"Mrs. Bernal—it is Mrs., correct?"

Ana Bernal nodded but remained silent as she looked from Parks to Milo and back again, appearing confused and not quite sure what was going on or what she should be doing.

"Mrs. Bernal, did you happen to ever speak with the person who resides at these peoples' address?"

"No. Never. All correspondence was done through email."

"Okay. And did this person ever contact you. Outside of the three transactions you had with them."

"As a matter of fact, they did. They wanted to know if I had anything else connected to the Palisades Poisoner case. Particularly anything that may have been handled by the Palisades Poisoner himself."

"Lewis Hayward?"

"Correct."

"And?"

"I told them I didn't. But that I could try and get ahold of something if they wanted. They said money was no object. That they wanted whatever I could get ahold of."

"When was this?"

"About a month ago. Maybe a little longer."

"And have you heard back from this person since?"

"Once more. I told them that I still didn't have anything and that I wasn't sure if I could get anything else, and I haven't heard back from them since. All emails I've sent in the last month have been bounced back saying the email address is no longer active." Ana Bernal suddenly looked concerned as she clutched the necklace around her neck. "Am I in danger?"

"Not likely. But to be honest, I'm not sure. We can place you into protective custody, though the reasons why we would be doing it would most likely land you in jail." Parks let this comment hang in the air between them.

Parks nodded to Milo, and the two immediately stood up. "Can you give us a moment?"

"Oh, uh, sure," Ana said as she leaned back in her chair, while Parks led Milo toward the front doorway.

"What do you think?" Milo whispered.

"I'm not sure just yet. What did you find?"

"I've found the emails she sent back and forth from hacking into her home line. I'll try to trace the original email account she had contact with, but I'm not sure I'll be able to get anything out of it if it really is a dead link. Other than that, I think she's holding out on us. But I'm not sure we're going to be able to get more out of her based on her grasp of reality. Think she's really in danger?"

"If there's a possibility she actually could identify the person who's been buying her items, then definitely. Especially if that person is aware that we're onto them through this trail. Which seems slight. But I do think there's a chance that if we leave her be, she may reach out to her fellow group members and spill about what happened here today."

"And is that a good thing or a bad thing? I can't tell what you're thinking right now."

"If our killer is communicating with her via this group I don't want him to know we're onto him through this avenue. The warrants are all in order. Can you cover every form of communication Ana Bernal may use? Her phones, computers, etcetera?"

"We've got them all monitored now," Milo confirmed. "You want to use her as bait?"

"At the least, she knows nothing and will say nothing to anyone and no one will ever be the wiser," Parks surmised as he mulled over her options. "On the other hand she may blab about it to the world, and that could lead to the person collecting these items, or at the very least to a person who knows a person who knows a person...if you catch my drift."

"I get you. But what if this puts her life in danger for knowing too much?"

"We can ask her to come with us. We can't force it at the moment as there's no actual proof that she's in danger. Other than that I can leave a patrol car out front to monitor the neighborhood and make hourly calls into us that all is secure."

"Kinda sucks all around," Milo admitted.

"This entire scenario sucks all around," Parks agreed. "But this woman put herself in harm's way by getting herself involved with this group in the first place."

Milo nodded in agreement as Parks dismissed him and turned to Ana Bernal, who jumped to her feet to face him, afraid he was about to leave her without a parting gift.

"Mrs. Bernal, you have two options. One, you can come downtown with us and we'll place you and your family into protective custody. I'm not sure how long this will last though, and you will be questioned further about your activities concerning this Post Vitae group."

"If they ever found out I was a member or that I said anything about it..."

"That leaves us with option two. You can remain here and I'll post a patrol car outside for the next forty-eight hours to make sure all is okay. And you have to promise me not to reach out to any of the members of your group if you want to remain safe." Parks felt lame, like he was reprimanding a five-year-old.

"I'll never tell," Ana Bernal promised. "Cross my heart."

"We were never here," Parks said as he retrieved the evidence bag that he could tell she was dying to get ahold of. She could care less what danger she may have been in. All that mattered was her souvenir.

"Never," Ana Bernal replied. "Never."

Parks handed over the evidence bag and quickly left the house.

"I can't believe you did that," Milo said from the porch as he followed Parks to their vehicle.

Parks held back a smile as he stared at the kid over the hood of the car.

"That wasn't actually a key card from the room that Kyle Oni..." Milo didn't finish as he got into the car, mentally scolding himself for having ever thought Parks would have actually removed a piece of evidence from the evidence room. "What was it then?"

"A key card from the Roosevelt Hotel," Parks shrugged. "No idea what room it went to. Or when it was ever used."

Milo grinned as he began typing away on his keypad.

"I'll start looking up the names of those—"

"The names are bogus," Parks said as he started up the car.

"How do you know—"

"Lacy Yardmen, Clayton Dects and Caleb Denny are anagrams for Mary Delancy, Scott Delancy, and Ben Delancy. Which means we're on the right track. This is just Lewis Hayward messing with us. See if you can find anything connected with those names, both the original and the anagrams, though I doubt they'll lead us anywhere. I think that address may be more important. I want to know who is living at it. Or more likely, *was* living at it. We're on the right track. I can feel it."

SUNDAY

TWENTY-EIGHT

David Parks awoke to knocking at his front door. He looked around his bedroom and saw his electronic clock blinking at a steady 3:14, suggesting that the power had gone out some time during the night.

Parks stumbled his way to the front door and opened it to find his downstairs neighbor staring up at him, all bright-eyed and ready to face the day, cup of coffee included.

"I had a feeling you'd slept through the power outage, and I wasn't quite sure if you had to be up early or not this morning," Tracy Scott smiled as she offered over the cup.

"Actually," Parks started as he rubbed his hands over his face, "we've had sort of an eventful past week. They're giving us time to recuperate."

"So you actually get a weekend? Well, lucky me, then," Tracy beamed as she entered Parks's apartment.

Tracy found her way to the kitchen and sat down at the table, fiddling with a few pieces of the latest puzzle Parks had been working on. He had the four corners and a fourth of the center already completed.

"Look, Tracy...I appreciate the coffee, but I'm just waking up. And

I wanted to talk to you, but I really hadn't planned on it—"

"That was her, wasn't it?" Tracy asked, cutting him off. The tone of her voice was one of genuine curiosity without the slightest hint of jealousy.

"Her who? What?"

"The other day. The redhead. The one who broke your heart a while back. That was her, wasn't it?" Parks didn't reply, and Tracy continued, "It's okay. I figured as much. I could tell by the way you behaved around her. I mean, I only saw through the window, but a girl can tell these things. She's really beautiful. I can understand why you fell for her."

"Look, Tracy…I, well, it—"

"It's okay, silly," Tracy said, throwing on a smile but still unable to completely mask the slight pain she felt. "I mean, we're just a fling. Two lonely people who are there for each other when we need it. It's okay. It's nothing serious. I get it. I understand that kind of happiness. And Lord knows I wouldn't want to be the one to stand in the middle of it."

Tracy stood up and walked over to Parks, who still hadn't moved more than a step or two from his front door.

"That's why I stopped by. To make sure my instincts were right. It's okay. I get it. I hate it…but I get it. No hard feelings, okay? Still good neighbors?"

Parks stared down at the woman with a slight tilt to his head as he studied her.

"You know, you're one in a million," Parks finally said.

"Yeah, yeah," Tracy smiled as she kissed her hand and placed it over his mouth. "I'm still gonna call you when I need my faucet fixed. Lord knows Mr. Turvey never has time to fix it himself."

"You better," Parks replied.

"She here? Right now, I mean?" Tracy asked in a sudden whisper as if she had been caught somewhere she shouldn't have been.

"Who? Her—oh, her? No. No, she's not."

"Well, then let me give you some womanly advice," Tracy said as she exited his condo and started down the steps.. "If this is the only day you get off this week, you might want to call her. Better yet, just show up. Women love surprises and especially a man who takes initiative."

Parks took Tracy's advice. He showered, changed, popped a few more of his doctor prescribed pills, and was about to hit the road when he saw just how early it was. Though it wasn't so early for a time-zone difference.

"Hey, Dave," said Susan Levinson as she answered her Facetime call on her phone. "You look tired. What's up?"

"Thanks. I hope this is an okay time, but I was wondering if you could put Joshua on for me."

"Did he call you again?"

"Earlier this week. It's okay."

"He's just gonna throw the phone."

"That's fine. I just wanna say hi. You never know."

"True. Okay," Susan said as she began to walk into another room, calling out her son's name. Parks could barely make out some mumbling as Susan Levinson entered a child's bedroom; suddenly, the phone was passed over and Dave found himself staring up at the seven-year-old son of his former partner.

"Hey there, buddy. You remember me?" Dave asked with a smile on his face. After fifteen seconds of no reply, Dave decided to continue on. "That's okay. I understand if you don't want to talk. I hope you remember me though. I sure do remember you. I know you've been calling, and it's okay, that's not a bad thing. You can call me whenever you want and I'll always pick up. I promise. Okay?"

The little boy simply looked to the side, as if his mother was just off-screen, monitoring the conversation.

"How are you doing, little buddy? You okay?" The boy looked back to the screen on the phone but remained quiet. "You miss your dad?" Parks could see a hitch in the boy's chest. "Yeah, I know. It's okay. I miss him too. You know it's okay that you miss him. That's a good thing."

"I don't wanna die," the little boy said in a barely audible voice.

"The bad men, huh?" Parks said as he felt his heart tighten within his chest. He knew how the kid felt. And suddenly he felt this might be a much longer conversation than he had originally anticipated.

It actually hadn't been a long conversation, as Joshua had done no more speaking. He simply listened as Parks spoke. Thirty minutes later Parks realized that there was nothing more to be said that morning, and he promised Joshua that it was okay for him to call and promised he would call back the next Sunday morning and talk with him again. Even if he had nothing to say.

Feeling better about the day already, Parks drove for the Venice canals in hopes of surprising Jackie. It was when he got there that he realized he might get a surprise himself if the woman was not in fact home.

As Parks walked up to the white picket front gate that sealed off her property from that of her neighbors, he saw that she was just about to leave.

"Guess you had plans for the day, huh?" Parks called out, almost startling Jackie into a small scream.

"You...I swear," Jackie said, trying to look pissed but only managing a smile. "What are you doing here?"

"Day off," Parks answered, as if that explained everything. "I could have spent the day doing one of my puzzles. Or working out or lounging in front of the TV. Or back downtown working the case in some peace and quiet. I considered them all...but then thought there was somewhere else I'd rather be." Parks shrugged. "I just hadn't considered that you might have had plans yourself and realize now that I should have called."

"It's okay," Jackie smiled as she walked up to him. She pulled one of his shoulders down to bring his face closer to her as she planted a kiss on his cheek. "I do have plans."

She walked past him to her car, turning off the alarm. Parks stood there staring up at her house, the brief memories of the last time he had been there flashing back to him—*of Lewis Hayward and her son Ricky and of them barely surviving with their lives. Him being injected and his body becoming paralyzed with*—

"Hey, Mr. Daydreamer," Jackie said, snapping him out of his thoughts.

Parks turned around and saw her smiling at him, her bright white teeth calling to him.

"I'm just heading to the farmer's market. Feel like helping a poor, helpless woman find some healthy eats for the week?"

They spent the next two hours at a nearby farmer's market, choosing various fruits and vegetables for meals that Jackie would make throughout the week. They talked with the local vendors and were taught how to pick the best pieces and what would last longer or needed to be cooked the soonest. About an hour into the shopping excursion, Parks noticed that in-between picking up fruits and vegetables, Jackie had gotten into the habit of grabbing his hand as they walked from stand to stand, and he found himself liking the feeling that came with the familiarity of her warmth.

They finished shopping and then stopped back by her house to drop off their purchases before heading to the beach to grab some lunch. They got drinks, perhaps one too many, but were enjoying themselves. They then walked along the sandy boulevard that lined the ocean and took in the sights that many of the locals barely paid attention to themselves. Gulls cried out as they flew overhead, and tourists bicycled along the pathways. Several games of volleyball were going on the beach, while sunbathers tried to catch the last few rays before winter finally came.

"What are you thinking?" Jackie asked, as they walked side by side, their hands holding onto one another.

"I'm thinking this...Nothing."

"No, really. What?"

"You'll think it's...you might take it...not how I mean it."

"I think I understand you better than you think, Dave Parks," Jackie said, still looking forward. "Try me."

"I'm thinking this is weird. In a good way. Normal, I mean. I'm not used to it. But I feel like this is what it's like to live a normal life. To have someone to spend time with. Your life with. You do things like what we did today. I don't have many days like that. In case you didn't realize that."

"Oh, I think that secret's out of the bag."

"Today was nice. No—it was better than nice. But also...strange."

"Because you're not used to it."

"Because it's not a world I know."

They stepped off the beach and walked the paths toward the canals and eventually Jackie's home.

"I only know murder and assault and the scummy things we as people do to one another. And I like it. I mean not what we do to one another. But that I'm good at handling that. Dealing with that. It's what I know. I know how to be around that. How to compartmentalize everything in my life. But this...this is all foreign to me. Different. It's strange, and I'm not sure if I'm doing it right or not."

Well, I have a news flash for you, Detective Parks. There is no doing it right or not. You just do it. For some people it may work. For others not. That's why we as people do this thing called dating. It's how we find that perfect fit. That one person who accepts us for how we are, flaws 'n' all. Sometimes it works out. Sometimes not. But we keep on going. But you can't be doing it wrong as long as you're being yourself. As long as you try to be happy yourself, then I truly believe that happiness will spread. Be contagious, so to speak. It's all the more anyone could or should ask from another person. For people to be happy. And to be themselves."

"But where is this going?"

"Us? You mean today? Or in general? Because to be honest, Dave, I've no idea. I don't know where this—us—is going. I'm just taking it a day at a time. I've had such a long year...I'm just trying to enjoy this happiness right now while I've got it. Is that okay? Or do you need more right now?"

"Right now? Right now this is all I need," Parks said as he pulled Jackie over and gave her a kiss.

"Good," Jackie nodded, taking Parks's hand and leading him over a bridge. "Because even though I know you've always got a case to work on, maybe once this one is over, maybe then we can take a moment or two to figure out something more. Like what's next."

"That sounds good to me."

They spent the next ten minutes walking in silence, listening to the gulls and taking in each other's presence.

"I've got work to do," Parks said, finally breaking the silence.

"Excuse me?"

"I'm sorry. I've had Milo pulling case files and searching for online documents for me left and right, and he gave me a pile of stuff to go over, and I just realized I haven't thought about the case once today. While I was with you. I think you're a bad influence."

"Oh, really? Well, you don't happen to have those files with you, now, do you?" Jackie smiled and held back a small laugh. "Who am I talking to? Of course you have them. Why don't you go grab them, I'll do some kitchen work with the stuff we bought today, and you can spread out on the table. Bounce some ideas off me. I'd like to see how you work again. You know? To help prepare me for my own detective work one day."

"Oh, right. The detective's exams. You took them, right? How did you do?"

"Honestly, no idea. I'm still waiting for my results. I think I have another week to wait. Truth be told, that's part of the reason I agreed to work this case. It's keeping my mind busy. That and I figured I could keep learning out in the field until I know one way or the other. This could either officially be the first or last case I work as an LAPD detective."

"You know you made it, right? I mean, you did. You passed. I know you. There's no way you didn't."

"Oh? And what makes you say that?"

"It's my keen detective skills at work here. I just know. Besides, you're one in a million, you know that?"

"Awww," Jackie said, smacking Parks's arm. "I bet you say that to all the girls."

TWENTY-NINE

An hour later Jackie finished washing her purchases from earlier that day, placing everything into its proper bin in the refrigerator or up on the shelves in the cupboards while Parks spread out, deep in thought, reviewing Milo's findings. Even Milo hadn't been sure what he had been looking for, or what he had found, simply copying everything on every subject he had been told to by Parks and handing it all over.

"That helping?" Jackie asked, startling Parks who must have been deeper in thought than either one had been aware.

"What's that?" Parks asked, looking up.

Jackie nodded at the murder books for the Palisades Poisoner case spread out in front of him.

"Oh, I'm sorry," Parks said closing the first folder. "That was thoughtless of me. I never should have brought these case files in here to—"

"Nonsense," Jackie said, placing a hand over Parks's. "I told you to bring them in here. Tell me pictures and paperwork about dead bodies spread out all over the dinner table wouldn't offend any other woman you know? Truthfully, if you think the crime-scene photos you look at are bad, you ought to see the ones I stare at all day." Jackie smiled and tousled Parks's hair. "Truth is I knew being called for this case we would have to review and possibly revisit certain aspects of that case. I'm okay with it. I have to be. I need to be. I need to move on. This helps. It's closure. In a way. I don't mind. I mean, part of me does. But it doesn't matter. I need this. And if I have to go through it, I might as well go through it with you. And, dammit, this is my job. And I'll be damned if I'm going to allow that man to take away one more thing from me. *So...*What do we have so far?"

"I thought I had a lead on an address in Marin County where our killer was staying," Parks began. "I had Milo research it. Was a month-to-month motel with no video surveillance, and whoever had stayed there checked out two weeks ago. Or so says the manager. Had been there four months. Always paid in cash, in advance. Always left it at the front desk in an envelope. Couldn't say if a man or a woman had stayed there. Though he did remember a man paying the first month's rent and accepting the room key. It's been five months though, so he couldn't recall what the man looked like. I've got the Marin County sheriff's department investigating, but it's looking like a dead end. They have their tech people going over the room, but it's been rented out in the last two weeks, so that's going to be a dead end too. Figured it might be. If our killer is down here in L.A. now carrying out Lewis Hayward's orders, then it would make sense he wouldn't be up north anymore. Although, I feel we were on the right track. Marin County's just an arm's length away from San Quentin. Our killer, whoever he is, wanted to be near Hayward."

"At least you're making progress. You're on the trail of our killer. Might be a few steps behind, but you're gaining on him."

"Or her," Parks smiled.

"Or her." Jackie smiled back. "Oh, did you check to see if Hayward had any visitors at San Quentin so far? I mean, since this person you're looking for lived or lives so close to there."

"We have. We've had Hayward on the highest levels of security and monitoring since he arrived at San Quentin. Other than his lawyer, there's been no outside contact."

"What about his cellmates?"

Parks looked questioningly at Jackie. "What do you mean?"

"Well, if I was a super evil and devious villain and I knew I was being watched and wanted to get information out into the world, then I'd think of a way to do it. And it seems pretty simple to give any messages to my cellmate for him to pass onto whomever he was talking to during visiting hours. I mean, unless you've been monitoring him as well?"

Light seemed to come to Parks's face as he stood up, grabbed Jackie's face, and kissed her. "You're freaking brilliant, you know that?"

"I know. I'm a woman. Kinda born that way."

Parks's cell phone began to vibrate on the table, and he picked it up and looked at it. "I need to take this. I'll just be a minute. Okay?"

Jackie smiled at him, and he got up and left the table. She stared down at the files and turned one around, staring down at the mug shot of Lewis Hayward. That man had done so much damage to so many people. She flipped the page and began reading the file. Five minutes later Parks made his way back to the table.

"Setting up your next date?" she winked.

"Actually, that was my former partner."

"From your patrol days?"

"The one and only. Been trying to get a hold of him since we started this case. See if he remembers anything more about Mary Delancy.

He's apparently been out of town on a family vacation, but he's agreed to come in tomorrow afternoon and talk to us."

"Well, that's good," Jackie smiled. "Detective…?"

"Ballard," Parks answered. "Ryan Ballard. He was a good man."

"He was your partner for four years. But you haven't stayed in touch all these years?"

"I, well, things happen. Life, I mean. No one thing. Not everyone stays in touch with everyone."

"I didn't mean to attack you," Jackie said. "I just wondered if there was a reason?"

"No," Parks answered curtly. "No reason. I transferred from patrol to GND. He stayed on in patrol. We saw each other from time to time at crime scenes. Then a few years after I moved on to detective, there was an incident. On a case. He got shot. Got early retirement. His wife forced him to leave early. He has two daughters. And I know he wants to be there for them, so I don't think he put up much of a fight after that. Transferred to the far side of the valley for a nice life of simplicity. Or something like that. I've seen him on and off over the years, but nothing steady. Why do you ask?"

"No reason," Jackie shrugged. "Just trying out my new detective skills on you. Seeing how well I do with the interrogation aspect is all."

"Word of advice?"

"From you? Always."

"Might want to stick to poisons," Parks said playfully.

"Oh, is that so?" Jackie looked for something to throw at him and then gave up.

Parks had gone back to the file in front of him when he noticed Jackie still staring at him.

"What?"

"Wha…? Oh, nothing. Sorry, I was staring," Jackie turned and got up from the table.

"What is it, Jackie?" Parks asked, leaning back in his seat.

"If it's not too personal a question, how many partners have you had? Over the years."

"Oh, well now…traveling down memory road now. Let's see; Ballard was my patrol partner. Had Bollen back in my GND days."

"Gangs and Narcotics Division," Jackie said with a nod, showing that she had paid attention to his story the first time.

"Yep. Then in Robbery-Homicide I had Fincher, then Markowitz before they joined us with the Investigative Analysis Section that put us into our little multiple-people groups where I was more or less paired up…" Parks paused for a moment as he got caught up with his memories. "Um, where I was partnered up with Aaron Levinson for five years as they tried to merge me with Homicide Special Section."

"Aaron Levinson. I've heard that name before."

"From me."

"From around the department as well."

"Yeah, well…Levinson kinda put a bad light on the department. Like another Furman. Just not as racist."

"Still, a corrupt cop who plants evidence isn't taken lightly by the public. Not nowadays."

"Regardless if he *was* trying to put a child killer behind bars. Imagine trying to prove you were the naïve partner of said corrupt cop. Trying to prove—*fuck*."

"Oh, my," Jackie said, somewhat stunned by Parks's about-face. "Something wrong?"

"Oh, oh nothing," Parks said, hand against his face.

"What is it?"

"Nothing. Really. I mean that I can help. I just forgot about something. I have it under good authority that I may be hit with a lawsuit tomorrow. Or the day after at the latest."

"Who's suing you?"

"The Kozlov brothers. They're hitting the LAPD and me in separate lawsuits, claiming that we were each responsible for Aaron Levinson's duplicitous behavior toward Peter Kozlov that resulted in him being locked up."

"Um, I know that Peter Kozlov was arrested for harming those children, but wasn't he actually sentenced to prison for having his brother murder his wife so she couldn't testify against him?"

"Yes. And apparently he's blaming us—the LAPD and me since Aaron's no longer around to take the blame—for forcing him to have to kill his wife. Saying if we hadn't put her in that position of having to testify against him, blah, blah, blah."

Jackie looked as if she was trying to hold back laughter.

"Are you shitting me? Really? It's your fault he had to kill his wife?"

"Blame-shifting. It's a twenty-first century miracle excuse for everything. You're not really surprised that this lawsuit is going forward?"

"Oh, I've heard of some seriously stupid lawsuits in my days. But this one takes the cake. You're not seriously concerned about it, are you?"

"No, not really," Parks admitted as he slumped in his chair. "Lawyers say we shouldn't be. This is just another thing to take up my time and possibly smear my name. But what the hell? It's only my reputation, right?"

"I'm sorry," Jackie said taking his hand. "Truly."

"It's okay. Just another day in the life of Detective Parks."

"Can't say this life has been a cakewalk for you, Detective Parks."

"No…" Parks muttered. "No, you can't. But I thank you for asking. More than you know."

MONDAY

THIRTY

At 8:50 a.m., Chief Hardwick walked onto the floor and instructed Milo to turn on a computer that would link up with the cor-
rectional facility north of San Francisco for the video conference that
was to take place at nine o'clock. Dave couldn't say he was surprised
that all communication with inmates at San Quentin was being done
online, both to save the department any travel expenses and to save
Parks's group from having to deal with him being away. At the moment it would just be Milo and Hardwick with Dave as he interviewed
Nicholas Vaquier, though Rachel Moore's morning appointment with
Dr. Black was at eight and she would most likely be joining them just
as the interview began. Jake Fairmont's appointment with the station-
appointed shrink was at nine; thus, he would have to catch up on the
morning's events, pending the doctor's approval stating him fit for
work, after all was said and done.

As Milo worked on his end of the project, Hardwick went over the
rules of engagement with Parks; how he would be the only one on the
monitor to communicate with the convict and what to ask him and go
over as per the rules set up by Nicholas Vaquier's lawyer.

Ten minutes later, they were ready.

Nicholas Vaquier was not what Detective Parks had expected. Though they were meeting through the technology of video conferencing, Parks was more than able to take in all the physical attributes the man had to offer. The convict was in his late forties, thin, with the usual signs of having aged the last decade behind bars showing up on his face. He was lean yet strong, hours of pumping weights evident by the man's forearms. His tar-black hair was long enough to hang in his eyes. He had tattoos along both forearms and around the parts of his neck that Parks could see. Various images of women doing sexual things to inanimate objects appeared to be the theme, along with eyes, which were tattooed everywhere on the man's body. If he had been out in the world still peeping in on people, there was little he would have been able to do to hide the fact.

"Are you the reason I've been summoned away from my one-hour-a-day yard privileges?" Vaquier asked as he glared into the computer screen.

"Nicholas Vaquier?" Parks asked into the microphone.

"What. Do. You. Want?" Vaquier looked around his room, which appeared to be the an office in the prison of some sort, barely paying attention to the computer monitor before him.

"This is about Mary Delancy," Parks snapped, finally getting the man's attention.

Nicholas Vaquier's head turned to the computer screen so quickly Parks thought it would just keep on spinning around.

"Miss Mary? What's she want now? Isn't she happy enough that I'm locked away in this hellhole for all eternity?" Vaquier backed away from the screen and spread out his arms as if to show off all he didn't have. "Or has she finally come around and decided to set me free and ask for my forgiveness?"

"Why would she do that?"

"Shit," Vaquier hissed. The word coming out 'shee-it.' "You don't know nothing. What the hell do you want?"

"You don't seem to like Mary Delancy all that much."

"Is that a question, Officer? Because I don't hear one. And why shouldn't I be pissed at that woman? She's the reason I'm in here."

"It's Detective. And aren't you sure it's something you did that got you put in there?"

"Shee-it," Vaquier spat. "My fault? Piss on that. Miss Mary done put me in here. All her. And that asshole she was wit. His fault. Both them. Sure I done did stuff to be ashamed of in the eyes of the good Almighty. And He knows I'll answer for that. But I dun't do what they said I done did to get put in here. No, sir. Not me. I's innocent. But I've found resolution. I'm at peace now thanks to Mehen's protection. It's all come full circle. Ouroboros."

As Vaquier said these last words, he made a circle with both of his index fingers, causing Parks to take a pause at the words and gesture. The word had come out 'Roar-o-boar-us' but Parks figured out what the man was talking about.

"So—" Distracted by both Vaquier's words and the sudden appearance of Rachel Moore, Parks tried to collect his thoughts, as he looked at the sheet of questions before him. "So you weren't sending Mary Delancy letters with particular portions of your various being in them?"

"The hell you just say?"

"Did you or did you not send letters to Mary Delancy describing various erotic situations you'd like to find her in? Letters that contained...fingernail clippings? Hairs? Other bodily secretions?"

"I told her I'd like to see her naked and have relations with her—

252 | TYLER COMPTON

biblically speaking—if that's what you're asking. Have you seen the woman? Don't tell me you wun't like a piece of dat ass?"

"Did Mary Delancy make it known that she was not appreciative of your so-called gifts?"

"What the hell you callin' me for, Detective? Time is money. Time is money."

Parks looked to Hardwick, who motioned for him to continue.

"Have you spoken or had any contact with Mary Delancy since your incarceration?"

"The hell you say? Why the hell would I ever have any contact with Miss Mary? She the reason I'm in here. I told you dat. Naw man. I ain't seen her. But I'm okay with that. Resolution. Ouroboros. We all get what's comin' to us. But I've been baptized in His glory and am now reborn and protected. I know the truth. Ain't no one listening, but I know it just the same. You tell Miss Mary that from me. Okay?"

"Mr. Vaquier..." Parks paused for a moment, looked over at the eyes of his team staring back at him, and continued. "Mary Delancy was found dead in her home last week."

"The hell you just say?" Parks wasn't sure if the man didn't believe him or really wanted him to repeat himself.

"She was found dead in her bed last week," Parks repeated.

"Miss Mary wasn't that old, was she?"

"I didn't say she died of natural causes, Mr. Vaquier."

"Well *shee*-it. Guess Mehen musta abandoned her. She done forgot to pay the toll. But He still lookin' out for me. But Miss Mary...I didn't do it. The Man can't pin this one on me. You *know* where I was. I got the most air-tightest alibi on tha planet. Ya hear?" When Parks didn't reply, Vaquier repeated himself. "*Ya hear?*"

"No one's questioning your alibi, Mr. Vaquier. You're not a suspect. We're simply talking with you this morning to get your take on the situation and see if you can't shed some light on your past associations with the deceased."

Vaquier remained quiet and stared at the camera as if he wasn't sure what Parks had just said to him.

"How do you feel about this news, Mr. Vaquier?"

"Miss Mary is dead. Always a shame when a good-lookin' woman like that goes too early. I loved her. And she loved me back, I know it. That was our story. We were destined to be together. So I'll just keep my mouth shut and say the Lord done work in mysterious ways. Amen to that."

"Mr. Vaquier? What did you mean by saying you don't belong in prison? Can you elaborate on that for me, please?"

"Why the hell should I? I know you ain't gonna believe me. None of them ever did. Or do. Cuz I'm a felon. I know. But just cuz of that don't mean you gotta go around blaming me and framing me for shit I didn't do. Don't I do enough of it on my own to nab my ass? Oh, wait. No I don't, cuz I'm in-*no*-cent."

Vaquier stretched out the word innocent, pronouncing each syllable.

"Mr. Vaquier, according to your arrest record, you broke into the Delancy house and attacked Scott Delancy. The police arrived and arrested you. Found you holding a knife and threatening the Delancys. Are you saying this wasn't true?"

"*Shee*-it, man, I was asleep in my own bed when the po-po come breakin' down my door and hauled my ass to the dead woman's house. Then they arrested me and that's that. That's bull is what that is."

"Scott Delancy had to get fifty-seven stitches that night. Mary Delancy had a sprained wrist, two broken fingers, and a blackened eye.

And a man named Thomas Cream was found dead in Mary's kitchen," Parks continued as he flipped through the photos from Vaquier's arrest file. "You saying you didn't do that?"

"*Shee*-it, naw, I didn't do that," Vaquier spat. "I was framed. Framed by the po-po for a crime I didn't commit. I would have neva hurt that woman. She my woman. I would done cut the fucker who did that shit to her. I just don't understand why she felt she had to blame me. Didn't she know? I loved her. I would've done anything for her. I would've killed the sombitch who did that to her. Maybe she was scared. I don't know. Maybe I was the only way out for her." Vaquier sat quietly and thought this over. "Maybe that's what it's all about. You see? She did what she did to me to save me? And save herself? I'd have done all this again if it meant saving her. I love her, Detective. Don't you know that? I love that woman and she loved me back."

Parks took in Vaquier's words, trying to decipher the truth from fiction. Vaquier's delusions were growing by the second, and Parks knew he was simply feeding them. The man's hatred for Mary Delancy might be rooted deep inside, but his obsession was too grave for him to be able to hold her fully accountable. He would find a way, no matter what anyone said or did, to twist everything around to mean that Mary Delancy loved him and did this all so they could be together.

"Had you ever seen Thomas Cream before that night?"

"You mean the night he was killed? Yup. I seen him around her house from time to time. From my place out—he was just a kid. Ain't no threat. Just a piece of ass Miss Mary was getting her jollies off on. Can't blame the woman for that. Woman's got needs. I understand that. Only can blame Miss Mary for other things."

"If you feel that Mary Delancy was the reason—"

"Against her will," Vaquier interrupted.

"Against her will. But that she was part of the reason you were put in there? To help frame you for Thomas Cream's murder? Then who is the person to blame?"

"Some other, new asshole hanging around. He the one who convinced her I was poison and that I needed to be locked up. I knew she didn't believe him, but she was a'scared of him. Had to go along with what he told her to do, lest she wanted to be found six feet under. Now you want to talk about obsessed? There was a man who was obsessed. I done seen him over there all the time. From my spot out...well, he had a thing for Miss Mary. That's the gospel truth there. Didn't like no one else out lookin' in on Miss Mary. No, sir."

Parks soaked in all of the information, some making sense and most sounding like pure gibberish.

"Just to clarify, you're not talking about Mary's sons, are you?"

"Sons? Shit. She only got the one, right?"

Rachel Moore leaned in and whispered to Parks. "That would make sense, timeline wise. The oldest son, Ben, would have moved out by the time Vaquier was stalking Mary Delancy. Scott would still be living at home. Her husband died in '82. Vaquier was around Mary from about '95 to '99 when he was locked up for the first time. He probably wouldn't know about her oldest son."

"Hey? You still talkin' to me?" Vaquier shouted into the computer screen.

"I'm still here. I'm still here," Parks said, reverting his attention back to Vaquier.

"No, it wasn't her pansy-ass son. Ain't got no fuckin' backbone, that one. Couldn't pull the wings off a fly, that one. Naw, I'm talking about the man she was seein'. I don't know his name. Called him the Duck-Man."

"Excuse me?" Parks shot out as he jerked his attention back to the video screen. "What did you say?"

"I don't know the man's name. But everyone around him called him the Duck-Man. Said his name was Duck or something like that. But like I said, you wouldn't never believe me."

"Duck tattoo?" Milo mouthed and Parks shook him off as he turned to Rachel Moore, on whose face he could read frustration and disappointment.

"The Duck-Man was around a lot. I remember seeing him over there all the time. Him and Miss Mary were getting might comfortable. But I know she didn't like him too much. She was a'scared of him. I know it."

"So what you're telling me is this Duck-Man is the person who murdered Thomas Cream and then set you up to take the fall for it?"

Vaquier simply wiped his mouth as if he had no other suitable answer.

"End this," Hardwick said softly yet with enough force that no one mistook her order.

"All right, Mr. Vaquier. I'd like to thank you for your time," Parks said as he looked to Milo to turn the computer off.

Milo barely had time to disconnect the monitor and audio feed before Hardwick cursed to the Gods above.

"So Nicholas Vaquier feels he's been set up," Milo wondered from his seat at his desk. "There's a shocker. Of course he said that. They *all* say that. I mean, we're not really surprised about that, now, are we? I mean, how's a person gonna kidnap and drag Vaquier out of his home, across the city to Mary Delancy's place, and place him at the scene of the crime without anyone being any the wiser? Who could do that?"

"We could." Parks stared up at Hardwick.

"What?"

"The police. We could have hauled a known criminal like Vaquier out of his house without a single question being raised. Vaquier was always being hauled away for questioning during that time. He was on parole. He could have been transported over to the crime scene and set up without anyone taking a second guess at the situation."

"This could all just be conspiracy theories being thrown around to get us off track," Hardwick offered to Parks.

"No, it's not, and you know it. This all makes sense," Parks said, rubbing his hands over his face and looking at his group. "Mary Delancy liked orchids. So he sent her orchids. But not just any. *Blue* orchids. To symbolize himself. To set himself apart from the others. Denise Jones told us that much before her death."

"So we're blaming an obsessive cop for all this?" Milo asked. "Again?"

"Who's the Duck-Man?" Rachel asked calmly, eyes directed completely at Parks. "The nickname's familiar, but I can't place it."

"It's what they used to call him around the station," Parks explained, speaking to no one in particular as he stared down at his desk. "To poke fun at him. One day the captain got his name wrong. It does sound like a duck's name. A mallard. So it stuck. I didn't. But that's because he was my superior. But I still heard it from time to time around the station. Out at crime scenes. Vaquier could have easily overheard someone call him that."

"Who? Who, Dave?"

"My old patrol partner. Ryan Ballard."

THIRTY-ONE

It had been suggested that pending Jake Fairmont agreeing to once-a-day visits with Dr. Black for the next week, the detective would be cleared for duty. Jake more than happily agreed, just so long as he could keep working the case.

Once Jake made it back to the station, Parks pulled him aside to his office for a quick one-on-one.

"While I'm glad to see you don't have any reservations about continuing to see Dr. Black—at least on the outside it's a smart move—I just want to make sure you're aware, right now, up front, so you don't feel blindsided, that once this particular case is over, you will be required to take a mandatory two-week stress leave. Understood?"

"Seriously? This is bullshit. I just got back."

"And this doesn't mean you're going anywhere or that they don't want to keep you around. But we are only human, and we do need to keep a careful watch of ourselves. Trust me. This is coming from someone who's taken several 'optional' work absences due to stress."

Both men knew Parks was talking about the two weeks he had taken after the Knott/Davis case and the one before that after his partner Aaron Levinson had died at the hands of Peter Kozlov, who nearly took Parks's life as well.

"Hey," Parks said, snapping to get Jake's attention. "Hey. You know I have your back, right? You're not going anywhere. Not on my watch."

Jake seemed to relax, and he breathed deeply and smiled.

"I hear you. I'm with you."

"Okay. Now let's catch you up."

The two made their way back out to the rest of the team while Parks caught Jake up with what they had discovered that morning.

"You really going to accuse your old partner of being obsessed and having an affair with a celebrity he was...what? Supposed to be protecting? To the point of framing an innocent man—who also happens to be a sick stalker, but was still innocent no less—for *murder*, no less? To what? Help her feel safer? To be with her? What? Tell me. What?" Fairmont's question was genuine and everyone knew it.

"No, I'm not," Parks answered. "But Ballard is coming in later today to help answer some questions about Mary Delancy, so maybe now we just have a few more questions for him is all." Parks caught Jackie hold back a smile and turned to her. "Something amusing?"

"Just the alleged affair between Mary and Ballard," Jackie smiled. "And then remembering how everyone thought her house was the old *Double Indemnity* house at first. That's all."

"I'm glad we're still finding humor in all of this," Parks said, standing up and walking to the murder board. "But we still have a case to go over. So until Ballard arrives...how about we go over everything else we have."

"But what about Ballard?" Fairmont asked. "Do we honestly think there's a chance he could be our killer? Another cop? And what exactly are we accusing him of? Killing this Thomas Cream person and then twenty-something years later going back and killing Mary Delancy and her son because, what? They were going to tattle on him or something?"

Parks turned to Milo and said nothing.

"Look," Parks sighed. "I don't know. My gut tells me no. But I haven't talked to the man in four years and haven't seen him for almost seven. Who knows? He might not be the man I remember. Who even knows what I remember. We proceed. We will investigate Ballard the same as we would any other lead. Fairmont...I want you and Rachel to start digging into his personal life. See about an alibi for him for the time of Mary Delancy's death. Okay? We'll start with the basics. Milo, we keep bringing up this murder of Thomas Cream at Mary's place, but I've never actually gone over that case file. Can you pull any and everything they have on it? I know it's more than twenty years ago, so I'm not sure what all you'll actually find."

"Do you mind if I ask what I think is an obvious-but-maybe-I-just-don't-know question?" Milo Tippin asked, raising his hand.

"Shoot."

"I've been rereading the case files from the Palisades Poisoner case, and I was wondering a few things."

"Which unfortunately is our first mistake, I fear. But go on."

"Wait," Fairmont interrupted. "What do you mean, a mistake?"

"Lewis Hayward was a member of the LAPD for two years before he sprung his little poison death spree. That's two years of patience and meticulous planning. Lewis Hayward is not an impatient man, nor is he trifle for circumstances."

"Meaning?"

"He'd had two years to access this department's files. If he had truly in some way been planning on killing the Delancys since before his incarceration, then how are we to know that some of the files concerning them haven't simply gone missing? That what's really important to be known about them to help us identify why they've been killed hasn't been erased?" Everyone remained quiet as they took in Parks's words. "Or worse."

"What's worse than missing case files?" Fairmont asked.

"Altered case files," Rachel Moore answered.

"Exactly. It's not only what isn't there but what is. How do we know that what we're reading isn't just manufactured lies put there by Hayward to drive us on a wild goose chase of chasing our tails?"

"How do we?" Fairmont asked.

Parks simply shrugged. He had no answer for that one. At least not a good one.

"Trust me. Lewis Hayward being a member of the LAPD has been one clusterfuck after another. IAD has been going crazy ever since his incarceration. They've been working on going over every case he's ever touched. Every person he's ever put behind bars has filed a motion for release, and some may even get it. As the leader of Hayward's team, Mark Wilkes has been in with IAD on an almost weekly basis, trying to help clear up this mess." Parks paused as he looked to Hardwick to make sure that while he was trying to keep his team in the light that he wasn't overstepping any confidential boundaries. "Trust me…as much as I hate to say it, Mark Wilkes has had nothing but shit heaped onto him since Lewis Hayward, and though I'll never repeat this aloud, he's been doing a hell of a job. Fortunately, that's IAD's job to deal with. Unfortunately, there's not a whole lot we can do about it but be aware of it. If there's a way to double-check any of our work with outside sources, then I suggest we do it. It's just something to keep your attention on when going over all of this. Sorry to interrupt, but you were saying, Milo?"

Milo had to think a moment about where he was going with his train of thought. "Oh, our killer this time? We're going on the assumption that he is more than just a copycat, that he is in fact somehow actually linked to Lewis Hayward, correct?"

"Correct," Parks said with absurdity. "What are you getting at?"

"And to refresh everyone's memories, what was the motivation for Lewis Hayward's series of poisonings?"

"Lewis Hayward was a nut job who killed people he blamed for his daughter's death," Fairmont offered. "Messed up thing was Hayward was the one who killed her himself. Just couldn't take the blame, so he shifted it on to other people."

"Or so we've been able to best piece together," Rachel reminded Jake.

"Or so we think," Fairmont said, waving her off.

"Punishment," Parks said to himself as he stared up at the murder board.

"Bingo," Tippin smiled.

"What are you getting at?" Jackie asked.

"The Palisades Poisoner poisonings. Those people were chosen and punished based on crimes they had committed. The Ten Commandments. That was what we figured out. Right? That's happening here too. In a way, these people are being punished as well."

"But punished for what?" Rachel asked. "People do things wrong every day. Bad things. Some more than others. That doesn't make us all worthy of death."

"Maybe not. Maybe so. According to Lewis Hayward's way of thinking, it might," Parks corrected. "But this all stems from Mary Delancy. *She's* the start of this case, so she's our origin point. Everything else grows from her. She's our main focus point. Everyone else is just collateral damage. She was the main target."

"So then what did Mary Delancy do?" Rachel asked.

"False idols?" Fairmont offered. "That making one a false god commandment?"

"No, no," Parks said shaking his head. "This isn't about the commandments again. This is about someone's personal vendetta against Mary Delancy. Someone personally feels that Mary Delancy did something wrong. Against him. Somehow. But what...?"

"Vaquier?" Rachel Moore asked. "He said he had been falsely imprisoned. What if someone found out and agreed?"

"So we think this is Nicholas Vaquier getting revenge from behind bars?" Fairmont asked. "I could see Lewis Hayward being able to do that, but not Nicholas Vaquier. And if Hayward was doing that for Vaquier...I mean, *why*? What's the connection between those two? Other than being cellmates?"

"Maybe Hayward's using Vaquier's problems as a way to continue on with his...message? Crusade?" Jackie suggested.

"It's a possibility," Parks said. "But I don't see it. Hayward feels himself holy. He wouldn't touch Vaquier, despite his wrongful imprisonment, because of his past. Vaquier may be innocent of whatever Mary Delancy framed him for, but he's still too...*dirty*. Contaminated. Hayward would feel that Vaquier would only corrupt his cause. If Hayward is pulling the strings here, it's not for Vaquier. Vaquier is simply a coincidence. Collateral damage."

"So what then? What's the purpose behind all this?" Rachel asked.

"Mary Delancy's death was punishment because of something they did. Back then."

"Her son too?" Rachel Moore added. "Why him? Was he just as

guilty?"

"The eyes may see the truth, but what the tongue won't reveal is just as sinful," Parks replied. "Or something like that. Scott Delancy witnessed this blessed event. And then said and did nothing."

"Or said the wrong thing. Lied about what really happened," Jackie suggested. "Their throat is an open grave, with their tongues they keep deceiving. The poison of asps is under their lips. Romans 3:13."

Everyone thought about this for a moment.

"But a child? They're blaming a child?" Rachel continued.

"You're assuming this is to make sense to us? Because if you want that, then you're in the wrong line of business. And hell, we might even be wrong about this. But I don't think so. Something happened years ago. Something that caused Denise Jones to quit being Mary's publicist. Why? She knows the truth. Hence the reason she too was poisoned. Not from stopping us from finding out the truth. The truth will out itself. Whoever's behind this wants the truth to be known. She was poisoned for keeping quiet about it for so long. Like Jackie said, she lied. She felt guilty, which is why she quit, but she still went along with whatever happened. So our killer's out to get revenge for whatever happened against everyone who helped cover this event up. We just have to be better and faster if we want it. Remember, we're dealing with poisons here. There's no official timetable to work off. Poisons are not an exact science. But we all know Hayward to be a very patient person, so he's got this down as close to exact as I think someone can get when dealing with uncontrollable substances."

"Mary Delancy's husband? His death?" Jackie asked. "Probably the second oldest crime in the book. After Cain and Abel of course. And you all keep coming back to the double indemnity thing. What if it was her husband's death? What if it wasn't natural? How did he die after all?"

"Heart attack," Rachel answered. "Natural causes. Or at least that's what's on the coroner's report. But it was known he had heart problems. His doctors were aware of it. Though there were rumors that he may have possibly induced and/or worsened his condition himself. He was a big-time believer in homeopathic remedies. And back in the seventies and eighties when some of them may not have been aboveboard. The Delancys were big pushers of several different forms of self-help types of medication. One that he pushed and was apparently taking quite a bit for his heart condition was some form of a...colloidal silver. Whatever that is."

"Silver?" Jackie asked, suddenly alert.

"What is it?" Parks asked.

"Tanaka and I have been talking, and according to the tests we've run, we believe our killer is mixing the strychnine he or she is using with some form of silver."

"Silver?"

"Yeah. In a powder form. It's called argyria. That's what's giving the bodies that extreme bluish condition and might even be speeding up the reaction time. We're still investigating and running a few more tests though. I'll get back to you on it. We're close."

"Well, the silver thing would connect all this back to Mary's husband," Jake offered up. "Seems plausible. I mean, what else happened that connected Mary Delancy to Lewis Hayward?"

"Well, if there was a cover-up, then we wouldn't know about it," Milo ribbed. "Hence the word cover-up."

"Don't think I won't hit you," Jake said without turning to face Milo. "Don't think I won't. But publicly, anything else?"

"Thomas Cream's murder," Rachel offered up. "But we know all about that. He was sleeping with Mary Delancy and was killed. Nicholas Vaquier was sentenced to prison for it. Even if he does say it's a cover-up. But even if it was, Nicholas Vaquier would be the injured party here, and why would Lewis Hayward care about his wrongful imprisonment?"

"Maybe—," Parks said, mulling over the possibilities in his mind, "it wasn't *who* killed Thomas Cream, but *why* he was killed."

"You're saying it wasn't because someone was jealous he was sleeping with Mary Delancy?" Jackie asked.

"What if he was simply in the wrong place at the wrong time?" Rachel asked.

"And saw something he shouldn't have?" Parks wondered. "Maybe that's what got him killed. Maybe he was killed to cover up what he saw. Maybe that's what Hayward's trying to expose. Hmmm."

"Boss," Milo called out as he pointed to his computer screen. Even during their brainstorming session, the kid was still working on other angles.

"What have you got, Milo?" Parks asked as he leaned into the kid's computer.

"These are the phone records from the Delancy residence for the last year. Take a look at the highlighted numbers."

Milo waited patiently while Parks looked at the several highlighted numbers and saw the familiar number three times.

"Is this who I think it is? Calling Mary Delancy?" "Three calls. All to Mary Delancy."

"And when were these calls—" Parks stopped.

He didn't need to ask as he saw the dates on the same three lines as the numbers dialed. They were from the same afternoon and evening as Mary and Scott Delancy's murders.

THIRTY-TWO

Five hours had passed and Parks was busy reading the pages of Mary Delancy's memoir when his phone rang. He answered it without looking away from the file in his lap, his attention completely focused on getting results.

"David," came the soft voice from the other end of Parks's desk phone. The voice had a calming effect to it, so that when he heard his name, Parks would have been put into a slight trance had it not been for the fact that it was his first name he heard, a name he wasn't all that familiar with hearing during business hours.

"Yes? What? Who—wha?" Parks replied, slightly dumbfounded.

"I was so saddened to hear that you had been so close to me and yet failed to contact me with questions about your current ongoing case," continued the man's voice.

"Hayward?" Parks spat as he suddenly placed the voice on the other end of the line.

He quickly swung his feet off his desk as he sat straight up, his attention at full alert. Neither Rachel Moore nor Jake Fairmont had heard the name Parks called out, but both had seen their boss's demeanor change dramatically since picking up the phone, and they exchanged concerned glances.

A chuckling came through the phone as Parks looked around the room, catching eyes with Rachel and Jake before locking on with Milo and silently snapping at him as he motioned to his phone. Milo had no idea who his boss was talking with but knew that Parks wanted his full attention on the situation at hand.

Rachel and Jake were already listening in on the conversation in progress.

"Hayward?" Parks repeated. "Is this really you?"

"You need to ask?" Lewis Hayward replied. "I think you know the answer to that."

"But you're under restriction. You don't have access."

"And yet logic would seem to defy your confusion and dictate that what you believe to be is not so. Don't concern yourself with the simple petty occurrences such as how or why and simply know that it is. This is happening. But again, I repeat, I'm hurt that you didn't reach out for my assistance. After all, since you were already on video conference with my current location of constriction, and while I've no doubt Vaquier had several interesting things to say, I was hurt you didn't feel the need to connect with me. Why was that? Feel you're already ten steps ahead on this case? Or getting there? Don't need a little extra helping hand? It does appear you are making progress."

While Lewis Hayward had been talking, Chief Hardwick had entered the room, a look of frantic confusion on her face. Parks noticed Milo typing away on a hand-held device, no doubt the way he communicated with her as to the situation at hand. Hardwick picked up a phone, but Parks didn't hear her join the conversation and knew that she was no doubt contacting the prison where Lewis Hayward should have been confined.

"No doubt Detectives Moore and Fairmont are on the line as well?" Hayward continued, the sound of glee echoing through the lines of communication. "And our boy, Milo? Huh?"

Parks shook his head from side to side, informing his team to remain quiet, no matter what Hayward knew or thought he knew. "And how is the Scooby Gang these days? Rachel and Jake still sneaking around? Or does that not matter now that you've done such a good job negotiating all of your returns."

"What do you want, Hayward?" Parks asked as he controlled his rage. *How* was he doing this? *Why* was he doing this? Simply to show he *could?* But to what purpose?

"And what about the lovely Doctor Jacqueline Isley? Is she there as well? If so, I would like to take this time to apologize to her personally for having to harm her son, though in my defense—"

"What do you want?" Parks repeated, his temper beginning to flair. Jackie was at her lab digging through her records on strychnine. Regardless, Parks didn't want to hear what Lewis Hayward had to say to or about Jackie Isley or her son.

"Why to help you, of course, silly," Hayward laughed. "What other purpose could there be for my calling you?"

"Oh, I don't know. Maybe to relay another threat."

"I'm assuming you're talking about my letters? I see the big brass finally thought highly enough of you to inform you of them. Too bad they probably waited too late to do so. It's okay. Things have changed since their creation. Several pawns on the board are changing location. Rooks have been moved into play ahead of schedule."

"Their creation? Rooks?" Parks said mostly to himself as Hayward continued.

"Yes, things have changed. I hear you're doing quite a job on your current case. Mary Delancy. Yet, you're no closer to solving said case, is that true? No true suspects? I mean sure you have a few likely candidates, but no true line of direction? Would it help you to know that this case echoes several other cases you've recently worked?"

"Hayward, you—"

"I mean, of course there are the obvious connections to my case from last year," Hayward interrupted, amused and not at all distracted by Parks's questions. "That is true. There is *that* connection. Then there's also the Knott/Davis connection." Hayward laughed as he figured Parks was confused, while everyone on the team looked to one another. "No. No. I don't mean this case is in any way directly related to that case. Do you remember what we talked about last time you paid me a visit?"

Parks thought about their conversation as he looked around at his team members. While he had gone over what Hayward and he had discussed last spring when he last visited, he had ended up dismissing most of what the man had said as gibberish. He hadn't even gone into great detail about it with Hardwick, whom he knew he should have.

"You mean about you being an ouroboros and protected by Mehan?" Parks shot out.

Hayward paused for a moment. "I am impressed. I had forgotten that I had mentioned that to you, and yet I think I'm more surprised that you recalled those words. I assume you know the meaning behind them?" Before Parks could answer, Hayward continued, "But of course you do. Even if you do deny it. I know it to be so. Otherwise, you wouldn't have the cyber geek out searching on the path that I have no doubt you sent him on. No, that's not what I meant. Actually, I am referring to what I said about the case you were working on at the time. About the motivation behind the deaths?"

"You said that the person who killed Fredrick Knott and Kelli Davis did it for one reason, not realizing he was being set up and killed those two for a completely unrelated purpose altogether," Parks finally answered. "Are you admitting that you've fooled some innocent into killing Mary Delancy and her son for one reason, while your true ulterior motives remain all to yourself?"

Hayward laughed.

"Oh, my. My dear Parks, I do love the way your mind works. As if I could have ever convinced someone to kill for me. No, no. I assure you. The person who killed Mary and her son did it all of his own abstract thoughts. Perhaps though, you are blinded by the thought that Mary and her son are the end game?"

"Death isn't a game," Parks replied as he tried to process Hayward's words. He may have thought the man spouted gibberish, but he knew Hayward too well to know it was all nonsense. His words had meaning behind them. He knew that much. "It is final, though. So it is the end. No matter what the reasoning behind it. But what you're saying is that there's more to come? That what happened to Mary Delancy and her son was simply a set up...?" Parks paused as he mulled this thought over. "But for what reason? For whom? The killer was trying to get in contact with someone that he otherwise couldn't have without being obvious? Or were their deaths...perhaps, payment of some sort? For services rendered? To you? In exchange for something else?"

"Hmmm," Hayward replied with a smirk that Parks could hear in his voice. "Maybe you're finally getting warmer. I think I've set you on the right path. But before I go, a word of advice. Speaking of the ouroboros, I'm sorry for what has happened to Ana Bernal. She broke the sacred covenant and spoke out of turn. So she has been dealt with accordingly. And Dave, despite what you may think, her blood is not on your hands. She was aware of the path she had chosen. I truly am sorry for what had to happen. But get Tippin off the path you've got him plowing through unless you want to see *him* suffer some unfortunate consequence. You and he have some suspicious thoughts going through your minds, and it is going to get someone hurt. I wouldn't like to see that. Not to any of my former teammates. So trust me on this. Back off."

Everyone listening to the phone conversation turned to Milo, who immediately turned a bright shade of red. Rachel and Jake had no idea what Hayward was talking about but knew it was something they'd be informed of in due time. Parks had a plan for everything. Everyone had their place in it and did as told. They might not have always liked it, but they did as he instructed, as they had learned to trust his guidance. Unfortunately, at the moment Parks looked like a rabid dog constricted to a tethered pole.

"What the hell did you do?" Parks all but yelled through the phone.

Milo was already off the line and was most likely calling in on the patrol car positioned outside of Ana Bernal's home.

Hardwick was frustrated as she glared at the phone in her hands while her body tensed up. She tried pacing but was restricted by the phone cord that kept her at the nearby desk. She got nowhere as she was transferred from location to location. Parks wasn't sure how Hayward did it—he was sure the man was still locked up inside San Quentin—but he knew he had pulled strings to get this call made. But no matter, time ticked away for Hayward no matter what accommodations he had made to achieve this conversation.

The room was silent, and Parks breathed into the phone, not sure what to say. He contemplated simply hanging up on the man and wondered why he didn't. It wasn't like they were tracing him to find out where he was. They knew where he was. What was his motivation to stay on the line? Why not just be done—

"Lewis," Parks said, addressing the man by his first name, something he rarely ever did. Parks could hear the man's breathing take a hitch from the other end as the joyfulness of his being took pause, the realization that they were getting serious taking over him.

"David," Lewis Hayward replied.

"Lewis...what do you want? With me? With all of this? What do you want?"

There was a pause, and Parks could hear Lewis Hayward breathing on the other end of the line. The sounds of metal grinding and doors opening and closing continued in the background. If Lewis Hayward was not at San Quentin, then he was somewhere that sure sounded an awful lot like a prison.

"Your city is a modern-day Sodom and Gomorrah. 'For their vine is from the vine of Sodom, And from the fields of Gomorrah; Their grapes are grapes of poison, Their clusters, bitter.' You see, sin fills the streets, the homes of its so-called citizens. Good people go on being harmed in ways nearly imaginable—punished, day in and day out—while evil continues to grow rampant, unpunished for being nothing more than sin. But it must be stopped. Someone must take control. Must be willing to make the sacrifice needed to make the change for the better. There is always dark before the light. I accept that. Losing my Julie was what was needed for me to see that light. That change. I accept that now. As hard as it was, I was called, and this was what was needed for me to heed that calling. There will be change. This city is filled with an infection that will ruin the eternal lives of all its citizens unless something is done. And so I will do it. I will carry out this change. To poison the evil that plagues its streets and cleanse the lives of those who so deserve it. Every man, woman, and child, no matter the cost, in order to be saved must accept that their actions have consequences. And they must pay for their sins in order to survive. Without that there is no surviving. There is nothing else. Nothing more to come. No next."

There was only silence between the two men as Parks took in Lewis Hayward's words. His explanation. His excuse for his thirst—his *need*—to kill.

"And who chose you to carry out this so-called cleansing?" Parks asked.

"I was chosen. This is my calling in life."

"So you've turned religious? That seems a change, even for you."

"You'll see. Sooner or later. You'll see you have no choice but to accept. Those who fall in line with what I have to offer will be spared. All others...who fall to the wayside...they will see and reap the consequences that have been chosen for them."

"How do you really—?"

"Looks like my time is up. I'm assuming Hardwick finally got through to the proper authorities," Hayward interrupted. "It's been nice chatting again, Dave. I hope we get to do it again. Until next time."

With those words, the line went dead, and Parks and his team were left with just as many questions as before.

Even with sirens blaring, it had taken Parks and his team almost thirty minutes to arrive at the home of Ana Bernal. The aroma of a batch of freshly made chocolate-chip cookies still wafted through the air as the plate of them sat on the table next to Ana's body. Whatever Ana had put into the batter, or perhaps had been slipped into it without her knowing, had done the trick most efficiently and quickly.

While the crime scene was being processed, Parks discovered that Ana's husband had taken their children to visit his family in Sun Valley the day before, and they weren't due back until that evening. He would now be coming back sooner than planned and sans children. Parks had questions for the confused husband, though he had a feeling not even he knew about his wife's extracurricular affairs concerning the memorabilia of killers and crime scenes.

Parks questioned the two patrol officers stationed outside the Bernal residence, and both men repeatedly assured him that no persons had been to the front door of the home, let alone let inside. There had also not been any deliveries or packages dropped off since their posting. Though he wanted to be frustrated at the two men, he knew it was not their fault. If Lewis Hayward had wanted in, he would have found a way. And no one would have been able to stop him.

More than likely, Ana Bernal had already possessed the toxin that she had used, no doubt on herself. Then, Lewis Hayward had most likely contacted the woman in some way and given her the option: Take yourself out of the equation, or your whole family will have to be taken out instead. And to a devoted wife and mother like Ana had appeared to be, how was that even a choice?

"How long?" Parks asked Amy Tanaka.

"Not sure, but based on the oven, the cookies, her body, everything, I'd say less than two hours. Max."

"How did he get to her?" Rachel asked Parks quietly.

"No idea. That's just the way he works." Parks sighed. They had to carry on. "All right, everyone. We know what happened here, but we still process this like any other scene. Okay?"

Everyone was already hard at work at his or her duties when

Parks's phone began to ring.

"How's it look?" Hardwick asked without a greeting of any sort.

"Exactly what we expected," Parks answered. "At least it was just the woman and not her whole family with her."

"It's sad when that's what we've to be thankful for," Hardwick retorted.

"I know," Parks said. "But we take what we can get. It could have been worse here. A lot worse."

"Speaking of…you ready for some more bad news?"

"Lord. What now?"

"Your old partner, Ryan Ballard?"

"Yeah? What of him?"

"He's in the hospital. Seems he's fallen ill. Quite ill."

THIRTY-THREE

After Parks was sure his team had the Ana Bernal crime scene under control, he then made the fifty-minute trek to Simi Valley Presbyterian Hospital, where his former partner, Ryan Ballard, had been admitted just a few hours before. Once he figured out where he was headed, he finally found Ryan's wife, Mary, red-eyed and distraught as she tried to figure out what was going on. After the initial shock of her husband's former partner of twenty years before having shown up, she accepted him with open arms and scolded him for looking too thin and needing to eat more. As well as the lecture about finding a nice woman to settle down with.

"They won't tell me anything," Mary admitted. "I'm trying to find out what happened, but they won't tell me anything more than it's his heart. I don't understand. He walks five miles every day. He's healthy. It just makes no sense. See if you can't find something out, will you, Dave?"

"Are you the doctor in charge of Ryan Ballard?" Dave asked a fifty-year-old man whom he was finally able to determine was most likely the chief doctor on the floor.

"Are you David Parks?" the doctor asked as Dave took out his ID and flashed it for the doctor. "I'm Doctor Bensinger. Normally I'd say you wouldn't be privy to this information, even as an officer of the law, but Mr. Ballard has insisted I inform you of what's going on."

"What is going on?"

"It appears that while Mr. Ballard is on several different medications for his heart and whatnot, the majority of them are vitamins. But it appears that something else may have been slipped in with his daily vitamins. He's not saying what, and we're not getting the feeling that it was accidental or unintentional."

"You're saying he took something intentionally that got him here?"

"I'm saying he shouldn't still be alive, whatever it was he took."

"You don't know?"

"Not yet. He's not telling us what he took, and while we're running tests, it takes time to get the results back. Time I'm afraid he doesn't have. It's like he's not getting enough oxygen to his system and it's shutting his body down, organ by organ. And I can't help but wonder if that's intentional. Now he refuses to let his wife in to see him or for us to let her know what's going on. But whatever he took is beginning to affect his brain, and he's starting to be out of it. I'll be honest; I'm not sure how I feel about all this. Or that I'm even sure what's going on here."

"Can I see him?"

"Only for a minute or two. He hasn't got long, and I'd like to let his wife in to see him one last time, despite his objections."

"I'll talk to him. I'll make sure she gets in there."

"Okay," Dr. Bensinger finally agreed. "This way."

When Parks first entered the room, it took him a moment to place his former partner. He knew the face was familiar, sort of like seeing a celebrity you are used to only seeing on TV would be if you saw her face to face for the first time. He was older than Parks had remembered, but so was he. Almost twenty years older. Parks had only been in his early twenties when he last worked with his partner, still a baby in the eyes of all those around him, while his partner had been nearing forty. Now he had to be over sixty. The man had a shaved scalp where there had once been a mane of golden, straw-colored hair. He still had his mustache, though it was now completely gray. He appeared fragile and thinner than Parks had remembered, and Parks wondered how much of it was due to whatever the man had taken that had landed him here. His eyes were grayer than Parks remembered, surrounded by more crow's feet and a drooping sadness both over and under the eyes, though they appeared to be just as alert and attentive as in the old days. Parks made his way across the room to the side of Ballard's bed, and when he finally reached the man, he saw a smile come across the man's face.

"Damn, Parks." Ballard crackled, his voice sounding as if he was talking through a mouthful of gravel. He continued to stare, not sure what to say. "Damn."

"Yeah, you too," Parks replied.

"My ass. So, what's up? How you been? You look like shit."

"What's going on here, Ryan? What happened? Why are you here?"

"You got a wife? Kids yet? Or are you still heartbroken over the first one?"

"No," Parks said calmly as he cared to. He wasn't in the mood to discuss his personal life, but he did want to get the man relaxed. "No, no. No wife. No kids. Still just a bachelor."

"Smart is what you are. And I should know. I got kids and grandkids coming out my ass. Trust me on this one, partner. Stay a bachelor. It's cheaper."

"Right. Ryan, what happened?"

"I knew why...why you had called me. Earlier...this week. I knew what it was about...truth was you scared...the hell out of me. Even though this was twenty years ago. Shit, you probably remember more than I do. Younger guy like you...you probably still have all your brain cells. Most of mine...have packed up and vacated the...if you get what I mean?"

Parks stared at the folder in his hand, not that it had any significance to anything but because he would rather be looking at anything other than his former partner. Would have rather been anywhere but there with the man.

"Truthfully, I think we've sort of figured out and pieced together most of what we were looking for," Parks said as he looked up at Ballard.

"Look, I don't know what it is you think I can—"

"If you remember me at all as a patrol cop and have any imagination of the kind of detective I've become, or had the potential to become, then you should be more than aware of what I should know right now." Parks hoped that the seriousness and intensity with which he delivered his words would help set the tone. "Concerning Mary Delancy. I'm aware of what I need to be. And what I'm not, I believe you can help with. I don't know how bad this is about to get; I'm trying not to let my imagination get ahold of me. But I know what the human condition is capable of. Hell, I've seen it. Over these past seventeen years. You know what I mean."

Ballard did know, and he cracked his knuckles in all ten fingers to show what he thought of Parks and what he was doing. He glanced around, probably considering his options, years out of his prime on the force, wondering how far he was willing to go and at what cost.

"I knew it would all come to this. One day. I knew it would. What goes around comes around. Always. Karma. Even if you don't believe in that shit. It's true. It works itself out in the end. Always does. I always told you that. I wasn't sure what to do when you called. Or what I was going to say. I have a family, dammit," Ballard hissed through clenched teeth. "A wife. Children. Grandchildren, dammit. Don't do this to me."

"You did this to yourself a long time ago," Parks replied matter-of-factly. "Just tell me the truth and you can spend whatever time you have left with your family. Speaking of which, why did you do this? Whatever this is? Why would you?"

Both men stayed silent for a moment. He knew why. Whatever Ballard had been trying to do was so that his family would never have to find out the truth. Truth was he should have gone into his office and blown his brains out like so many other men did rather than whatever it was he had let Lewis Hayward talk him into.

"This was Lewis Hayward's doing, right? Whatever it was you took? That got you here today?"

"I didn't know what you wanted to know about," Ryan Ballard crackled. "But I knew it was bad. I knew it was because of all...that. So I called him. Asked for his forgiveness. But he said the truth will out. Nothing he could do once the ball was put into motion. But he said he was a forgiving man. That the sins of the father did not necessarily need to fall on the sons. That he would make sure that the truth stayed where it was and that the repercussions of my actions did not fall on anyone else so long as I played the game his way."

"That's why you're here today. In this room. Suffering. You have to for his satisfaction."

As if on cue, Ballard immediately winced in pain and jerked his back up as if he had leaned against something sharp.

"It's penance. For their protection," Ballard corrected. "For their survival. He can get to anyone and at any time in any place. Don't forget that. That man is a snake. I knew it the moment I set eyes on him. Years ago...even before all that Palisades Poisoner bullshit."

"You met him? Lewis Hayward? Before all this?"

"He was around the department for two years before all that Poisoner bullshit. I saw him. I knew something was wrong with him. You could just see it in his eyes. No matter how hard he tried to hide it. Some men are just born wrong. That man is one of them."

"So what happened? What happened that you have to suffer for? Mary Delancy? Nicholas Vaquier? What?"

"Mary Delancy? So I slept with her. So what?" Ballard asked, leaning back in his bed and crossing his arms. "That's not a crime. Shit. People have affairs every day of the year. If it was a crime, they'd make divorce illegal just so they'd have someone to prosecute."

"How did it begin?"

"You mean you don't know?" Ballard laughed. "Shit. You were there. With me, I mean. House calls. Shit, that woman called about every little damn thing. But she was a looker. Got to give her that. Woman knew how to take care of herself. Doing yoga and shit like that before the rest of the world even knew what that shit was. However, she did drink. That was her one weakness. Her one downfall. Woman loved to drink. But hey, who doesn't like a good one every now and again?"

"Who approached who?" Parks continued. He needed to keep this moving along, before Ballard lost his motivation and nerve.

"She approached me. One time when you were out at the car getting something. I don't remember what. Woman was like an animal. Pounced on me the second you were gone. Surprised she didn't go after a little pup like you. Young. Inexperienced. Shit, she would have chewed you up and devoured you. But then again, she probably knew I wouldn't leave a young'un like you out of my sight around a woman like her. But me, shit, she probably thought she could 'handle' me. So she tried."

"And then what?"

"Then what, what? I went back one night on my own. It all went on from there. We had our thing. Lasted a little while, then it ended. Shit like that always does. The end. So what?"

Parks was silent for a moment as he collected his thoughts as best he could without his notes in front of him.

"Tell me about Thomas Cream," Parks said. "Who was he?"

"Who?" The look on Ballard's face suggested he really didn't know who Parks was talking about. Somehow Parks wasn't surprised. He might truly not know the man's name. But he still knew the man. If only by their interaction fifteen years ago.

"Thomas Cream," Parks repeated. "He was the man who was found with his head bashed in with a hammer in Mary Delancy's kitchen. We got the call about it. You and I. Remember?"

"Shit yeah, I remember that. Just some kid Mary was sleeping around with. So what about it? You're talking about that guy that that Vazquez pervert killed when he broke into Mary's house. I remember it."

"You mean Nicholas Vaquier. That's the incident I'm talking about. Though you and I both know that Vaquier is innocent."

Ballard let out a giant guffaw and almost fell out of his chair.

"What the hell are you talking about? Vaquier innocent? Shit. My ass, he was innocent. That asshole was one sick fuck. We did the world a favor by putting that sick pervert behind bars. Fuckin' favor. And don't you forget it."

"There's a difference between stalking a woman and jerking off outside her windows and being locked up for taking a life you never took," Parks replied quietly. "Isn't there?"

"You don't know what the hell you're talking about," Ballard snapped.

"See, the problem is in the statements everyone gave that night," Parks began to explain. "It all might have worked out if you hadn't gone and complicated it. You got Vaquier at his home, brought him back to the Delancy house, and told everyone you had caught him there. Truth is he was never there that night. But he had been before. You knew that. Even I knew that. Hell, the news had reported it. So no one would question you saying he'd been there that night. And I never saw the reports back then. Everyone relied on you, the experienced and senior officer, for the final word. But Vaquier wasn't there that night. You went and got him and brought him there. If you had simply gone to his house and said you arrested him there after he fled the crime scene, then that might have been it. All these years later, I wouldn't have even questioned it. Even when I reread the report earlier today. But you had to bring him back to the crime scene. I still don't know why. I tried to figure that one out. Best I could think was to get his prints there or something along that line. It doesn't matter why. Just that you did it."

"So what?"

"So what?" Parks mimicked, not really shocked.

"Yeah. So *what?* I didn't kill Thomas Cream. But the person who did is already dead. So who's going to say anything to help get Vaquier sprung? Me? And so what if I do? So what if I go on record and say I helped cover up a murder and pinned it on a sex pervert? You think anyone's going to care?"

"You didn't kill Thomas Cream? Who did?"

"Fuck the truth," Ballard spat. "Truth doesn't do anything but ruin lives. People can't handle the truth, never have been able to, and never will. That's just a fact of life. You want the truth? You want to know who killed Thomas Cream? Look to that bitch's son. Another sick, little twist if you ask me."

"Scott?"

"The hell do I know his name? The younger one. The one she had wrapped all around her fingers. Had him convinced he was in love with her. Probably was. But when she had another man over and he saw him he lost it. That sick little shit went psycho and bashed that man's skull in with a hammer like nobody's business."

"And you agreed to cover it up?"

Ballard simply raised his arms in a so-what, you-got-me pose. What else was there? Ballard winced again and began coughing, wheezing for air that wasn't finding its way to his lungs. He was sounding worse.

"She really had *you* that wrapped up around her fingers?" Parks asked. "You were that infatuated?"

"She was a goddamn legend. A woman no less, but a God to men like you and me. We were simple people. She was of a completely different world. But it wasn't just her. *And* I was in love. Or so I thought. And she knew it. Enough to threaten my marriage. We both knew that. But it wasn't just her. Her child was involved. What would you have done? I couldn't just let them accuse the woman's son. She never would have looked at me the same way."

Parks flinched, though he doubted Ballard saw. It was true. He knew a thing or two about accusing the son of a woman he loved. He did know about the consequences that came with such accusations as well.

"They say you can do anything but love someone the same way twice," Ballard continued. "I truly do believe that. She probably could have still loved me. Even if I had let them take her son away. She might have been okay with that. But she wouldn't have been able to love me the same way anymore. Not after that. Not after what she would have known I was capable of doing."

"You had a wife. And children. You telling me you would have thrown all that away on the chance that a woman you had an affair with might not sleep with you anymore because her murderous son might be sent to prison for a crime he actually committed?"

"Look. You couldn't possibly understand—"

"Bullshit," Parks said firmly. "And you and I both know it."

"And what exactly is it we know?"

"She call you? Recently? Mary Delancy?"

"So what if she did? That's not a crime."

"True," Parks agreed. "Then why?"

Parks tried his best to read his former partner's face, older and more lined than he remembered notwithstanding. Parks could still tell when he was hitting a nerve and making a point. And the tubes and beeping going on all around the man probably weren't helping his concentration much either. The room was stuffy and reeked of contaminants and sterile tools just waiting to be used on the human body.

"No. Mary didn't call you. Recently. That was her son. Scott. Wasn't it?"

"What the hell are you going on about?"

"Fifteen years ago you and Beth were having some difficulties. *That* I do remember. You even stayed on my couch several times. Not often, but a few times. Sure, your true reasons for staying were hidden in nights of heavy drinking that you used to mask them, but just the same, I knew."

"What are you going on about?"

"Scott Delancy didn't kill his mother's lover. *You* did. *You* were the one snooping around her property when you spotted her with another man. *You* were the one who lost touch with reality and lost it. *You* were the one who went after Thomas Cream with a hammer. *You* were the one who covered it up and blamed Vaquier to cover your own ass. And why not? You were a *cop*. You commanded authority. And when Mary Delancy saw how easy it was for you to throw blame on Vaquier...well, she believed it when you 'convinced' her to keep her son in line. And she did. She never let him out of the house after that. Not for fifteen years. Didn't matter what others thought or said about her. Called her names. Said she had a weird relationship with her son. Spread rumors. All these years. Even her older son, Ben, thought she was just obsessed with Scott. Everyone did. You said it. Neighbors. Everyone who had a story to tell. But the truth of it was she was simply keeping him safe. Wasn't she? Safe from you. What did you do? Threaten him? Threaten to lock him up? To kill him? She was a single woman without a husband to help protect her. So when the stalkers started in for her, she went to you for protection. Only you turned on her. And not only did she keep her son from the world, I think eventually she even went a little crazy and began to keep herself locked up in that hose of hers just to keep them both alive. You even called her every now and again just to remind her of what was what. That you were still around."

Ballard tried to stare up at Parks in disbelief, even as he shrunk back in his giant hospital bed. Parks could tell the man hated being weakened and inferior to him. That he wanted nothing more than to jump up and pummel him.

"Her house was a mess," Parks said, looking and sounding as if he was simply talking to himself, forgetting the fact that Ballard was even there, just bouncing ideas off himself. "Why? Not the whole thing, mind you, just the bedroom—where they had been attacked—and the downstairs study. Her study. The room filled with books. Family history books. As if she had been studying up on her past. There was a desk, too, covered in papers. The room was trashed. As if someone had been searching for something in it. Obviously not Mary. She should know where everything in her own house is. But not someone from the outside. Someone who wasn't familiar with her place. Which got me thinking...Mary Delancy hadn't left her house in years. Decades even. But there was something in that room that someone wanted. What? And who? And how would they know it's in that room? Or what it even was they were looking for? She never had any contact with the outside world. Occasionally with her lawyer. We questioned him. He didn't seem right. He didn't fit all the right criteria. My former partner taught me all about that. No, she had no connection with the outside world. Except...except for the occasional call."

Ballard flinched. Parks caught it. He was on the right track.

"Mary Delancy was starting on her memoirs," Ballard finally admitted. "Her agent confirmed it. Not that she was planning any sort of a comeback. It's just what her agent asked of her. People write their memoirs nowadays. She was asked for hers...and she agreed to it. Times are changing. People don't remember like they used to. A good memoir helps to keep the money flowing. Or maybe she just had some unfinished business to get off her chest." Ballard sneered. How dare this woman do this to him? "Only her son had a different idea. See, she never would have revealed what really...happened fifteen years ago. I made sure she wouldn't. But Scott was a different story. He was tired of the life he had...he wanted more. His brother helped with that. But the brother didn't know the whole story. So he began...writing his own chapter to his mother's memoirs. And when he was finished, and when his mother was finished, he slipped it in there without her knowledge. This was a few months ago. So it went off to the agent and the publishers, et cetera, et cetera. Then last week I got a call. Probably some fact checker. Gotta check all those facts nowadays. Can't just go around slandering people. And after that phone call, I called Mary up myself."

"You called her three times last week. None of the three calls were that long, so you couldn't have gotten ahold of anyone. So then you did the next logical thing. You went over to her. You knew where she lived. She never left the house. You had made sure of that so many years ago. So you went there yourself. And the rest, well, you know what happened next."

"I didn't murder that bitch," Ballard all but hissed. "I swear to you, I didn't."

"You went over there and you lost it again and you killed Mary and her son and—"

"No, I didn't! I swear to you! When I left them, they were both alive," Ballard jerked back, realizing what he had just admitted to. Parks had him.

"Dave, I swear to you. On my wife's soul. I didn't murder that woman or her son. I went there. Sure. I lost my temper. I'll agree to that. And yeah, sure, I searched the place when she denied having written that chapter or even having it. But I never laid a hand on them. I didn't kill those two. I never would have. I loved her. I loved her, dammit!"

Ryan Ballard began coughing again, this time harder, his chest heaving in and out.

"And they just let you do that? Ransack their house. Trash their home? While they were both alive? They never put up any sort of resistance? Because the funny thing is there wasn't a single bruise on either of their bodies. Defensively, I mean. Sure, there were bruises from what they did to themselves physically after they swallowed the poison. But there were no defensive marks on them as if they had put up a struggle with an intruder. Yet, I don't see either one of them doing nothing, simply standing by idly as their home—where they'd both been imprisoned for the last seventeen years—gets ransacked. I think they would have fought you. I think there would have been at least some sort of evidence of self-defense against you."

Ballard opened his mouth and bit back his tongue; his eyes rolled and he began convulsing. Suddenly, the machines began beeping, and a doctor and two nurses immediately ran into the room.

"What's going on?" Parks asked as he backed away from his former partner.

"Out of the room. *Now,*" Doctor Bensinger ordered as he went back to work on Ballard.

Seven minutes later the doctor informed them that Ryan Ballard had passed without another word due to oxygen being cut off from his brain. Dave Parks stood there silently as he held Ryan Ballard's crying widow in his arms.

THIRTY-FOUR

"What's bothering you?" Parks asked as he stared across his desk at Jackie, while she concentrated on the report in front of her.

"Probably the same thing that's bothering you," she replied without looking up. "And don't deny it, I know something's bothering you."

"And how do you know what's bothering me?" Parks thought about this a moment. "Or that anything is bothering me?"

"Because you're a damn good detective. So I figure if something's bothering me, then it has to be bothering you."

"Because one plus one is *always* two."

"Always. One plus two plus two plus one."

Jackie winked at Parks as he looked at her with confusion on his face.

"So what is bothering you?"

"The poison."

"The strychnine? In particular? Or just that poison..."

"That Mary Delancy and her son were poisoned. I know what Ballard admitted to you earlier today, but he still protested he didn't kill Mary and her son. Could I see him being capable of killing them? Yes.

With a gun maybe. But poisoning them? Really?"

"I think Lewis Hayward has more than proven that a man is more than capable of committing murder with poison. In fact, if memory serves me correct, you even sent me an article once, saying that more poisoners are male than female? Correct?"

"That's not what I mean, and you know it. And if my memory serves me correctly, I believe that same article said that most poisoners are calculating and manipulative."

"Yeah, but haven't several sources said that before?"

"What I mean is, does that sound like Ballard to you?"

"A man who covered up a murder by threatening, possibly black-mailing, a former lover and her son into keeping quiet about it for him? That doesn't sound calculating or manipulative to you?"

Jackie sighed, trying her hardest to contain her frustration.

"Breathe," Parks said calmly. "Now just think it out. Where are you going with this?"

"You already know where I'm going with this."

"Yes, I do," Parks admitted. "I've already come to this conclusion hours ago. But you haven't. And what kind of a detective would you be if you didn't come to the same conclusion on your own? You need to believe you can do this. I do. It's like any other muscle in your body. The more you use it, the better it gets. So...what do you have?"

"If you already knew this, then—"

"What do you have?" Parks repeated.

"Was Ryan Ballard calculating and manipulative over the years? Yes. Is he a calculating and manipulative person? Over all? No idea, but I wouldn't say so. You know him better. But I'm going to say with what little I witnessed and have read that he is not—other than when it comes to his own personal well-being. He's what I would call less threatening and more menacing. If that makes any sense?"

"Why else would someone be calculating or manipulative if not for their own well-being?" Parks asked, and Jackie gave him a look that forced him to sink back in his chair.

"What I mean is he's an instinct man. Has to be, because that's the way he's learned to survive as a cop on the streets for thirty years. He doesn't act; he reacts. If we believe he murdered Thomas Cream, then we would also believe that wasn't a calculated thought process. He didn't hunt the man down and figure out the best way to not get caught. He saw the man with a woman he was obsessed with and he reacted. He attacked Cream and killed him. Brutally. With a hammer. Most likely a nearby weapon of opportunity. Not his police-issue weapon. Not something he had to go out and buy from a store. Something that was close and available. Then he reacted to that action by covering it up. With threats. Again, with and by brutality. This isn't a delicate, thoughtful, or thinking man. He's more old school. He doesn't think out several steps ahead, like Lewis Hayward did. He simply reacts. There's no way Ryan Ballard came back twenty years later, under the threat of exposure for his past crimes, and calculated a way to poison a woman and her son to...what? Make it look like a murder/suicide? That's too much. If Ballard had done this, he would have simply made it look like a home invasion robbery with gunshots to both their heads. And you know it."

"If I don't have to think for myself, can I just stay home tomorrow and have you come in and be me for the day?"

"Smart ass." Jackie smiled.

"Actually, I do agree."

"Then what was the whole point of speaking to Ballard earlier?"

"Confirmation. A theory is just that. A theory. I figured this out about the same time I made the accusations at the hospital. Maybe a little before that. There's no way Ballard is a part of Hayward's group of followers. He's no follower. He'd rather strike out on his own path. Plus, he'd think the painted symbols on walls and whatnot are silly and childish. He hated it whenever in TV shows or movies the killer always left calling cards like that. Called it cheap and unrealistic."

"So then why did you make the accusation?"

"Kind of like a multiple-car collision. Throw it all at you at once, and it's hard to react. I got him on the Thomas Cream murder. That one he did commit. That was what I set out to get him for. That's what whoever Hayward's got doing all this for him wanted. This was his endgame. He wanted to catch a dirty cop who had gotten away with murder for twenty years. Since Lewis Hayward was caught for carrying out his own personal vendetta last year, then all others be damned."

"Plus, it fits in with that whole law and order and punishment thing."

"That it does."

"Was Mary Delancy really writing her memoirs?"

"She was. Checked with her agent. Had a deal worth several million. And there is the secret chapter Ballard spoke of that Scott had probably snuck in about what Ballard had done to them. Agent confirmed it. Writing was different than the rest of the book."

"Then if Ballard was going to be exposed anyway, why did Hayward have them killed? They were going to do what he wanted accomplished anyway."

"That's where our ulterior motives come into play. And that is an answer I don't quite have for you yet. And probably won't until we identify Mary and Scott Delancy's killer."

"So what's next?"

"Next? Next we get some sleep. Then we come back tomorrow to see where we're at and what we've got. And hope it's enough to give us some direction."

TUESDAY

THIRTY-FIVE

The first packages had arrived via FedEx, were signed for by the receptionist at the front desk, and passed on to the hardworking detectives of the Homicide Special Section before anyone on the team had even arrived for duty that morning. There was one for each member of the team: Parks, Moore, Fairmont, Tippin, and even one for Jackie Isley, each placed on the respective detective's desk, with Jackie's placed on a free desk near Parks's.

"What's this?" Fairmont asked with a smile on his face as he slightly shook one of the twelve-by-twelve boxes in his hands. Each box was somewhat light in weight, weighing only a few pounds; obviously, something was inside as was evident when Fairmont shook his.

"I'm sure it can wait, no matter what it is," Parks said, looking back up at the murder board before him. When he heard nothing but silence from behind him, he turned to see nothing but Bambi eyes all around staring pitifully up at him.

"Maybe they're the new handheld devices that someone ordered for the team?" Fairmont asked suspiciously as he eyed Milo, who simply shrugged innocently.

"Fine. Go ahead and open them. Okay? Then let's focus on the case and work. Okay?"

Parks sat down in his chair, swiveling between the murder board and his team as they opened their packages.

"Hey, boss? Aren't you gonna open yours?" Fairmont asked as he ran a pair of scissors across the top of his box.

Parks smiled. "I'll live with waiting to open mine."

"But what if yours has some kind of a bonus—" Fairmont let out a yell that startled everyone as he flung his hand away from the box and immediately fell over his chair, colliding with it to the floor. As he did so, the box on his desk fell to the floor and several snakes of various colors and sizes immediately slithered out. A small snake, the color of oil, no longer than eight inches, had bitten Fairmont and still held on, its fangs tethered deep into his hand.

"Shit," Milo yelped as he stopped opening his box and stepped back from it.

But it was too late as he had already punctured the seal and the first head, covered in copper-colored diamonds, poked its way out through the box flap, flicked its tongue at the world around it, and slithered out of the box. The snake was approximately sixteen inches in length, the diamond pattern continuing down its back, as it began to slither across Milo Tippin's desk.

"Everyone stop!" Parks yelled as he jumped out of his chair, motioning everyone to step back from their boxes. "Get Fairmont up! Get him up!"

Rachel rushed to Jake's side and stared down at him as he wrangled on the floor, jerking his hand back and forth as the snake held on to him. She looked around when she saw Parks eyeing her, holding a pocketknife he always hand on him. He tossed it to her. She caught the knife, flipped the blade open, and ordered Fairmont to stop moving as she forced him to the ground, her knee on his arm as she cut the snake in half. The tail began flopping around on the floor, while the head remained attached to Fairmont's hand. Rachel slipped the knife between the snake's mouth and Fairmont's skin as she pried it from his hand. She flicked the head to the side and hugged Fairmont as she helped him to his feet and up onto a desk to avoid the several snakes working their way toward them.

Jackie had stepped off the elevator and made her way down the hall to the Homicide Special Section area, not paying attention as she looked through a file in her hands. "Hey, what do you all think about—"

"Stop where you are!" Parks shouted at Jackie, startling her into dropping her file. "Call animal control!"

"What?" Jackie asked, confused as she looked around, trying to piece together what was going on.

"Call animal control *now!*" Parks repeated when Jackie finally saw the snakes slithering around the floor.

As Milo tried to maneuver his still-unopened box to the center of his desk so as not to disturb it, he stumbled over his chair and fell to the floor. He slammed his head and arm against the floor; dazed, he tried to collect his bearings. Parks noticed a red-, yellow-, white- and black-ringed snake slithering toward the boy and started across the room toward him when Jackie yelled out at him.

"That's a coral snake. Be careful; they're poisonous!"

Parks made it to the snake when it was only a few feet from Milo's hand and slammed the heel of his work boot down on the snake's head, killing it.

"Don't lose sight of any of them," Parks ordered. "We don't need them lost in here for weeks. Okay? Don't anyone get bit, but if you can trap them, then do it. Try not to kill any of them either. Did someone call animal control?"

Everyone had managed to work his or her way up onto a desk and out of harm's way, as Parks surveyed the room for damage.

"How many of them are there?" Jackie asked from the nearby desk.

"Looks to be about a dozen or so per box. Luckily, only Jake and Milo got theirs opened, so only two dozen or so to keep an eye on and catch. But who knows? Are they all poisonous?"

"From what I can tell, they are," Jackie surmised. "I see a coral snake. A copperhead. Some puff adders. Pit vipers. A couple of cottonmouths. But they all fit inside the boxes, so none of them look that old. Makes them more dangerous. These are all younger snakes. Highly dangerous. Where the hell did they all come from?"

"Where do you think?" Parks said as Jackie looked questioningly to him. "Lewis Hayward."

The EMTs showed up and, with Jackie's help, administered the proper medication to Fairmont's snakebite before whisking him off to a nearby hospital for some further treatment. Rachel accompanied Jake so as to relay any further news.

Detectives Parks and Tippin were cleaning up the mess made during the disruption, while three members of the L.A. Animal Control did their best to collect each of the snakes. They also took possession of the other four unopened boxes, emptying the contents into their own containers to be able to leave the boxes with the LAPD, who would run its own tests on them.

"What the hell was Lewis Hayward thinking?" Hardwick cursed.

"Probably thinking he could have taken out a few of us," Jackie suggested. "Guess we showed him, huh?"

"I don't think so," Parks said, shaking his head.

"What do you mean? Those were boxes of poisonous snakes. They could have killed us. What if we had each taken our box home and opened it alone? Or in the car on the way home? Any one of us could have been killed just now."

"Agreed," said Parks. "But I don't think that was Hayward's intention. If Hayward wants to hurt us, he does it. Plain and simple. This was more like he was trying to help us. Give us a clue. In his own demented way."

"What the hell do snakes have to do with anything?" Hardwick asked. "Neither Mary Delancy nor her son were poisoned by snakes. Or by snake venom. From what I've been told, at least. And there have been no snakes associated with this case whatsoever. What's this have to do with anything?"

"The guy's just a sick wacko, and that's it," Jackie disagreed. "No hidden messages or meanings behind it. He's messing with us. Plain and simple. Throwing us off our game."

"I think we got the last of them," one of the animal control officers said to Parks and Jackie, as he showed off the plastic container holding several snakes captive. "Just a few more things and we'll be out of your way."

"Thank you," Parks said politely.

"This is starting to become a weekly thing, huh?" the officer said with a wink at Jackie as he filled out some paperwork and then handed it over to Hardwick to be signed off on.

Jackie simply half-shrugged, too exhausted to do anything else, and offered a half-smile that still would have knocked the socks off most men.

"At least this time there's no dead bodies, huh?" the man continued.

"Guess that's an improvement. Oh, well. See you next time."

"Wait!" Parks shouted as he spun around, startling everyone around him. "What do you mean this is a weekly thing? We haven't seen you before."

"Yes. Well, I did," Jackie explained. "Last week. At the Delancy house. This was before you took over the case."

Parks showed confusion across his face as he stared at Jackie.

"Mary's bird," Jackie continued as she looked to the animal rescue guys for help. "That...what was it? That mynah bird. We were glad when these guys showed up and took it away from us. Was a loud thing. Always squawking."

Even that stupid bird of hers—every time it squawked, I could swear it said her name—

"They took it away...?" Parks said, starting to daze off into his own world.

"Yeah, of course. They do that. When you call them. That's what they do. Mary Delancy and her son were dead, so who else was around to take care of the bird? We hadn't contacted her other son yet. Didn't know about him, actually."

"Before we took over the case," Parks said quietly. "I've never even seen the bird. Except in pictures."

Even that stupid bird of hers—every time it squawked—

"That's because they took it away," Jackie repeated herself. "Before you took over the case. So what? Who cares about the stupid bird? It's not like the bird killed anyone."

"So Benjamin Delancy never saw the bird either," Parks continued.

"I just said that," Jackie said, not sure where Parks was going with his line of thinking. "I mean, I highly doubt he went and got the bird from animal control. I couldn't see him caring. If he even knew his mother had the bird. Animal control took all the bird stuff along with it."

"Or her," Parks added.

"Her who?" Jackie asked.

Even that stupid bird of hers—every time it squawked, I could swear it said her name—

"How'd *she* know about the bird? It was taken away before they got there. Unless she was there when the bird was? Back before it was removed. Back before the murders..." Parks smiled. "Or *during* them."

THIRTY-SIX

Parks dashed off without another word, before anyone could stop him or ask him what he meant. No one had any clue or idea as to what went on in his brain.

Jackie stayed behind to help organize the mess made by the commotion the snakes had caused. Desks had been shoved aside, chairs overturned, papers and files thrown left and right, all in the name of avoiding poisonous snakes.

"What is all this garbage?" Jackie asked as she picked up several newspaper and magazine clippings, the edges of them frayed. Each piece was wrinkled and yellowed with age, even with proper storage over the years.

"Paperwork and clippings from Mary Delancy's house," Milo explained from behind her.

"But why?"

"Who knows? It's all just clippings of her that she had collected over the years."

"Ugh," Jackie said as she flipped through a *Life* magazine interview from the eighties. "She and her son were like a modern-day *Grey Gardens*." Jackie realized the reference she had made and looked to Milo.

"*Grey Gardens* is—"

"Believe it or not, I do actually know what you're talking about," Milo interrupted. "And for the record: I agree."

"I mean, just look at all of these," Jackie continued, tossing aside several more newspaper clippings. "Interviews with her. With her husband. With neighbors and—"

"With neighbors and what?" Milo asked, looking up and noticing Jackie staring intently at a magazine article about the actress. "Jackie? Jackie, what is it?"

"It's an article interviewing Mary Delancy's neighbors, one year after she had moved into her house," Jackie began, mostly murmuring as she read the article. "Asking about how she affected the neighborhood and whatnot."

"Yeah, I remember that article," Milo shrugged. "I mean not from when it came out. I wasn't even born yet. But Parks had us read over everything to try and get every aspect of Mary Delancy's life down to see if anything would lead…Jackie? What is it?"

"Rosemary Gibson," Jackie answered, staring at a picture of the actress's neighbors. There were eight of them, four couples, lined up in two rows as if posing for a high school group photo.

"Oh, I remember her," Milo said as he glanced at the picture and then went back to sorting papers. "She still lives next door, doesn't she? Hey, didn't you interview her? With Wilkes, I mean?"

"How accurate do you think this article is?"

"What do you mean?"

"Could they have misprinted someone's name in it?"

"It's possible. It happens. But I can check with the DMV. Why?"

"Because the lady in this picture, that this article claims is Rosemary Gibson—Mary Delancy's neighbor. That's not the same lady I interviewed with Wilkes."

Parks arrived at the Stay on Main Hotel and marched straight for the clerk at the front desk, who informed him that Katrina Thompson had not yet checked out but that she had also been moved to a different room, being as her former room was still sealed off. Parks made his way up to the proper floor and went to knock on the door when he saw it was ajar.

"Hello?" Parks called out as he slowly swung the door open. "Katrina? Detective Parks. LAPD. Hello? Anyone here?"

The room was empty, clean and put together as if she had never been there. He slammed his fist against the doorframe and walked out into the hallway, when he saw the yellow police tape at the other end of the hallway. He paused, and then marched down the hallway and tried the door to find it unlocked. The room had been cleaned of all evidence that a homicide had occurred there.

As if Benjamin Delancy's life hadn't been taken in that room.

He glanced quickly over the pristine and empty room and was about to leave when a single photo, propped into the border around a mirror hanging on the wall opposite the beds, caught his attention. He made his way across the room and snatched the photo out from its holder.

Parks stared intently at the picture on the front, then turned it over to find the Japanese character for nine written on the back next to the words: next time.

"Dammit," Parks cursed. He thought for a moment and then whipped out his cellphone and called Milo. "Yes, Milo, I know. Don't talk. Just listen. I need to know if it's possible for you to ping a cellphone for me. Katrina Thompson's. Ben gave me both of their cellular numbers. Hers in case I couldn't get a hold of him. I need you to trace it. I need to know where she is. Find out and call or text me with the location as soon as you get it. You hear me? Yes, now. Immediately. Thanks.

"He thinks Katrina's our poisoner?" Jackie asked.

"Sounds like it. He's desperate to find her. Not sure why though. Didn't say. Anyway, are you sure about this?" Milo asked.

So far Milo had only been able to zero Katrina Thompson's location down to currently being in the Hollywood area. He was hoping to have it more localized within a few minutes and promised to keep Parks updated. While Milo had been working on that for Dave, Jackie had asked for a patrol car to be sent out to the Gibson's home to see if anyone was around. She had a feeling no one would be. But if an old lady happened to be around, she wanted her picked up and brought in for questioning regarding the homicide at her neighbor's home.

"Anyway. You sure about that?" Milo repeated.

"Well, you're the one who found her ID through the DMV," Jackie said, as if that explained everything. "Guess we'll just have to wait and see. What other paperwork have you got sitting around here that I haven't seen yet?"

"Nothing, really," Milo said, gesturing to the mountains of paperwork lining one of the nearby tables. "Case files. Palisades Poisoner murder books. Files about Mary Delancy, her kids, family, and others. Thomas Cream's murder book. Kinda lucky we have that though."

"Oh?," Jackie said as she picked up the Thomas Cream murder book and began perusing through it.

"Yeah. It was misfiled actually. If I hadn't been looking in the wrong area for the right file who knows if I would have ever found it.

I—oh." Milo stopped as his computer began to beep.

"Oh?" Jackie repeated, not really focused on Milo.

"Yeah. Looks like I got a location on Katrina Thompson's phone. Looks like...looks like she's at the—what's she doing there?"

Parks drove down Santa Monica Boulevard, past Paramount Studios and up to the front gate of the Hollywood Forever Cemetery. He flashed his badge and ID at the guard resting in the front booth.

Ten minutes later, with a map of the cemetery grounds in his hands, Parks set off on foot to find his poisoner.

"Nothing," Jackie said as she hung up the phone.

"What?" Hardwick asked. She had walked onto the floor some five minutes before, and Jackie and Milo had caught the woman up on what was going on. Including Parks's disappearing act and that he was currently headed to the Hollywood Forever Cemetery.

"No one's home at the Gibson's home. Figures. Didn't really think the old bat would still be hanging around. Especially if she's not who she says she is. Maybe..." Jackie spaced out as she stared at an old black-and-white photo that had been inside Thomas Cream's murder book.

"Maybe what?" Milo asked as he stood up to see what she was staring at. "Oh, that."

"What is this?" Jackie asked.

"Family photo. Thomas Cream is the little boy. Well, the older of the two. Foster kids, I think. Thomas Cream was a foster kid. Bounced from house to house until that one. I think that was the final place he grew up in. At least from what I could gather from the notes we had on him. Notes which we only had because they're all pre-computer, so we know Lewis Hayward couldn't have altered them. Everything was handwritten. Why?"

"What's wrong, Jackie?" Hardwick asked as she looked at the photo.

"The woman in the photo," Jackie began. "The foster mother. That's the woman who was posing as Mary Delancy's neighbor that Wilkes and I interviewed. That photo may be forty years old, but I recognize her. That's her."

"Do we have an ID in the murder book of her?" Hardwick immediately asked Milo.

Milo was about to start searching for an answer when Jackie stopped him.

"I know it's her. Regardless of her name. But she's not what caught my attention. The children in the photo."

"Two girls and two boys. What of them? We know the older boy is Thomas Cream. So what? They'd all be grown by now. So what?"

"The other boy," Jackie explained. "Next to Thomas Cream. Do you see it?"

"See what?" Hardwick asked, as she focused on the photo once more. Even Milo tried to zone in on what Jackie had noticed. "I don't see anything." Milo shook his head in agreement. Nothing.

"My God," Jackie sighed. "Really? I get that seeing a picture of a five-year-old boy and the grown man he's become side-by-side wouldn't turn a head. It's hard to make a connection. Maybe a picture every five years along the kid's life, and you could. But since none of you on this damn team are parents, I guess you don't see it. But I do. I can tell. Maybe it's from looking at baby photos myself."

"What? What don't we see?" Hardwick demanded to know.

"The little boy. Look at his eyes? Do you see it?"

"What? They're eyes. On a five-year-old boy. In a forty-year-old, black-and-white photo. What are we supposed to see?"

"That little boy? Thomas Cream's foster brother? That's Lewis Hayward."

Parks walked for ten minutes before he saw the woman, sitting on a concrete bench in front of a headstone, the pond behind her as if she were posing for one of Fairmont's pictures. He continued toward her, wondering why she was there, when he began to remember Katrina's story about her sister having died in L.A., though he thought she would have been buried back wherever her family had come from.

As Parks finally got closer, Katrina turned her head, catching sight of him though not directly looking at him, tears running down her cheeks, leaving behind streaks of dark mascara.

"This is your sister's grave?" Parks asked quizzically.

"My father said she had dishonored our family with her death. A fitting death for a woman who marries a man like she did," Katrina said as she turned back to the grave. "My father told her from the first day she came home with him that he was no good. That his soul was blackened from within, nothing but evil inside. That he would spread his torment onto her if she married him. But she did not listen. Instead, she married him. In the church. And then ran away here to be with him."

"What's your sister's marriage have to do with you poisoning Mary and Scott Delancy? Who are they to you? To all of this?"

"Them? To me? Nothing. I had never met them before the night I took their lives," Katrina admitted as she sighed deeply. "They were simply a means to an end." She looked up at Parks, reading the confusion on his face.

"You think you can tell me a story that will excuse away your actions?" Parks asked as he stared at Katrina, her beauty still haunting him even though his eyes hadn't yet left her. She was tortured, the pain of loss etched across her face, her eyes forever echoing the loneliness she felt damned to suffer through for the rest of her life. "I don't know what you think—"

When Katrina continued to stare at her sister's grave without looking at him, Parks finally turned and looked at the giant slab of marble, the name etched in the stone immediately hitting him like a bullet from a gun: Natalia Malkov.

Suddenly the pieces of the puzzle, though not yet fully put together, began to form a much larger, and more understandable, picture that even he had not expected.

"Where is it?" Milo asked to no one in particular as he began scrambling through the mountains of paperwork on his desk. "Where is it?"

"Where is what?" Jackie asked as she tried to stay out of the line of fire of flying papers.

"It. *It!* Where is it?"

"In the sewers where Stephen King left him? What the hell are you talking about? What *it?*"

Milo stopped rummaging, looking almost exhausted, as he concentrated and thought for a moment.

"What?" Jackie asked.

"The rest of the file," Milo finally explained. "I know I had it—yes! I got it."

Milo jumped up and started out of the room.

"Stop there, Mister," Jackie ordered. "I will not let two of you do this to me today. Where are you going?"

"Just to my car. I left the rest of a file I need you to see. I'll be right back. Promise."

"You're Natalie's sister," Parks said as the realization of the facts hit him like a slap of cold morning air. Natalia Malkov. Only he had known her as Natalie Kozlov. Married to Peter Kozlov.

"Natalia," Katrina corrected without looking away from her sister's grave.

"Your father was right. Your sister's husband was a sick man. Very sick."

"I know."

"What he did to those children..."

"The boogeyman. You understand?"

"Yes. We have the boogeyman here. You were right. Peter Kozlov was the boogeyman. What he did to those children..."

"He did the same back home. That was why he fled."

"I know." Parks stood there for a moment, trying to piece everything together. The Kozlov case had been his last case before tackling the Palisades Poisoner. After Parks had captured Kozlov, he had sworn around-the-clock protection to his wife in exchange for her testimony against him. But Parks had failed. "You know, I had no idea Peter had a brother. Or that he was here. In the U.S. Or I swear to you I would have never left your sister unguarded like that. But she never—"

"I do not blame you for Natalia's death," Katrina said. "That is solely on Pitor and Viktor Kozlov." Katrina spat on the ground after having said both men's names. "I was told you lost your partner to Pitor as well."

Aaron Levinson.

"And you did not come away unscathed either, from what I've been told."

Katrina faced Dave and reached up and ran a finger over several of the scars that Peter Kozlov's razor blades had left when he and Dave had tussled.

"You have suffered much at the hands of Pitor Kozlov. I am aware of that. I do not blame you for Natalia's death. I'm not so petty."

"Then…what's this about? Why are you here? Why are you doing all this?"

"Justice," Katrina replied matter-of-factly. "Justice, Detective Parks."

You're missing something, Parks thought to himself. *This doesn't make sense.*

"How is taking Mary and Scott Delancy's life justice for your sister's death? What did they have to do with it?"

"Nothing. With my sister. Not that they were so innocent. Not from what he told me."

"Lewis Hayward?"

Katrina shrugged and turned back to her sister's grave.

"Why? Why's he doing all this? What's this mean to you? What's—" Parks stopped, the final pieces of the puzzle finally coming together.

Peter and Victor Kozlov were currently serving time up in San Quentin. He should have seen it. Had he only known. Was there still time? Or was Lewis Hayward's plan already too far in motion?

"He's going to do something, isn't he? To them?"

"It's not revenge," Katrina continued. "Revenge is so petty. So empty. So unfulfilling. I wanted justice for my sister's death. For all those people whom those two bastards hurt. *He* promised me that. It wasn't much he asked for in return. Not really. Not when you think about it. I was willing to sell my soul to the devil himself had I been asked."

You have no idea, thought Parks.

"He contacted you? Lewis Hayward. You know what he's capable of, right? You know what he's done here? In my country. To our people?"

"I only know he promised me justice. And after what he told me, I believe him. Justice will be served."

"He contacted you?" It was all the more Parks could think to say as he stumbled, his mind racing as he tried to figure out what to do next. How to handle this situation.

"Yes. Just after my sister's death. He promised me justice. He spelled out what he planned to do. I knew he was a cop, but he still had no access to Pitor or Victor. They were public figures in the news by then. How could he do it? He told me not to worry. Said that he'd have day-to-day interaction with them before the end of the year."

"And with no trial he was quickly and quietly allowed access to the prison of his choosing," Parks said, groaning on the inside as he continued to figure out Hayward's seemingly never-ending plan. "That's why he avoided a trial. Otherwise, he'd still be in the middle of it."

"And if he didn't keep up his end of the bargain, I wouldn't keep up mine," Katrina confirmed. "When I saw he was transferred up there with them before the end of the year, I knew he was a man of his word. So I became a woman of mine. And began my steps in completing what he asked for."

"You sought out Benjamin Delancy. Although I'm sure Lewis Hayward instructed you on how to find him. You knew who his mother and brother were. But why?"

"I never asked," Katrina admitted. "He made it known it wasn't my business. But he told me that they had hurt him much like Pitor had hurt me. That they had done someone he loved wrong and that justice was needed."

Justice? For Lewis Hayward? Someone close to him had been hurt by Mary Delancy? But who? Nicholas Vaquier? Thomas Cream? But who were they to him?

"But Peter and Victor are still alive. I know it. I would have been informed if something had been done to them."

"They won't be by the time you leave my side," Katrina smiled. "I admit I don't know how he does it, but the man is good with timing. He told me what to do. Where to do it. When. How to go about it. He said all steps would lead to here. I had to end up here. So you could see. So you could understand. What good would it do for him to kill them with you not knowing the reasons why? Or that he had done it himself? I know he promised to do this for me. And I will have my justice. Of that, I am sure. But truthfully, I don't think he's doing this for me. I think what he's going to do to Pitor and Viktor...is for you."

"I never asked for any of this," Parks practically screamed as he faced Katrina.

"You didn't have to," Katrina smiled. "He already knows. He knows everything. You know what?" Katrina leaned in and whispered to Parks. "I think that man is the Devil."

THIRTY-SEVEN

Jackie hadn't realized she was tapping her nails against the desk until a minute later when she heard the clock up on the wall click to the next minute. That was the only other sound she had heard around her. Despite being in the middle of a busy police station, there was no one else around, everyone out to lunch or conducting interviews on another wing of the building. Hardwick had gone back to her office to make sure that backup was arriving at Parks's location and that warrants were being filled out and signed for.

She looked around and could see the last few telltale signs of the destruction the snakes Lewis Hayward had delivered earlier that day had left on the floor. A chair was still over on its side off in the corner. Papers were still strewn about the floor near Parks's desk. And the ones that had been picked up were haphazardly disorganized along the various desks they currently lay on.

Jackie turned and looked up at the clock; then she looked around and realized she was still alone.

Where was Milo? How long had it been? He had said he'd be right back. How long did it take to get to the parking garage and back while also looking through one's car for—that's when Jackie saw Milo's phone resting on the corner of his desk.

Never in a million years could Jackie have ever explained to anyone why that particular piece of information set her on edge but it did, and she immediately got to her feet. She was just being paranoid, right? He was in the LAPD parking garage. Nothing was going to happen to him there. Just the same...Jackie reached down and felt her gun on her hip.

He'll be right back. You're being foolish. You'll probably run into him on the way down.

Fine. Then run into him. Just get moving.

And with that, Jackie started for the elevators.

"Who's helping you?" Parks asked as he looked around the cemetery. They were alone, no one else within viewing distance. The sound of traffic moving along outside the walls of the cemetery. There were no mourners at any other graves nearby nor was there a groundskeeper in sight.

She turned from her sister's tomb and smiled up at the detective, both confident and secure with the knowledge of what she had pulled off: everything coming together just as planned.

"We both know there's no way you could have pulled this all off on your own. Who's helping you?"

"I do not know her name. Only seen her once or twice. But he told me to trust her. That she would help me when I needed it. She hasn't let me down yet."

Parks paused for a moment as he thought about this when he heard a slight buzzing sound coming from Katrina's coat pocket.

"And that," smiled Katrina as she stood, "is a my reminder. I have a flight to catch."

Katrina reached for her coat pocket not waiting for a reply from Parks, who wasn't giving one either way. Parks realized the woman truly thought he was just going to let her walk out of there, and that's when he figured she was hiding something in her coat. A gun, most likely. Parks reached for Katrina's left arm and when he began to spin her around, she struck out with her right and cut Parks with a razor blade. He jerked his hand back, more out of reaction than from any sort of physical pain, the cut a simple line across his palm. As he focused on his hand, he momentarily forgot about Katrina, and by the time he looked back up at her, she was already next to him, her face in his, and he felt the puncture in the side of his neck.

Because this wasn't the first time he had been attacked by someone holding a syringe, Parks may not have been aware of what she was about to do, but somewhere in the back of his mind he knew to be prepared for anything, and he had his guard already up the second she struck him with the razor. Before she could inject whatever was in the syringe into his bloodstream, he had already hit the woman back and she flew to the ground, hitting the corner of her sister's gravestone on the side of her head, just above her right eye. She let out a deep moan, a guttural sound as if the wind had been knocked out of her as she fell to the ground.

Parks hadn't been able to completely stop Katrina from getting to him, and as he plucked the needle from the side of his neck, he could start to feel himself warming up. He stared down at the syringe and though it appeared to be mostly full, he could tell she had still gotten him. He dropped the syringe as he started to get up. He walked a few steps before falling back to the ground as he felt his legs begin to shake. Parks pulled himself up and supported himself against a stone bench not far from the gravesite. He turned and saw Katrina starting to pull herself up with the aid of her sister's tombstone.

The woman stood and turned, staring at Parks but not really see-ing him, as if she couldn't focus on him so far away, though he was only a few feet from her. The side of her face was covered in blood, the gash along the side of her face deep and possibly fatal without im-mediate medical aid.

"Katrina," Parks whispered as he felt his throat begin to constrict. The woman turned from him and began to stumble throughout the cemetery. Parks wasn't sure where she was heading, only knowing that it wasn't in the direction of the parking lot. "Katrina."

Jackie exited the elevator and walked past the few people she saw standing in the lobby as she headed out for the underground parking garage. There was a guard on duty near the entrance, and she waived to him as she continued on for Milo's car. That was when she realized she had no idea where the kid was even parked or what kind of a car he drove. Jackie looked around quickly and didn't see Milo. She fin-ished checking the three rows then remembered where Parks usually parked and figured the rest of his team may have parked nearby. She quickly made her way to the stairwell at the end of the level and head-ed down one flight, where she stopped dead in her tracks at the sight of the woman claiming to be Mrs. Gibson standing over Milo's body , which was leaning against what she assumed was his car. The boy looked to be unconscious, his glasses smashed on the floor next to him, the side of his face covered in blood. Jackie looked up and noticed the rear passenger window had been shattered, and she figured the woman had snuck up on the kid and slammed his head into the glass. But why had she even been there in the first place?

Jackie stood in the stairwell, took off her jacket to reveal her fuchsia-colored blouse, and wiped her hands off on her skirt.

Jackie could feel her heart beating, her head an echoing reminder as she stood posed; her SIG-Sauer P230 aimed out in front of her as she started out of the stairwell and headed for the older woman.

She wanted to brush the strand of crimson hair out of her face, away from her emerald eyes as she tried to focus, making sure her attention wasn't diverted. But both hands were currently on her weapon, trying her best to steady its aim.

A sheen of light sweat began to build along her forehead and above her lips, and she could smell the pungent salty odor as her body dealt with the uncomfortable situation she was in. She knew what she had to do. This was it. There was no turning back. Now or never.

Jackie Isley calmly sucked air in through her nose. She could do this. She knew what she needed to do and how to do it.

She was a professional. Always had been, and always would be.

She exhaled gently.

"Police! Freeze!" Jackie felt like a moron for shouting those words, but dammit, that felt great.

"You!" Jackie heard the woman shout as she turned toward Jackie.

The old woman immediately reached into her purse, pulled out a gun, and fired twice at Jackie, who ducked behind a car. Jackie started to rise when another bullet ricocheted off the top of the car and another shattered the window above her head. As the old woman stormed toward the vehicle, Jackie lowered herself to the ground, aimed her gun at the woman's leg, and fired twice, hitting her once in the shin. The woman's leg snapped and gave way below her, as the bullet ripped through her leg. But she had not lost her grip on the gun, and as she began to aim it, Jackie fired three more times, both hitting and killing Lewis Hayward's foster mother.

THIRTY-EIGHT

"You just like to scare the shit out of people, don't you?" Jackie Isley teased from her chair next to Dave's hospital bed.

He had just woken up some ten minutes before, and after the doctor's initial inspection, concluding that he would be all right, had been left alone. The doctor had promised—nay, threatened—to be back later for further testing.

"What's going on?" Dave asked.

"Well, you were found half unconscious at the Hollywood Forever Cemetery. You were rushed here. It was just a temporary muscle paralytic, so you're ok now. No other toxins in your body. I'm sure they'll release you soon enough."

"What about the woman—"

"Katrina Thompson?" He had no answer for that. Even he wasn't sure what her real last name was. "She was found in the cemetery. Fitting, really. She was dead. Nasty gash along the side of her head. Cracked her skull. Died of blood loss. The higher-ups still want to question you about her, though. Who was she? I mean, in this whole mess."

"You remember the whole Kozlov debacle?"

Jackie tensed for a moment but wasn't sure if Dave could tell from his angle. "Sicko child predator who attacked you and killed your partner?"

"And had his wife killed by his brother."

"Lest we forget."

"Kozlov's wife? Natalie...Katrina Thompson was her sister."

"Oh, no shit?" Jackie leaned back in her chair and processed this information.

"I think that's how Hayward was able to manipulate her. Promised her things."

"Like the deaths of Peter and Victor Kozlov?"

Dave jerked to Jackie. She had gone from barely knowing who the two child predators were to saying their names. Something was up.

Jackie exhaled and began.

"I think someone higher up wants to make it official to you. You've only been in here about three hours, but Peter and Victor Kozlov both died less than sixty minutes after you were found at the cemetery. No one's sure how it happened, and though we all know Lewis Hayward is somehow responsible, due to his stunt of calling you the other day, he's been in solitary confinement ever since. So he has an alibi."

"Of course," Dave said, lying back in his bed. He was tired already.

"Of course, twenty other inmates also got sick from some sort of contamination during dinner. Of those twenty, only two were raced to the emergency ward of the prison. The other eighteen are doing okay. Cramps and diarrhea, but otherwise okay. Unfortunately, the prison doctor could do nothing for the other two, who were then rushed off to the local hospital."

"Do I want to know the rest?"

Jackie shook her head. She had talked to the doctor personally herself. She knew the story. That the whole way to the hospital their bodies had swelled up and their veins pulsed through their bodies, appearing as if they wanted freedom from the skin that contained them in their owners' bodies. That ten minutes after leaving the prison, both men began screaming as their eyes and ears began to bleed, their eyes becoming sensitive to light while their ears echoed everything they heard as if gongs were being banged in their heads. Five minutes after that, both men began choking on their blood.

Ten minutes after arriving at the hospital, both men had died.

No. Jackie didn't want to tell him about that. Couldn't.

She already knew that most likely the autopsies would fail to identify the poison both men had been intoxicated with, though when opened up it would most likely show their insides, including all organs and their brains, had become nothing more than a gooey mush.

Jackie was more than aware of the toxins available out there and what damage they could do.

"Anything else?"

"They let Jake go a while ago. He stopped by to see you, but you were still out. He's been ordered to stay at home and recuperate for forty-eight hours. I think Rachel took him back to her place. You know...if you ask me, I think those two are going to move in together real soon."

"Anyone else injured I should know about?"

"Milo."

"Milo?"

"Yeah, but he's fine now. Just a few stitches on the side of his head. I told him it made him seem badass. That the chicks will dig it. He seemed okay with it. Other than the scar it will most likely leave. Then I told him it was a battle scar, just like you have. I think that cheered him up a little. I think the kid really looks up to you."

"Yeah…" Dave reflected. "How did Milo get injured?"

"Oh, well, that's a fun one. While you were out tracking down Katrina Thompson, we figured out who was helping her."

"Oh?"

"Well…we don't know her name yet. We're gonna try and track her down through state records, but they're kinda old and I'm not expecting much. She was Thomas Cream's foster mother."

"That explains the rage at the Delancys. I think."

"There's more, though…" Jackie said as she reached into her purse and removed a photo. "Seems as if she was also a foster mother to some other kids. Including…" Jackie handed the photo over to Dave. "Lewis Hayward."

Dave stared down at the photo, taking it all in, seeing with his eyes the truth that Jackie spoke.

"That explains a lot," Dave agreed.

"Thomas Cream, her baby, was killed. And then was unjustly covered up. She wanted revenge. And her other son was able to provide that," Jackie said, summing up.

"Exactly. But an older woman like that probably needed some help."

"Hence…Katrina Thompson. Just another pawn. You kill mine and I'll kill yours. Like *Strangers on a Train*."

Dave looked questioningly at Jackie, and she brushed him off.

"That's who Ana Bernal was selling the memorabilia to."

"What?" Jackie asked.

"Nothing. One of our leads. She was selling memorabilia from the Palisades Poisoner case. It was to her. Their mother. As a way of being closer to her sons. Most parents display Little League trophies. This one wanted souvenirs from his grand scheme. Bet she was so proud."

"That's kinda weird."

"Whole family is kinda weird."

"Can't argue with that."

"I'll need to call Hayward. Eventually."

"Can't question him about the Kozlovs. He'll deny everything. Can't prove anything."

"What about that nine? That Japanese nine?"

"Does it matter why? Or for what reason?"

"No. Not now it doesn't. Maybe later it will. I'll ask later."

"Good boy," Jackie said leaning back in her chair. "You know he put himself out on the line for her?"

"Who? What?"

"Lewis Hayward. For his mother."

"How so?"

"We know next to nothing about that man. Since he skipped his trial and all that. Can't find nearly anything about his past. But now we have somewhere to start." Jackie held back up the family photo of Lewis Hayward and Thomas Cream. "We may not know who she is quite yet, but it's a start. And we never would have made the connection if it hadn't been for these murders. He had to know that was a possibility. Even if he did try to erase every trace of himself during his time with the LAPD."

"We sacrifice a lot for family."

"Tell me about it," Jackie said, shaking her head as she grabbed the remote.

"What's going on? Why are you here?"

"Someone's gotta make sure you get back up to snuff," Jackie said, as she began flipping through channels. "Can't have bad guys out roaming around the streets of Los Angeles without someone there to stop them. Gotta get you better."

"And you're gonna help with that?"

"I'm here to help with everything," Jackie winked. "Whether you like it or not. Oh, look. *Murder, She Wrote* is on. How about that?"

"Do I look like a housebound sixty-year-old?"

"Well, you are eating Jell-O. There's always a *Law & Order* marathon."

"There's one on?"

"That shows been around since before TV was even invented. There's always an L&O marathon on some cable channel or other. It's a proven fact. I think there's one about the different hairstyles of the lady detective or the different ties of the guy detective."

"Stabler?"

"Of course, you'd call the guy one stable. Male chauvinist..."

"His name's—you've never actually seen the show before, have you?"

"Do you know how many hours of my life I'd have to give up to watch that show? Cuz you know I can't just watch one and then stop. And I have to see them all in order...and then I'd have to rate them all on both entertainment value versus reality based...and then..."

Parks began to laugh. And despite the pain in his throat, it felt good. Better than he could remember in quite some time.

ACKNOWLEDGEMENTS

I'd just like to take a quick moment to thank the many people who have helped make this novel possible. To my two editors, Gabe Robinson for his many helpful suggestions with plot and characters. You've helped tremendously. And Christine Pingleton for trying to spot every typo and grammatical error. If there's any still any in here it's my eyes to blame and not hers. There were numerous people and websites and forums who helped try to get the logistics of the LAPD and the forensic toxicology as accurate as possible. Any errors are entirely mine, include those made purposely for the sacrifice of the story over facts.

A special shout out/thanks goes to Tyler Dille (and his family) for helping me with the covers for these things as well as the web site design and other promotional pictures, ads, etc that he's helped me with along the way. This wouldn't be possible without your help.

I'd like to thank my parents any my brothers and their wives for their endless support. For the people who supported and kept asking when the next book was coming: Rita, Cindy, Lori, Eric (and his stepfather), and the many others who I am sure I am forgetting at the moment, thanks. And especially to all of the faceless people out there who I have not met but have supported me online and in book clubs where one of my books was chosen. I thank you immensely.

ABOUT THE AUTHOR

The son of a prison guard, Tyler Compton graduated from CSU, Sacramento in 2002 with a BA in Theatre Arts and a minor in Film Studies. An Eagle Scout, he has worked in the pool industry for over 15 years, as a server, bartender and (for one hilarious evening) as club security. He currently resides in Los Angeles where he has witnessed various forms of crime, including someone breaking into his apartment while he was in it.

His first book, *The Poisonous Ten*, was released in June 2013 and was named an Award-Winning Finalist in the Fiction: Mystery/Suspense category of the 2013 USA Best Book Awards, sponsored by USA Book News. His second book the the Detective Parks series, *Wicked Games*, was released later that same year. *The Blue Condition* rounds out the Det. Parks trilogy, although Tyler has plenty more cases for Det. Parks and his team in mind. Tyler has finished his first YA novel (also a mystery), *The Fast Out*, due out early 2017. He is currently at work on a new stand-alone mystery.

Follow @tscompton on Twitter or visit TylerComptonBooks.com for the latest news and details about future releases.

www.ingramcontent.com/pod-product-compliance
Lightning Source LLC
Chambersburg PA
CBHW020329180626
46812CB00001B/124